Praise for
Echoes on a Corn...

'A beautifully atmospheric time-travel story set in the magical landscape of Cornwall's Tamar Valley. I was hooked from the very first page and drawn into this mystical tale. There is romance, danger and ancient magic – perfect! Loved this enchanting story!'
Christina Courtenay, author of *Echoes of the Runes*

'Kate's storytelling has a rare magical quality that carries you away. I was genuinely bereft when the story ended, and it was in my thoughts for a long time. Romantic and mysterious, this is my favourite by this author so far!'
Nicola Cornick, author of *The Winter Garden*

'A wonderful timeslip, a tale of love across the centuries, in an exquisitely described setting. I loved every page!'
Kathleen McGurl, author of *The Girl from Bletchley Park*

'This is a real find of a book. I stayed up half the night to finish it. It gripped me from the first word to the last . . . A gorgeous read, highly recommended'
Elena Collins, author of *The Witch's Tree*

Also By Kate Ryder

Summer in a Cornish Cove
Cottage on a Cornish Cliff
Secrets of the Mist
Beneath Cornish Skies
Into a Cornish Wind

Echoes on a Cornish River

Kate Ryder

embla books

First published in Great Britain in 2023 by

Bonnier Books UK Limited
4th Floor, Victoria House, Bloomsbury Square, London, WC1B 4DA
Owned by Bonnier Books
Sveavägen 56, Stockholm, Sweden

A CIP catalogue record for this book is available from the British Library.

ISBN: 9781471415661

This book is typeset using Atomik ePublisher

Embla Books is an imprint of Bonnier Books UK
www.bonnierbooks.co.uk

For my husband, Martin

Hireth (Cornish):
Something in your bones;
a longing for home;
a yearning for something lost;
the essence of a place never yet known.

Prologue

The overhead lights are bright as Ellinor Forrester takes her seat. She feels a headache coming on and wishes she were anywhere but here at the airline's headquarters. In fact, all she wants is to lay her head on a soft pillow, close her eyes and drift off into oblivion.

'We realise this is difficult for you,' one of the male airline officials says, giving her a kindly smile, 'but, if you could describe what happened on board the flight.'

She stares at the two men sitting on the opposite side of the conference table, along with Helen Matthews, the woman from HR. Desperately, Ellinor looks around the sleek office, but there's no chance of escape. She *has* to do this.

She takes a deep breath, determined to be as unemotional, but descriptive, as possible.

'The flight started uneventfully enough, with no hint of what was to unfold.'

She pauses, trying to gain control of the emotion rising in her throat.

'In your own time,' the man says. 'Would you like some water?'

She nods. 'Please.'

Helen rises to her feet. Pouring water from a carafe, she passes a glass to Ellinor across the table with an encouraging smile.

'Thank you.' Ellinor makes brief eye contact with the woman. Attempting to still her shaking hand, she takes a sip of the cool liquid and tries again. 'I was working business class and as a seasoned flight attendant, with extensive training in passenger safety, I believed I'd be able to effectively deal with emergencies of any nature. However, three hours into the flight a man singled me out from the rest of the cabin crew. I was unaware of him until he was immediately behind me. It was as if he'd come out of nowhere.'

She stops and grits her teeth. If she can imagine it happened to someone else, maybe she'll be able to survive this interview without breaking down. Attempting to distance herself from the incident, Ellinor relays the order of events.

'The first moment I knew something wasn't right was when he wrapped his arm tightly around my neck and dug a hard object into the small of my back. He was a large man and towered over me and I was powerless to prevent him from forcing me along the aisle towards the cockpit.' She closes her eyes briefly and composes herself. 'It was only when he turned me to face the length of the cabin and removed the object pressing against my spine that I caught sight of a flash of steel from the cold blade of a knife as he brought it up under my jawline. The man was sweating profusely and I picked up on his unhinged emotions.' She glances guiltily at her interviewers. 'My legs threatened to buckle and I'm sorry to say that all my safety training deserted me.'

She takes another sip of water. It's as if the floodgates have opened, and now that she's started talking she can't stop.

'My captor's arm pressed against my windpipe and I struggled to draw breath. I was consumed with a sense of helplessness, and the passengers' expressions quickly turned to shock as the seriousness of the unfolding drama dawned on them. That was the worst of it – my complete lack of control over the situation. It was as if I was watching actors in a disaster movie. I saw my colleague, Karen Tate, walking calmly down the aisle towards us and, outwardly, she seemed unconcerned by what was happening. Despite being consumed with terror, I was full of admiration for her composure.'

Ellinor stops and gazes out of the window, but she doesn't see the colour of the sky, or the bank of trees bordering the land surrounding the building. She's back on board . . . a captive.

'What happened next?' the other male official prompts.

Ellinor's eyes flick to the man. 'Karen said, *Enough! What is it that you want?* The man braced his arm more tightly around my neck and I gagged, and fought to draw air into my lungs.'

Closing her eyes, Ellinor pinches the bridge of her nose. 'He shouted, *Come no further. If you do I won't hesitate to slice and dice . . . and it won't just be this pretty young thing that feels the sharpness of my blade.* As if to emphasise his determination, he increased the pressure of the blade on my neck and I felt it pierce my skin. I remember thinking, is this it? Am I going to die? You see, my husband, Simon, and I have so many plans yet to fulfil and it was incomprehensible that I would never know my future children. But a deep anger bubbled up in the pit of my stomach and I summoned all my inner strength, knowing that I had to keep my wits about me.'

She stops again, breathing hard as the memories she's tried so hard to push away take up residence in her mind once again.

'This is good, Ellinor,' the first official encourages. 'Take your time.'

She nods, pausing for a moment before continuing, 'Karen did as the man suggested and stood motionless in the aisle, staring at me with a mixture of responsibility, terror and pity playing in her eyes. Calmly she repeated, *What is it that you want?* The man laughed callously and said, *You'll find out soon enough.*'

Ellinor stares down at her hands. They're shaking and she clasps them together.

'I had a deep sense of dread as I realised that this was it; none of us were getting out alive. The assailant then dragged me backwards towards the cockpit and forced me to gain entry.'

The first official interrupts. 'How did he do that?'

Irrational guilt swamps her, and Ellinor takes a calming breath. Could she have done more to prevent him from entering the cockpit?

'I saw him glance up at the wide-angled flight-deck camera,' she says quietly. 'He knew what he was doing and stepped out of range, and threatened that if I didn't gain entry for him he would kill me. So, I stood directly in front of the camera, picked up the interphone and requested access. As soon as the door unlocked, he ran at me; slammed me against the galley wall and barged his way in. As I ricocheted off the wall, I heard my ribs crack and I ended up sprawled on the cabin floor.'

Ellinor's hand flies protectively to the side of her body.

'Minutes later, a loud grinding sound emanated throughout the cabin and the plane shuddered violently. I pulled myself up off the floor and staggered towards the nearest empty seat and gingerly strapped myself in. Karen quickly joined me. I asked her what the hell the noise was, as it wasn't turbulence, and then it happened again, and the aircraft started to climb steeply. The oxygen masks dropped and suddenly the plane went into freefall. As it plummeted out of the sky, the overhead lockers opened and spewed out their contents, filling the cabin with flying objects. I will never forget the sound of the passengers' screams, and in the seat behind me I heard a man praying.'

She takes another sip of water.

'As I glanced out of the window, my heart dived into my stomach, even as my mind failed to fully comprehend . . . and then I did. I think I said, *Oh, my God! The plane's upside down. We're going to crash*! Thoughts crowded my brain, tumbling over each other to gain importance, and I realised that I would never see my husband again. And then the idea that life doesn't always begin at forty popped into my head . . . I'm not even thirty! But then Karen's calm voice cut through my fear as she said, *Time to put on our life jackets, I think*.'

Ellinor gives a small laugh.

'It was so understated and bizarre that for a moment I had to fight a fit of irrational giggling. And then a sudden movement in the aisle made us both turn. A burly man staggered . . . half-crawled . . . along the cabin ceiling towards the cockpit, and as he wrenched open the door we saw a struggle taking place between the co-pilot and the deranged assailant. Immediately, the passenger threw himself into the enclosed space and the door slammed shut behind him. I turned to Karen, terrified, and then a few seconds later the plane levelled off and righted itself.'

Ellinor swallows hard.

Oh, God, I'm not going to be sick, am I?

'Do you want a break?' the second male official asks.

She shakes her head. She's almost there. Deep breaths, and soon she'll be out in the open again . . . Away from *people*.

'Suddenly, the intercom crackled into life,' she continues. 'Captain Andrews' voice came over the speaker, breathless, and he said, *Sorry about that, folks. A man tried to kill us all, but we're going to be OK.* My fingers flew to my neck; it was sticky and wet, and when I removed my hand I saw that my fingers were smeared in blood. But I felt weirdly calm. Karen undid her seatbelt and hurried up the aisle, and then the cockpit door flew open and the madman's figure filled the doorway. Instinctively, I cowered in my seat, but he was securely restrained between the co-pilot and the brave passenger, and they managed to get him into the galley. When the captain's voice came through the intercom again, he sounded much more composed. He explained that a deranged man had broken into the cockpit and tried to kill himself and all on board, but that he had been overpowered and was in a passenger restraint kit. He added, *For those with ongoing flights, rest assured we'll be landing only ten minutes behind schedule.*'

Ellinor gives a wry laugh. 'I was so relieved. And I half-expected him to wish the passengers a pleasant remaining flight, and again I had to suppress a burst of hysterical laughter. I undid my seatbelt, and even though the pain in my ribs was agony, I stood and turned to face the traumatised passengers and then slowly worked my way along the aisle and offered reassurances. After feeling such palpable, abject terror, the atmosphere in the plane was now buzzing. Everyone talked and hugged each other, even strangers. And when Karen announced that breakfast was cancelled because it was all over the cabin, a nervous titter resounded around business class.'

Ellinor stops. Picking up the glass tumbler, she drains the remaining water.

'And what happened when you landed in Dubai?' the first official queries.

'Once the plane came to a stop, airport personnel rushed up and wrapped the disembarking crew in blankets, and we were quickly ushered into the main terminal building. My neck wound was dressed and then I was taken to the nearest hospital by ambulance where a doctor examined me and confirmed that I had three fractured ribs, and the three-inch knife wound was stitched.'

The officials glance at each other.

'Thank you, Ellinor,' the first man says. 'We know how hard this must have been. Your account is very helpful and we will add it to the incident log. I believe that Helen has filled out all the paperwork for your leave of absence on health grounds.' He looks at the woman from HR, who nods in confirmation. 'She will also arrange counselling for you, paid for by the airline. From here on in, Helen will be your point of contact.'

One

Six Months Later

Ellinor stands in darkness before the bi-fold doors that grace the ground floor of her executive Surrey home. She glances out at the shadows lurking amongst the trees and studies the lines in the freshly mown grass, a series of symmetrical tracks shimmering silver in the moonlight. Her gaze wanders to the neat borders filled with clusters of snowdrops and sumptuous, early flowering shrubs that appear ghost-like in the eerie light, and considers what Tim, their gardener, had suggested only that afternoon. A pond and water feature to one side of the expansive decked area *is* a good idea; it will break up the lawn. Suddenly her eyes are drawn to the far end of the garden where the shadows are at their most menacing. Anxiety immediately claims her, and her heart begins to race. As her mouth turns dry, her fingers fly to the ridge of skin scarring her throat – ever the reminder. As Ellinor's soul shrinks, her breathing becomes shallow and she watches the shadows take form. Stepping away from the window, she is instantly swallowed up by the dark interior of the living room.

Cautiously emerging from the cover of foliage, a fox sniffs the night air before lightly stepping onto the immaculate lawn. Within minutes it is joined by a larger vulpine. Suburban foxes; used to rich pickings in this desirable neighbourhood. As Ellinor watches the creatures, she becomes aware that she's never truly noticed them before. She knows that they visit the garden – Tim has often reported he's removed their droppings from the lawn – but she's always been too wrapped up in her career to stop and observe nature. But now . . . it's as if the *outside* calls to her, desperate to show her a different world. The foxes are in good condition, their bodies are sleek and their tails full, and as Ellinor's heart rate slows, she removes her hand from her throat, reassured that nothing sinister invades the private, safe space of the back garden.

The vixen and the dog fox work their way across the grass, examining the ground and tracking invisible scents. They stop to sniff the plants and gaze up at the full moon, and for a moment they glance warily towards the large bulk of the house. Suddenly light floods the room and Ellinor blinks in surprise at the brutal assault on her senses. In one swift movement the foxes flee, merging once more into the darkness of the surrounding trees.

'Having trouble sleeping again?' Simon, her husband, asks as he crosses the room towards her.

Ellinor doesn't respond and continues to stare out of the window into the black abyss beyond the glass.

'Did you have the nightmare again?' He wraps his arms around her cold body.

She nods, unable to prevent herself from flinching at his touch. She's had this reaction to him ever since the near-fatal flight. Even though she knows he's being caring and protective, each time he encloses her in a cuddle she feels trapped, and is instantly back in the grip of her attacker.

'You're safe now,' Simon whispers, close to her ear. 'No one can hurt you.'

Tentatively – as if in experiment – she leans into his body, attempting to gain some inner strength from his reassurance. But quickly she steps away.

'Come to bed,' he says softly.

'In a minute.'

He frowns. 'When is your next counselling session?'

She sighs. 'Not until Monday week.'

'Perhaps you can bring it forward?'

'Maybe. Go back to bed, Simon. There's no point in us both getting cold.'

He leans in to kiss her lightly on the lips and she braces herself, determined not to recoil.

'Don't be long, Elli.'

'Go on,' she coaxes. 'You've got to be up in three hours.'

His bright blue eyes are full of concern. 'If you're sure?'

She gives a small nod and gently pushes him away.

Simon retraces his steps across the room, but as he reaches the door he looks back. Silently, he regards his wife who, once again, gazes out of the glass doors into the darkness, and a small frown settles on his brow.

The light illuminating the living room only further accentuates the deep, impenetrable blackness beyond the glass. Ellinor gazes up at the night sky. Clouds shroud the moon and she shivers. How long will the horror continue to replay in her mind? It's as if it's on a never-ending loop. As her body remembers the three fractured ribs, she rubs her side gently.

It was a few weeks after *the incident* that she learned that the six-foot-five-inch assailant had attacked the pilot and tried to wrestle the controls from him. During the ensuing fight the autopilot had been disengaged, which sent the plane into a steep climb and caused the engines to stall. That was the awful noise they'd heard before the plane tipped upside down and plummeted twelve thousand feet. With superhuman strength, the co-pilot attempted to pull the madman away, only to suffer a broken jaw in the fracas. It wasn't until the brave passenger had appeared – a rugby player, as it turned out – that between them they were able to restrain the attacker, which allowed the pilot to restart the engines and level the plane, despite having had half his ear bitten off.

Ellinor shudders and rubs her arms. It was such a close call. She now knows that if the plane had fallen for four seconds longer, the pilot would not have been able to save them. Even now, months on from that fateful day, it feels surreal, and she finds it hard to comprehend that she'd nearly died. She's still reeling from the experience – despite having been laid off work on health grounds and receiving regular counselling sessions – and now it's left her fearful and questioning every decision in her life. If only she could put to rest the recurring nightmares. But she suspects that this one flight will remain clearly etched on her memory forever.

Running her index finger along the raised ridge of skin on her neck, Ellinor knows she was fortunate to get away with just a three-inch scar. It will fade in time, but the internal scars will be more difficult to eradicate. She sighs deeply and turns away from the darkness outside. Walking to the door, she switches off the lights and makes her way to the relative security of the bedroom.

Two

When Ellinor comes to, the bed beside her is empty. Dressing quickly, she makes her way downstairs, pausing on the half-landing when she hears her husband talking in hushed tones. She lingers just out of sight.

'Yes, again last night. I'm not happy leaving her on her own but I've called a meeting this morning and I can't miss it.' He falls silent. After a long pause, he continues, 'That would be helpful, Chloe. You're a lifesaver.'

Ellinor continues to descend the stairs and Simon glances up.

'I'll let her know. Bye for now.' He replaces the handset.

'Why is my sister a lifesaver?' Ellinor asks, stopping on the bottom step.

Their eyes are on a level as Simon walks across the hall towards her. 'She's coming over in half an hour, after dropping off Max and Tara at school.'

Ellinor shakes her head. 'She doesn't have to do that! She's got enough on her plate, what with the baby as well.'

Simon places his hands on either side of Ellinor's waist and, involuntarily, her stomach muscles clench.

'Chloe said she was happy to call by. Says she wants to catch up with you, anyway.'

Ellinor pulls a face. 'I don't want to be a bother to anyone. I can cope.'

He smiles at her. 'I know you can, but after the night you've just had, wouldn't it be a good distraction to spend time with your sister?'

'I guess so.'

Removing his hands, he glances at his watch. 'Sorry, but

must dash. Can't be late for the quarterly sales meeting, seeing as I've arranged it!'

'What time will you be home tonight?'

'I doubt I'll be much later than six, but if it's any different I'll phone.' Her husband drops a soft kiss on her mouth and Ellinor tries not to recoil. 'Take it easy today. I promise you, Elli, things will get better.'

What does he know of the terror I've faced?

She forces a smile and sternly reminds herself that it's kind of him to be concerned.

Crossing over to the hall table, Simon picks up the briefcase at its feet and walks to the front door.

'See you later,' he says, giving her a tender smile before stepping out onto the gravelled driveway.

Ellinor follows. Standing in the open doorway, she breathes in the quiet, still morning. There's a hint of spring in the air, and away to the east the sky is a beautiful, milky pink. She watches as her husband unlocks the doors of his Audi and slides the briefcase onto the passenger seat.

'Don't get cold,' he says, glancing back at her. 'The weather may seem fair, but it is only early March.'

She nods and gives him a wave, as he climbs in and drives towards the opening electric gates. The next minute the car sweeps out onto the private road . . . and then he's gone.

Ellinor glances across at the properties on the opposite side of the road. The houses in this gated, private estate are mock-Tudor in style, and each has a slight variation to its neighbour. Some are part-faced with terracotta tiles and several have large oak-framed extensions; all enjoy large grounds – a rarity in these days of infill – which are neatly manicured and orderly. A moneyed, organised air prevails on the estate. Nothing ever disturbs this quietly assured environment, and yet, as Ellinor looks around, she's aware how quickly this could change in the blink of an eye. Her neighbours have no notion of how fragile life can be as they go about their daily lives, ferrying children to and from school, commuting to work, and wives and house-husbands enjoying regular coffee mornings, not to mention the thriving book club in the community. She used to be involved with the 'Ladies that Lunch' club, when she was between flights, but she hasn't been able to face that since *the incident*. It all seems too much of an effort to put on a brave face when the slightest noise sets her on edge. And crowds! She now possesses highly attuned radar at a hundred yards to any unusual attitude or 'oddball'. No, she's better off taking it a day at a time, as she has been advised to do.

In her pursuit of leading a quiet, uncompromised life, Ellinor's recently taken up painting, but her art is not the pleasing, serene landscapes she'd hoped to produce. Mostly, it features dark, jagged, brutal images, which her counsellor assures her is all part of the healing process. And she's read *so* many books that she's become a bit of a celebrity amongst the members of the book club and can recommend a plethora of new authors whenever asked, although she finds it a trial to attend the get-togethers, however safe they are. It's the one social event she's attempted to continue with because, after all, where's the danger in exchanging ideas about novels over a glass of wine or two? But still . . . it's such a small life in comparison to the one she had, and she's ever impatient to reclaim her former self.

Sighing with frustration, Ellinor turns away and enters the house, firmly bolting the door behind her.

'So, sister Chloe is coming to babysit me!' Her voice echoes around the empty hallway.

It's not that she doesn't want to see her sister; they were close growing up. Ellinor just wishes she could be more dynamic and regain some of her lost confidence. She used to be so positive and full of life, but she's a mere shadow of that former woman. Simon must surely wonder who he's now married to! Walking through to the kitchen, she switches on the kettle and busies herself preparing coffee while waiting for Chloe to arrive.

* * *

Ninety minutes later, Ellinor watches her sister and baby Leo through the leisure centre's expansive, plate-glass café windows as they splash about in the toddlers' pool. Reluctantly persuaded by Chloe to attend her nephew's 'ducklings' swimming session at the local baths, Ellinor attempts to relax and ignore the loud and startling, echoing sounds around her. She'd tried to object, but Chloe was so insistent that Ellinor had eventually agreed to come, although she'd refused to bring a swimming costume and join in. The place is heaving with mothers, babies and toddlers, and the mix of heat and chlorine in the air makes her feel claustrophobic. In fact, she may have to slip outside to get some fresh air.

Standing thigh-deep in the pool, Chloe turns to look at her sister with a proud smile as she guides baby Leo around the pool. Encircled by bright orange armbands, his little chubby arms thrash the water. Ellinor smiles and gives her sister the thumbs-up. What different directions their lives have taken. With only two years between them, their childhood had been spent playing together – harmoniously, for the most part – and being the elder, Ellinor had looked out for her sister. Even now she feels a sense of responsibility towards her. But when Chloe fell for Duncan, a lad in Ellinor's class at school, an imperceptible fissure had crept into the siblings' relationship. At eighteen, Chloe married Duncan, and children soon followed to complete their happy family. Inevitably, the sisters' relationship changed, but Ellinor is happy in her role as Godmother to Tara, and she loves her niece and nephews and would do anything for them. But some days it's hard to remember that Chloe is the younger sister; her life is so full of grown-up responsibilities.

Ellinor picks up the cup of coffee from the small café table. Suddenly a hand lands heavily on her shoulder and she whirls around in her seat, watching as the hot contents of her cup fly in slow motion towards the perpetrator. For a moment she's transported back and can only see the face of her attacker on the plane. She cowers away from her assailant, but as her senses realign she cringes with embarrassment. The man is a stranger, and he stares at her in astonishment, as a large brown stain spreads across the front of his white shirt.

'I'm so sorry!' Ellinor says, quickly replacing the cup in its saucer and getting to her feet. Picking up a paper napkin, she dabs at his chest, noticing that his shirt is made of fine linen and expensive.

The man stands back smartly. 'Don't. It'll only make it worse,' he says, holding the front of his shirt away from his body.

'You took me by surprise.' Ellinor's face flushes with humiliation.

'My mistake,' he says. 'I thought you were someone else. I should have approached more sensitively.'

'Can I pay for your shirt to be cleaned?'

'As I said, it was my fault,' he says graciously. Holding up a sports holdall, he adds, 'I've got a clean T-shirt in here. I was on my way to do a few laps during the lunch hour.' He smiles awkwardly.

Ellinor breathes more easily. He seems pleasant enough . . . And it could have been so much worse.

'There's not much coffee left in that cup. Let me buy you a refill,' he offers.

'Oh, no,' she exclaims. 'I wouldn't dream of it.'

He hesitates. 'Well, I guess I'd better get on.'

But he doesn't move and Ellinor glances at him in surprise. Is he suddenly going to produce a knife and hold it to her throat? She steps away, increasing the distance between them.

'If you want to complete those laps in your lunch hour you'd better get on,' she says more confidently than she feels. She glances towards the pool but there's no sign of Chloe or Leo. Turning back to the man, she nervously fingers her scar. 'Don't let me keep you.'

He smiles politely and then turns away, striding purposefully towards the men's changing area.

Ellinor sits down with her back to the plate-glass window. Clasping her hands together, she attempts to stop the tremors and looks around for her sister. All she wants to do is go home. As her breathing gradually regulates, she cringes at her overreaction to the man. How mortifying to cover him with coffee! But then he shouldn't have slapped his hand down on her shoulder. It was all a silly mistake, but she's so jumpy and reacting to the slightest thing.

At last, she sees Chloe walking towards her with baby Leo in her arms.

'That was good,' says her sister, removing the holdall from her shoulder and placing it on the floor. 'Did you see how well Leo was doing?'

'I did.' Ellinor gives a brief smile.

'Fancy a spot of lunch?' Chloe asks.

'I'd rather go home, if you don't mind.'

'What? We've only been here an hour!'

Ellinor pulls a face. 'I feel claustrophobic.' She gets to her feet. 'Can we do lunch another time?'

Holding her baby up in front of her, Chloe pulls a sad face and says in a childish voice, 'Aunty Elli doesn't want to play with Mummy and Leo today.'

'Oh, for God's sake, it's not that!' Ellinor snaps. 'Let's just go.' Picking up her sister's holdall, she walks smartly towards the exit.

'What's got into you?' Chloe says, trailing after her with her baby on her hip.

Nothing! Just the little matter of a life-threatening encounter that has scarred me more deeply than people seem to realise . . .

She turns back and forces a smile onto her face. 'Sorry, Chloe, but I'm having difficulty breathing in here. Leo did well today. Bet he's going to represent the UK at the Olympics one day.'

'Did you hear that, Leo?' Chloe croons to her little boy. 'The Olympics, here we come!'

Three

Two days later, Ellinor stands in front of the easel where she's been for the past couple of hours. This particular painting is not proving the therapeutic experience she'd hoped for. Standing back, she scrutinises the canvas – an abstract comprising discordant shapes with angry, barbed edges and full of fury. She sighs in dismay. Even the colours she's chosen have blended and produced a depressing, sluggish brown.

'Disgusting. You're disgusting!' she growls, as she throws the paintbrush onto the palette.

Ripping off her paint-splattered shirt and sending buttons scattering in all directions, she storms from the conservatory and marches into the kitchen. Angrily, she grabs the kettle, fills it with water and switches it on.

'It's obviously a brown day today,' she mutters, as she takes down a bone-china mug from a cupboard.

Eyeing the jars of coffee neatly lined up on the shelf, she wonders if she can be bothered to make the real stuff. Her hand hovers over a canister of Colombian coffee beans, but instead she selects a jar of instant, just as the shrill sound of a ringing phone slices through the silence of the house. Crossing over to the cordless handset sitting on the kitchen counter, Ellinor picks it up and speaks into the mouthpiece.

'Hello,' she says in a flat voice.

'Hi, cuz!'

'Ian!' Her face breaks into a smile.

During Ellinor and Chloe's formative years, their cousin Ian and his family had lived in the neighbouring street of their leafy Hertfordshire village. They'd all attended the same school and subsequently spent a lot of time hanging

17

out together. He was two years older than Ellinor and she'd considered him the brother she never had. He, in turn, had looked out for her, especially when several of his classmates showed an increasing awareness of, and interest in, his attractive, vivacious cousin.

'It's so good to hear from you,' Ellinor says genuinely. 'How are things in Cornwall?'

'Good, thanks. Hectic, but all positive. Thought I'd phone and find out what you're up to.' When she doesn't answer, he quickly continues, 'How's that high-flying husband of yours?'

'High-flying,' Ellinor echoes drily. 'Unlike his wife. She's not flying anywhere.'

Awkwardness crackles down the line.

'Sorry, Elli. Bad choice of words.'

She sighs and walks back to the kettle. 'Oh, ignore me. I'm just being churlish. I've had a rotten morning and thought I'd do a spot of painting, but what I've produced may soon line the bin.'

'Don't be so harsh on yourself. I bet it's not that bad.'

'Believe me,' she says, with a self-deprecating laugh, 'it most certainly is!'

'You've had a dreadful experience,' Ian says sympathetically. 'It's bound to take time to recover from it.'

'You're right, but I wish my recovery would hurry up.' She sighs again. Wedging the phone between her shoulder and chin, she spoons coffee into the mug. 'But enough of this, let's talk about something more uplifting. How's Pippa?'

'She's well, thanks, although she's constantly telling me that I work her to the bone.'

'You'd better not drive her away.' Ellinor pours hot water onto the granules and watches them dissolve. 'I have no idea how you persuaded her to marry you,' she teases, 'but she's a keeper, that wife of yours.'

'I don't know how I did either, and duly noted,' Ian says with a laugh. 'Anyway, we wondered if you and Simon would like to come and stay for a weekend. We want to show you the improvements we've made to the farm, and I'd like some business advice from the man himself.'

'He'd like that,' Ellinor says, replacing the kettle on its base. 'You know how he loves to discuss ideas with you – and the wackier the better! When are you thinking?'

'The weekend after next?'

Ellinor glances at the calendar on the wall. 'There's nothing in the diary but I should check with Simon, in case he's organised something he's yet to tell me about. I'll ask him to phone you.'

Pulling out one of the bar stools neatly tucked under the kitchen island, she perches on the seat and sips her coffee. The cousins have always had an easy relationship and they talk for a while longer, but eventually she bids Ian farewell. Ellinor places the empty coffee mug on the draining board and returns to the conservatory.

'You're not getting the better of me,' she says crossly to the murky canvas propped on the easel. 'When you're dry you are having a new coat of paint, and then watch out. No browns in the next painting . . . you mark my words!'

She crosses over to the window, picking up stray buttons from the floor on the way, and stares out over the garden. There's no sign of the foxes today, but that's hardly surprising. Being nocturnal animals, they prefer adventures at dusk or under the cover of darkness. Her gaze wanders to the side of the raised decking where the grass butts up against the wooden boards. It won't be long before Tim makes a start on the new pond and water feature. A flicker of interest takes her by surprise, and she realises she's looking forward to discussing the options for marginal planting. The local garden centre has an extensive aquatics section, and she makes a mental note to buy half-a-dozen goldfish when the pond is finished. Yes, that's what she needs – a project to get her teeth into. As her interest increases, Ellinor carefully examines her reaction. It's the first time she's experienced any positive emotion since *the incident*.

* * *

Simon arrives home that evening bearing a large bouquet of flowers.

'What are these for?' she asks, as he hands them to her.

'No reason,' he says, with a smile. 'Just for being you.'

Ellinor sniffs the hot coral roses, indigo limonium, and daisy-like asters that together create a beautiful riot of colour.

'I promise I will be me again one day, Si,' she says quietly.

He reaches for her, but she takes a step back.

'Sorry,' he says.

'No, I'm sorry.'

'I'll not rush you,' he continues, masking his hurt, 'but I just want you to know that I'm here for you.'

She smiles, blinking rapidly as her vision mists. 'I know you are and thank you. I'd better put these in water.'

As she enters the kitchen she berates herself silently. Why can't she be natural with him? She misses their previous closeness and it's obvious that it pains him when she rejects his advances.

'What have you been up to today?' he asks, following her into the room.

'Oh, this and that. Mostly murdering a masterpiece.'

He laughs softly.

'Ian rang,' she adds, turning on the tap and filling a vase with cold water. 'He's invited us down to Cornwall the weekend after next. I checked the calendar and it's free, unless you have plans you haven't told me about?'

'I haven't organised anything.' His eyes narrow as he considers his wife. 'It sounds fun, but we'll only go if you feel up to a visit.'

'I'm sure I'll be OK,' she says, smiling reassuringly at him. 'I don't think they've arranged anything major. Ian wants to show us around the farm and ask your advice about the business. The most exciting thing will probably be visiting the local farmers' market, and I'm sure I can manage that without having a meltdown.'

But as she says this, a vision of the man at the swimming pool comes back to her, and the colour drains from her face as she recalls his look of shock as she'd drenched him in hot coffee. She'd been so close to falling apart.

'It'll be good to catch up,' Simon says. 'It's been way too long.'

'I agree. When Ian and Pippa first told us they'd decided to give up their careers in IT and buy a farm in Cornwall, it was a bit of a surprise. I mean, the closest thing Ian ever came to farming was working on his dad's allotment as a kid!' Ellinor skews her lips sideways. 'I'd taken it for granted they'd always be accessible, and I miss our meet-ups. It's hard to believe they've been gone for over a year.'

'It all happened so quickly,' Simon says. 'But the good news is that Ian and Pippa are only *just* over the Tamar Bridge, so it's not as if it's a marathon drive to get to them. Anyway, a change of scene will do us both good.'

'Yes.' A ghost of a smile registers on Ellinor's face. 'I've already laid the table and supper's almost ready.'

'Fancy a glass of vino?'

'Thanks,' she says, watching as he exits the room.

Later, once they've eaten, Simon asks, 'What do you want to do now?' He nods towards the sitting room. 'How about a film in the comfort of our private cinema?'

'Oh, you do take me to the most salubrious venues!' she says with a laugh. 'I'll clear away the plates while you find something on Netflix.'

'No, Elli. Leave the dishes. We can do it together later.' Pushing back his chair, he gets to his feet. 'This is *date night*,' he adds, in a corny American accent.

'What an exciting life you have with me these days,' she mumbles under her breath.

'Hey!' he exclaims. 'You don't hear me complaining, do you?'

Walking briskly around the table, Simon takes hold of her hands and Ellinor wills herself to remain calm. It's so easy for any unexpected moves to bring on heart palpitations these days. She looks up into his bright blue eyes, which, in some lights, appear almost sapphire. They were the first thing she'd noticed about him.

'OK, Simon Forrester, lead the way.'

Her husband pulls her to her feet and as they pass the open doors to the conservatory, he asks, 'What's with the brown painting?'

She glances in and grimaces. 'However hard I try, I can't find my creative flow. That's what came out. It's hideous but it's getting a makeover . . . soon as.'

He glances at her, a tease dancing in his eyes. 'I thought it was the ground that Tim's dug over for the pond!'

Playfully, she swipes his arm. 'I suppose I could try and rework it into that.'

A while later, as they sit on the couch absorbed by a TV drama, Simon casually places his arm around his wife's shoulders. Ellinor steadies herself, wishing she could snuggle into him as she used to, safe in the knowledge that nothing will harm her here in the privacy of their home. She's told her therapist that if there's one thing she can rely on, it's Simon. He is the lynchpin to her security . . . or so she'd believed.

'Are you OK?' her husband asks. 'You seem tense.'

'Sorry, Si.' Extracting herself from his embrace, Ellinor shifts and creates space between them on the couch. 'I feel trapped with your arm around my shoulders.'

Simon regards her for a long moment. With an almost imperceptible sigh, he turns his attention back to the TV screen.

Four

The room is pleasantly decorated in calming, muted pastel shades, and slatted window shutters are partially open, allowing clients glimpses of a playing field attached to the local secondary school. Taking up most of the far wall are four split-canvas prints, the whole depicting an exotic beach scene bathed in the soothing glow of a setting sun. In one corner is a large potted palm, and positioned around a coffee table, on which someone has carefully arranged a selection of healthy-living and wellbeing magazines, are three comfortable armchairs. The overall impression is of a neat, tidy lounge, not a psychotherapist's office.

Ellinor glances out of the windows, the partly open shutters presenting the view in a series of vertical slices. Although it's a crisp, clear day, the insubstantial sun struggles to gain any significant strength and she follows the vapour trails of a plane crossing the ice-blue sky, and considers where it's heading. America probably, judging by its direction. At the sound of the door opening, she turns.

'Good morning, Ellinor.' The therapist's voice is smooth and professional. Entering the room with a notebook in hand, she closes the door quietly behind her. 'And how have you been since we last met?'

'OK, overall,' Ellinor says with a polite smile.

The woman walks across the room. Sitting in the opposite armchair, she opens the book and scans her notes.

Ellinor observes her therapist. She's neatly turned out in a tailored white blouse and black-and-white houndstooth pencil skirt that hugs a trim figure and shows off her slim, toned legs to perfection, which she now elegantly crosses.

Tidy and carefully considered – just like the room. Randomly, Ellinor wonders if she had any say in its décor.

The woman looks up and smiles warmly. 'How are your sleep patterns? I know you have been experiencing difficulties.'

'I rarely sleep through the night. When I do, I often wake in the grip of anxiety.' Ellinor sighs. 'Palpitations and me . . . we're close friends.'

The therapist purses her lips. 'And do you continue to dream?'

Irritation bites.

'They're not dreams, Sarah,' Ellinor says, her tone impassioned. 'They're nightmares. And, yes, I continue to have them.'

'We don't want to grant them any unnecessary importance, Ellinor,' the therapist says, her voice unflustered and as silky as smooth milk chocolate. 'By referring to them as nightmares, we allow them to garner energy.'

We?

Ellinor sighs again. Everything annoys her this morning.

'But that's what they are,' she says simply.

Removing a pen clipped to the notebook, the woman jots something down and then glances up with a sympathetic smile. 'They may be vivid, but it's best not to give them the substance they most definitely do not deserve.'

Swallowing her exasperation, Ellinor wonders what this woman – despite her training – actually knows. She talks about the violent images that frequently assault Ellinor these days as if they are Disneyesque versions of naughty, wayward children and can be easily brought back into line! But since the airline continues to pay for her counselling sessions, the least Ellinor can do is attend the appointments. Hopefully, one day during their discussions, the therapist will hit her with an eye-opening revelation.

'Last time we met,' Sarah continues, 'we discussed various ways of counteracting the negative emotions these dreams conjure. How have you found our coping strategies?'

Annoyance bubbles to the surface. *Our* coping strategies! There's nothing shared about the trauma she's had, however much this woman spins her words and coats her voice in honey. This therapist would make the perfect politician!

Stifling a sarcastic laugh, Ellinor replies, 'I'm following the EFT techniques you recommended.'

The woman nods. 'That's good. But remember; don't abandon them just because you're not experiencing instant results.' Her gaze turns to one of assessment. 'And how is your relationship with your husband?'

Ellinor glances down at her feet. They look so large and inelegant compared to the therapist's neat pair. Raising her eyes, she meets Sarah's enquiring gaze.

'Much the same.'

'How do you feel about that?'

'Sad, angry, exhausted, guilty.'

The therapist nods and jots something further in her notebook. 'All these emotions are to be expected.'

'But I can't expect him to put up with not having the woman he married,' Ellinor says. She takes a deep breath. 'I mean, how much longer will Simon tolerate my fear of intimacy with him?'

'Don't be so hard on yourself, Ellinor. Give it time.'

'But will *he* give it time?'

Sarah's look is sympathetic and understanding, but she doesn't add anything to encourage further exploration of this line of conversation. Instead, she changes the subject.

'I know at first you wanted to abandon every commitment and social event, but it's good practice to continue those that you feel able to cope with.'

Sugar-coating and lip service! Where's the lightbulb moment, that nugget of pure gold that will make me sit up and realise counselling is, at last, helping me to turn a corner?

'How are you getting on with that side of life?' the therapist gently probes.

'I've continued with the book club. I figure that as I no longer travel anywhere, I might as well armchair travel instead.' She gives a wry laugh. 'I read so much that I've become the person other members turn to when they want suggestions for the next novel.'

Sarah smiles. 'That's good, Ellinor; both the armchair travel and becoming a figure of authority.'

'Oh, I'm not interested in becoming a figure of authority,' Ellinor says, rather more vehemently than she means to. She shifts uneasily in her seat.

'But it's good to have a purpose, don't you think?' the therapist says, inclining her head and surveying her client.

Ellinor gazes through the shutters again. The vapour trail has almost disappeared, leaving only a vague, fractured impression across the pale blue sky.

'Yes, it's good,' she responds in a flat voice.

'I hear a *but*,' Sarah says.

Ellinor turns back to the woman. 'It's not the purpose I thought I'd have. It doesn't compare to travelling the world, however thrilling a book may be. I loved my job, before . . .' Her voice peters away.

As the psychotherapist's pen scribbles furiously across the page, Ellinor considers what earth-shattering revelations are being recorded under her name.

Eventually, the woman's hand stills. 'I don't want to put you under any pressure, but do you feel ready to return to work?'

Do I?

Ellinor shifts in her seat again. The thought of being trapped on a plane with God-knows-who on board fills her with dread, but she hates not working. She has to have *something* to call her own. A vision of the deranged man fills her head, and instantly her fingers fly to the prominent ridge of skin on her neck. As if it's happening again, she feels the sharp edge of cold steel pressed to her throat and a shudder runs through her body.

'I . . . I thought I was,' she stammers, 'but now I'm not so sure.'

As the therapist patiently waits for Ellinor to expand on this revelation, only the distant sound of passing traffic penetrates the deep quiet in the room.

Eventually, Ellinor breaks the silence. 'I went to the leisure centre the other day with my sister and her baby. I sat in the café and watched them in the pool.'

She glances at Sarah. If she tells her what happened, the incident will be recorded in that notebook and her recovery may be considered even further down the line. But she shouldn't keep it to herself, should she? After all, that's what this woman is being paid for . . . to help her recover.

'That's nice,' the woman says, giving her an encouraging smile.

Ellinor gazes down at her hands. She's surprised to see them shaking and quickly she clasps them together. 'It was . . .' she looks up, '. . . but there was a situation.'

Sarah's expression doesn't alter. 'What sort of situation?'

Taking a deep breath, Ellinor explains about the stranger and the hot coffee.

'And what do you make of your reaction?'

Ellinor gives a derisive snort. 'I thought that's why I came here . . . for you to provide that!'

If the therapist is taken aback by her client's response, she makes no sign of it. Without missing a beat, she says smoothly, 'Of course, but you can make your own evaluations, Ellinor.'

Ellinor frowns. 'Sorry. I don't mean to be rude. I'm just out of sorts. What I assess from my reaction is that I'm not ready to return to flight-attendant duties. I would be a nightmare to work with, especially if I had a pot of hot coffee in my hands!' She laughs at her small joke, but Sarah doesn't join in.

'Do you think your reaction was shock at uninvited, physical contact?'

Ellinor considers the question. 'Yes . . . and no. Sure, the hand on my shoulder was unexpected and a shock, but when I looked at the man I saw that monster on the plane.' She shudders again at the memory. 'The stranger's face became my attacker's! It took a while for me to realise it wasn't him.'

The therapist writes several lengthy paragraphs before looking up with a smile. 'You're doing so well.'

Ellinor pulls a face.

'You are, Ellinor. There are bound to be glitches in your recovery, but little by little you are getting there.' Sarah uncrosses her slender legs. Placing her ankles neatly together, she sits forward in her seat. 'If you introduce further outings into your days, the anxiety and fear you experience in public will dissipate. I'm not suggesting stressful events, just something that requires a little more engagement from you.'

'Well,' Ellinor says with narrowed eyes, 'Simon and I are going to Cornwall at the weekend to stay with my cousin and his wife, so I guess I'll have to *engage* during my time with them.'

She shakes her head, embarrassed at her mocking tone. Why is she being so tricky with this woman? She's only trying to help.

The therapist doesn't react, and her countenance remains perfectly pleasant. 'That's good, Ellinor. Baby steps are what we are after.' Glancing at her watch, she closes the notebook. 'We've covered quite some ground this morning and I think that's enough for today.' Elegantly, she rises from her chair. 'Enjoy the weekend away with your husband and I look forward to seeing you again in two weeks.'

Five

Simon glances over at his wife in the passenger seat. Her head rests against the window and her eyes are closed. 'Almost there,' he says softly.

Ellinor's eyes snap open and she straightens up. 'That's strange, I must have fallen asleep.'

'You dropped off around Honiton.'

She stares at him incredulously. 'But I never sleep during the day. In fact, I *never* sleep!'

'Perhaps coming away for the weekend is a good idea and you're beginning to relax.'

She gives a brief smile.

'Here we go,' Simon says in a jovial voice. 'Hello, Cornwall!'

Peering through the windscreen at the fast-approaching suspension bridge, Ellinor reads aloud the plaque displayed between two towering concrete pillars. *Tamar Bridge, 1961.*

'And that,' Simon says, indicating a second bridge running parallel, 'is Isambard Kingdom Brunel's railway bridge, built in 1856.'

'Goodness. So many years before people could cross the river by car,' Ellinor remarks. 'Where's the next crossing point?'

Simon purses his lips in consideration. 'Much further upriver, I think. Probably the road from Tavistock.'

Ellinor looks beyond her husband at the wide expanse of river disappearing into the distance. Neatly moored sailing boats dot the Cornish side, and on the Devon bank, a couple of large cranes sit on a pontoon with three barges moored alongside.

'I wonder if Ian and Pippa have a boat,' she ponders.

'I'm not sure they have the time to mess about on the water,' Simon says. 'When I spoke to Ian, he said they're committed to long hours building the business.'

'I suppose that's because it's just the two of them doing it,' Ellinor comments.

She watches a motorboat make its way upriver, its wake leaving a clean, white scar on the grey water.

'A large undertaking that's for sure,' Simon agrees, 'but as it's their passion it probably doesn't feel like it.'

'Ah, yes . . . passion,' she murmurs wistfully.

Simon glances at his wife. Reaching out, he places a hand lightly on her thigh and gives it a gentle squeeze.

Ellinor freezes.

'Don't worry, darling. Your passion for travel will return. I know it will. When you set your mind to something, you always pull through.'

Feeling guilty at her reaction to his touch, briefly she covers his hand with hers.

'Thanks, Simon.'

But *will* her passion return? Will she want to fly again? And will she ever respond naturally to her husband without always having to steel herself? It's hardly conducive to making a baby if she never allows him anywhere near her. That dream seems further away than ever. She concentrates on the river. It's a slow-moving beast that opens out broadly, bordered on both sides by neatly hedged fields reaching down to the water's edge, and in the near distance it appears to split.

Ellinor glances back at the road. One westbound lane of the bridge is closed and the traffic moves at a politely sedate pace.

'What's that?' she asks, pointing to an eye-catching sculpture rising above the treeline.

'Looks like a modern take on a Celtic cross to me,' says Simon, glancing out of the window.

Set back from the road, a tall column of verdigris blocks reaches skywards. On the top is a spiked circular design interspersed with gold, giving the impression of a starburst or the rays of the sun.

'I like it,' she says quietly. 'It's vibrant and welcoming.'

He smiles. 'No doubt Ian and Pippa will be able to educate us about it.'

Having crossed the river, the road now leads into a tunnel excavated out of the hillside, but before the car disappears into the subterranean highway, Ellinor glances up at a row of houses straddling the ridge. She raises her eyebrows, thinking how odd it must be to live somewhere, knowing that beneath the foundations of your property is a man-made tunnel for traffic. Several minutes later, they emerge back into daylight again and soon the outskirts of Saltash are left behind. Continuing for a short distance along the tree-lined dual carriageway, Simon indicates right at the next roundabout and turns the car in a northerly direction.

'Just a few miles further,' he says, glancing at the satnav.

Settling back in her seat, Ellinor watches the countryside whizz by. Neat, green fields border each side of the road, but it's the stunning views that are so mesmerising. In the distance, beneath rolling clouds sweeping across a vast sky, are the bruised violet tors of Dartmoor.

Space to breathe . . .

Involuntarily, she takes a deep breath, unclenching her jaw, and instantly the tension lifts. She hadn't realised how uptight she was, but all at once she's aware of a welcome easing of knotted muscles. As Ellinor rotates her shoulders, out of the corner of her eye she notices Simon smile.

Soon they pass through a couple of hamlets where charming, traditional stone cottages jostle cheek by jowl with their more contemporary counterparts.

'I suppose infill happens everywhere,' Ellinor remarks.

'Progress,' Simon mutters, indicating right and turning onto a country lane.

As they head deeper into the Cornish countryside, the sun

breaks through the clouds and large brushstrokes of blue daub the previously sombre-coloured canvas.

Ellinor checks her phone. 'Ian says we should follow signs for Cotehele National Trust but take the turning before its entrance. Their farm is half a mile further on, on the left.'

Glancing up, she takes in the high hedges enclosing the lane. Stunted, lone trees lean at alarming angles in the hedgerows, and field gate entrances allow glimpses of sweeping farmland stretching away across a lush valley to a slice of river estuary, glinting silver in the sun. It's a vastly different landscape to the one she's used to in the Home Counties.

'Interesting mix of properties down here,' Simon observes, as they pass by a large, modern bungalow with accompanying cattle sheds, polytunnels and greenhouses that give away its function as a working farm.

Coming into view on the opposite side of the road are a pair of executive homes built of local stone, mirroring each other. Attractive dormer windows break up extensive rooflines, and herringbone driveways lead to smart entrance porches flanked by arches that support stylish glazed steel balconies.

'The architect had fun here,' Ellinor says. 'Those houses wouldn't look out of place on our estate.'

Suddenly the satnav springs into life, and the disembodied woman's voice directs Simon to take a turning on the left. A line of grass grows freely down the centre of a lane bordered by the obligatory high hedges, and a few hundred yards further on Simon slows the car at a closed five-bar gate, on which a sign announces Comfort Wood Farm.

Ellinor climbs out of the car. Opening the gate, she holds it back against the hedge and gazes up at puffy white clouds. As she draws the clean Cornish air deep into her lungs, a suggestion of something stirs in her soul. Perhaps it *is* time to shake things up and venture forth once more, and as she climbs back into the car she tells herself to be brave this weekend.

Simon drives the Audi carefully along the farm track, avoiding the deeper holes pitting its uneven surface, and comments, 'These could do with filling in.'

Suddenly, they round a corner and find themselves face to face with a mellow-coloured ancient farmhouse sitting comfortably in its surroundings. Tall, substantial chimneys rise from the extensive slate rooflines of varying levels, and a range of old farm buildings create a courtyard.

Ellinor stares through the windscreen. 'How old did Ian say the house is?'

Simon pulls on the handbrake. 'Fifteenth century, I think.'

All at once the front door flies open and a couple of black-and-white spaniels spill out onto the gravelled forecourt, their tails wagging enthusiastically. In their wake is a tall, slim woman wearing dungarees. She has an open face and a wide, friendly smile, and her mass of wild, curly brown hair is haphazardly contained by a scarf casually wrapped around her head.

Striding towards the car, she throws open her arms and says in a confident voice, 'Simon, Ellinor. Welcome!'

Six

As soon as Ellinor gets out of the car she is enveloped in a warm hug.

'It's so good to see you. It's been *waaay* too long!'

'Hello, Pippa,' Ellinor says, reminding herself to breathe slowly and not overreact at the sudden onslaught.

The woman holds her at arm's length and scrutinises her. 'You're looking well.'

Ellinor pulls a face. 'Getting there . . .'

Pippa's smile is empathetic. 'Good girl.' She turns her attention to Simon and pulls him into a friendly embrace. 'Simon, great to see you again. How was the journey?'

'The traffic wasn't too bad,' he says, returning the hug. 'The only hold-up was around Stonehenge.'

'Rubberneckers! They can't resist it when those standing stones come into view. And little wonder – it's such a spectacular sight.' Pippa links arms with Ellinor and Simon. 'You've arrived just in time for tea, but please excuse the state of the old pile. The builders are in and we're in chaos! We're having a few outhouses knocked together into what will become a letting annexe, but I'm not sure when it'll be ready to market. You know how it is . . . money dictates.'

Simon nods in understanding.

Stirred by their mistress's animated voice and the arrival of the newcomers, the dogs bark and run around as Pippa guides her guests across the stone driveway towards the farmhouse. As they enter the hallway, even though it's mid-afternoon, Ellinor notices how still and dark it is inside, and she glances back through the open front door at the bright, sunny courtyard.

'Come on in,' Pippa says, following the dogs through an open doorway. 'Simon, you may have to duck,' she warns.

He does.

Ellinor gazes around the entrance hall and immediately picks up on a timeless atmosphere as she regards the large slate flagstones on the floor, the exposed wall timbers and the substantial oak beams spanning a low ceiling. On a mahogany side table sits an arrangement of colourful cut flowers in a pottery jug, and dust motes quiver in shafts of sunlight that have found entry through a mullioned window at the far end. She follows Pippa and Simon into a dining room, in time to see the dogs scampering across the slate floor and disappearing through a doorway on the far side. A long oak refectory table has been laid for tea, and it seems to Ellinor that a thick, watchful haze lingers in the air.

'Ian, love,' Pippa calls out. 'Simon and Elli have arrived.' She turns to her guests. 'Take a seat, although perhaps you'd like to freshen up first? There's a cloakroom off the hall.'

Simon declines, while Ellinor retraces her steps. Once again she's surprised by how dark the entrance hall is, even though the front door stands open and the sun shines brightly in the yard. The air in here is heavy with something that she can't describe, as if the shadows toy with her. Frowning, she makes her way to the cloakroom, and by the time she comes back to the dining room, Ian has joined Pippa and Simon at the table. Immediately, her cousin springs to his feet and gives her a hug.

'So good to see you, Elli.'

'And you,' she replies, giving him a squeeze.

'I'm afraid our hospitality is a bit rough and ready these days,' Pippa says, pouring tea through a strainer into cups from a teapot attractively decorated with blue dancing hares. 'I have managed to maintain some standards, however, and I positively refuse to resort to dunking teabags!' She lets out a good-natured laugh.

Ellinor smiles and pulls out a chair next to Simon.

'Help yourselves to cake and biscuits,' Ian says.

'Homemade cherry cake,' Pippa adds. 'Sadly, not mine. I just don't have the time. It's one of Mrs Trewithen's, from the local farmers' market. She certainly knows how to bake.'

Easy conversation encircles the table. It's always been this way, from the moment Ian had first introduced Pippa to Ellinor and Simon. His girlfriend – now wife – had seamlessly slipped into their style of companionship, as if she'd always been there.

'What we thought we'd do this weekend,' Ian announces, as he helps himself to a slice of cake, 'is have an early supper at home tonight so that you can relax after your journey, and then tomorrow we'd like to show you over the farm. We have great plans for taking the orchards forward, and I'd like to discuss the marketing angle with you, Simon, if you don't mind. But I don't want it to be a busman's holiday, so tell me if you'd rather not.'

'Don't worry about that, Ian,' Simon says with an easy smile. 'I'm only too happy to discuss future developments and offer any advice that may be helpful.'

Ian gives a nod. 'Thanks. We're really excited by our vision of what lies ahead for the farm.'

'And if you like,' Pippa interjects, 'we can visit Cotehele on Sunday morning. It's a pleasant walk over the fields from here and the views down to the river are quite spectacular. You are National Trust members, aren't you?'

'Yes,' says Ellinor.

'Good. We've been over the property several times since first moving here and we notice something different each time.' Reaching for a biscuit, Pippa adds, 'It has a superb collection of textiles, armour and furniture.'

'Sounds interesting,' Simon comments.

'It is,' Pippa enthuses. 'It's a Grade I medieval house with Tudor additions, and the gardens and grounds are beautiful. There's a stone dovecote in a remarkable state of preservation, and a quay and a working mill, which are both equally intriguing.'

Suddenly one of the dogs gives a sharp bark from the outer room, and both Simon and Ellinor glance towards the door.

'Don't worry,' Pippa reassures. 'That's probably just one of the builders entering the kitchen.'

The next minute a large figure looms in the doorway, and Ellinor's eyes open wide in terror. Her hand flies to her throat, and as her heart rate rockets, her breathing becomes laboured and beads of perspiration prick her forehead. Hurriedly getting to her feet, she sends the chair crashing over backwards onto the floor as startled faces turn to her.

Standing in the doorway, blocking out the light from the kitchen, is her assailant. As the man leers at her, she observes the knife in his hand, its blade glinting in a shaft of sunlight penetrating through a diamond-paned window into the room's dark interior. A strangled cry escapes from her throat and she backs away, never once taking her eyes from the man's face.

In an instant Simon is on his feet. 'Elli?'

He moves towards her, his arm outstretched, but she bats him away.

'It's only Jake, our builder,' Pippa says in concern.

Ellinor's heart hammers furiously against her ribcage, as Simon takes another tentative step towards his wife.

'Don't,' she growls, hating that she's the cause of his look of hurt and confusion.

Wild-eyed, she stares at the large man. Her dramatic outburst has made him take a step back inside the kitchen, and now that she looks at him properly she realises her mistake. This man has red hair, whereas her assailant was fair-haired, and the knife in his hand is no more than a screwdriver. Relief floods through her as her legs suddenly give way. Immediately Simon is at her side and he manages to hold on to her as she collapses to the floor.

'Oh, my God,' Ellinor groans, holding her head in her hands. 'I thought he was that man on the plane!'

Sitting down beside her on the cold flagstone floor, Simon draws her to him. 'It's OK, Elli. He's not here,' he says soothingly. 'It's only the builder. You've probably shocked him more than he has you.'

Ellinor's body shakes uncontrollably, and tears begin to flow.

'Here you go.' Ian holds out a glass of water to his cousin and glances inquisitively at Simon.

When Ellinor doesn't respond, Simon takes the glass from him and mouths, 'Later.'

'I'm so sorry,' Ellinor says, gaining some composure. 'You must all think I'm nuts.'

'No,' Ian says quietly. 'You've been through a very difficult experience. None of us can imagine what it must have been like.'

She looks up at her cousin's concerned face. 'You're very understanding,' she mumbles in embarrassment. Taking the glass from her husband, she sips the water.

'Do you think you can get to your feet?' Simon asks.

'I think so.'

Supporting herself on his arms, she allows him to lift her up from the floor.

'Would you like to rest in your room for a while?' Ian suggests.

She nods.

'I'll show you up, then,' he says.

'I'll grab the bags from the car and follow you,' Simon announces.

Ellinor turns back to the man now standing well back from the kitchen doorway with an awkward, bewildered look clouding his face.

'I'm so sorry,' she says in a small voice.

He grimaces. 'I didn't mean to frighten you.' Then, as if to make light of what has just occurred, he adds, 'I usually have a more positive effect on the ladies.'

Ellinor smiles weakly and follows Ian and Simon out of the room.

Seven

Later, after sharing a companionable supper with Pippa and Ian, during which there are no further unexpected incidents, Ellinor and Simon bid their hosts goodnight and make their way up to the guest room. It's a comfortable space that hints at the age of the farmhouse, with its intriguingly differing ceiling heights and exposed timbers that criss-cross the walls.

'Must remember to watch out for low flying trees,' Simon says, ducking under a substantial ceiling beam.

Ellinor smiles. Removing her jewellery, she lays it on top of an oak chest of drawers.

'Just listen to that,' her husband continues, as he stands at the open window and gazes out into the courtyard. 'Not a sound.'

'It's so peaceful,' Ellinor says, crossing over to the bed. 'Even when it's quiet back home there's always a distant hum of traffic from the A3.' She slips beneath a generously plump duvet.

Simon half turns to his wife. 'Hopefully you'll have a good night's sleep here.'

She sighs. 'That would be nice.'

Taking hold of the curtains, Simon starts to close them.

'Leave them ajar a bit, Si. I'd like to feel the breeze.'

Quickly undressing, he climbs into bed beside her and propping himself on one elbow, looks inquisitively at his wife. 'Are you feeling OK now?'

She'd rather not be reminded of the earlier, embarrassing incident with the builder, but reluctantly she responds. 'Yes. It was a shock, that's all. I wasn't expecting anyone else to be here, apart from Ian and Pippa.'

Simon frowns.

'Don't worry.' She gives him a smile. 'Baby steps, the therapist says.'

He nods and leans in to kiss her, but she averts her face. 'Sorry,' she mumbles.

Simon swallows the sigh forming in his throat. 'No, I'm sorry.' Rolling away, he reaches for the switch on the bedside lamp. 'Sleep well, Elli.'

Ellinor chews her lip and stares into the darkness. She knows she should reach out and offer her husband some reassurance that intimacy will return to their relationship, but it feels a Herculean effort and she hasn't got the energy. Just sharing the same bed with him is hard enough. She watches shadows play across the different ceiling levels and listens to the sounds of the Cornish countryside settling in for the night, and it's not long before she hears Simon's breathing deepen. As gentle snoring emanates from his side of the bed, Ellinor expels a long, silent breath and turns to gaze at her husband's strong profile. He doesn't deserve this aloofness from her. Although she's explained the fear and terror that has taken up residence in her mind, she's not sure he fully understands. How could he? Unless he's been through the horrifying experience himself, how could he possibly know what it was like to be in her shoes? Leaning towards him, she runs an affectionate finger down the side of his cheek before turning away.

As the night closes in, cloaking this peaceful pocket of south-east Cornwall in a blanket of tranquillity and silence, moonbeams enter through the large gap in the curtains and spill their soft silvery light across the floor. Ellinor wonders if she'll get any sleep, but before long her eyelids droop. In the near distance, a barn owl softly hoots. Unseen by the slumbering occupants of the farmhouse, it alights from a nearby farm building and swoops across the courtyard on silent wings in search of prey. Ellinor stirs. Mumbling something, she shifts position and drifts into welcoming deep sleep.

The next thing she's aware of is a hand gently shaking her shoulder.

'Morning, beautiful.'

Ellinor prises open one eye and sees Simon smiling down at her. She stretches, luxuriating in the cosy softness of the bed. 'What time is it?'

'Early. Seven thirty. I've brought you tea.'

She draws herself up into a sitting position and takes the cup from him. 'Are Ian and Pippa awake?'

'Yes. Pippa's making breakfast, but she says you needn't hurry and to come down when you're ready.'

Ellinor gazes towards the window where pale gold shafts of sunlight now stream through the gap in the curtains.

'Looks like it's going to be a good day,' she comments.

'Ian wants to show me over the farm after breakfast,' Simon says.

'I'll come with you,' Ellinor says, blowing on the surface of her tea. 'I could do with the exercise.'

His tender gaze rests on her face. 'You look so much better this morning.'

'I suppose that's a compliment,' she says, giving him a lopsided grin. Suddenly her eyes open wide, and she straightens up. 'Simon . . . I slept well! Can you believe it?'

He smiles. 'As I said, maybe coming away was a good idea.'

Rejoicing in the realisation that she's had a good night's sleep for the first time since *the incident*, Ellinor leans back against the oak headrest and smiles broadly at her husband.

'Si,' she says, holding out her hand to him. 'I know things are odd between us just now, and I'm so sorry.'

Sadness clouds his eyes.

'I don't understand it,' she continues, 'but all will be well in time. I promise.'

Taking hold of her hand, Simon squeezes her fingers. 'Take as long as you need, Elli. I'll be here, waiting.'

'Thank you,' she whispers.

But as he leans in to drop a kiss on her forehead, Ellinor's jaw tightens, and once again she wills herself not to flinch.

'Let's just relax and enjoy the weekend,' Simon suggests. 'It'll be good to immerse ourselves in Ian and Pippa's new lifestyle. You never know, maybe some of their enthusiasm will rub off on us.'

Eight

The fields beyond the farmhouse sweep down the valley in a series of paddocks bounded by Cornish stonewalls and natural hedges. To Ellinor, the sky feels huge. She, Simon and Ian stand at the top of a sloping, south-facing field with panoramic views towards Plymouth and the sea; and in the near distance, the silver river languidly snakes its way through the landscape towards the ocean.

'As you can see,' Ian says, motioning towards a large, neighbouring field on the other side of a stone hedge, 'there are varying stages of planting. The fruit trees in Penrose Orchard were planted several years ago by the previous owner and they provide our commercial fruiting crops. This traditional orchard' – he indicates the smaller trees in the immediate paddock – 'is our latest project.'

'What's the difference between traditional and commercial?' Ellinor asks.

'Traditional orchards are far better for wildlife,' Ian explains. 'We don't need this one to produce large quantities of fruit to sell so we've planted the trees further apart, which allows wildflowers to grow, thereby encouraging pollinators to pollinate the blossom.'

'Clever,' Ellinor remarks, as she eyes a dozen russet-coloured chickens scratching beneath the immature boughs.

'We're focusing on old Tamar Valley varieties,' Ian continues, 'such as Pig's Snout, Colloggett Pippin and Slack-ma-Girdle. However, each tree is precious because it provides a home for birds, bees, butterflies and insects. We've already seen lesser spotted woodpeckers, bats and mistletoe moths.'

'Biodiversity . . .' Simon comments.

'Exactly,' Ian says enthusiastically. 'Worryingly, these creatures are in sharp decline. Did you know that due to changes in agricultural practices and pressures from development, orchard numbers have fallen by sixty-three per cent since the 1950s?'

Simon and Ellinor shake their heads.

'Both Pippa and I agree to make it our life's purpose to preserve and protect this rare and valuable habitat and encourage the wildlife that depends on it. We want to build on the wonderful diversity of life found here, and there's an amazing number of apples and other varieties of traditional fruit that we can plant, like cherries and plums.'

Ellinor glances at her cousin. It's been a long time since she's heard him sound so enthusiastic and fired up.

Ian grins at her. 'Bet you don't recognise this former computer programmer.'

She smiles.

'Moving here has given us a new lease of life. I can't deny that it's hard work establishing the business, but neither Pippa nor I would go back to our previous existence.'

'It's wonderful seeing you so committed to something,' Ellinor remarks.

He laughs. 'I tell you, Elli, I may not look it, but I feel ten years younger! I'd forgotten what it was like to be passionate about something.'

His words hit home. When had she last been passionate about something? Travelling the world used to tick that box . . . to a degree.

'So, what are your plans?' Simon asks, as they wander through the orchard.

'Well, we have several . . . and they're fairly ambitious . . . but the most pressing one is to upgrade the apple-pressing facility. Old man Penrose – the previous owner – was born in the farmhouse and he inherited the farm from his father. He diversified away from keeping a herd of cows and milk production and established the old orchard. He planted the first apple trees about twenty-five years ago.'

'Is that why it's called Penrose Orchard?' Ellinor asks.

Ian smiles. 'It wasn't called that when we bought the farm. We called it that, as a nod to the old boy.'

'That's nice,' says Simon. 'Does *old man Penrose* know he has an orchard named after him?'

'We did tell him, but he has dementia, and I don't know how much he retains. That's why he had to sell the farm, so he could live in a care home near his daughter in North Devon.'

Having reached a five-bar wooden gate on the opposite side of the orchard, they turn to look back up the sloping land. Suddenly, loud squawking erupts, and the chickens scatter as two farm cats stealthily appear in their midst.

'Giles and Agatha,' Ian comments with a grin.

Ellinor gives him a quizzical look. 'Would that be a reference to Farmer Giles?'

Ian chuckles. 'And his wife! You know how mad Pippa is for all things Tolkien.'

They watch as the cats swagger through the group of chickens, which indignantly regroup and resume their scratching amongst the grass at the base of the trees.

Turning to gaze at the pastoral scene with its glittering river, Ellinor takes a deep breath of the pollution-free spring air. To her left, a large swathe of woodland extends across the hillside and beyond that, on the opposite side of the valley, rise the majestic tors of Dartmoor. As she allows the view to absorb deep into her being, she has only half an ear to Ian and Simon's discussion about the farm business.

'We need to inject more capital into the commercial side,' Ian says, 'and I've been looking at loans, although I'm reluctant to add yet another burden to our ever-growing list of financial commitments. However, needs must. We all know one has to speculate to accumulate and we want to upgrade the apple press. I'll show it to you later. It's located in the barn next to the farmhouse.'

'Is there any other way you can raise immediate capital?' Simon asks.

'As you know,' Ian replies, 'Jake's currently remodelling the old dairy and a couple of small outhouses into a holiday let, but I doubt it will bring in an income much before late summer at the earliest.' Plucking a long blade of grass from the base of the stone wall, he weaves it through his fingers. 'We plan to offer an apple-crushing and bottling service in the autumn when the public can bring us their windfalls or purchase our own apple juice. We're also considering the idea of having open days so that people can come and relax in these gorgeous surroundings and picnic in the orchards. We may even provide picnic baskets ourselves, full of delicious, locally sourced food, or possibly hold barbeque days. Pippa's also keen to set up a farm shop. We're well placed for these sorts of enterprises, what with having Cotehele as an immediate neighbour and having high numbers of visitors consistently passing the end of the lane. With clever marketing we could tap in to that.'

Simon nods. 'I can help there.'

'I hoped you'd say that!' Ian says gratefully. 'But none of this is an immediate fix.' His eyebrows knit together. 'That's why I'm considering loans, although, as I said, I hesitate to go down that path.'

'I'll put my thinking cap on,' Simon promises, taking a step towards his wife. 'Enjoying yourself, Elli?'

She turns to him with a smile. 'It's so peaceful and beautiful here. I'm sure it's just what the therapist would have ordered.'

He smiles at her with affection.

'Ian, what's that over there?' Ellinor asks, pointing to an area of woodland away to the east.

Ian's eyes follow the line of her finger. 'Do you mean the stone chimney poking out above the trees?'

'Yes.'

'It's an old, dilapidated cottage on the edge of our land. Barely more than walls now.'

'It's well hidden,' she says.

'It is. You don't know it's there until you suddenly come upon it, and not many people know it exists. It's only visible now from up here because a large tree came down recently.' He turns to her. 'If you like, on our way to Cotehele tomorrow we can visit it.'

'I'd like that,' Ellinor replies.

'We applied for planning permission on it a few months back. Happily, there were no objections, and it was granted. But as far as developing it . . . that's for a time in the future when we've got some capital.' Ian turns to Simon and Ellinor. 'Come on. Let me show you the beating heart of the business – the apple press.'

Nine

Soon after breakfast the following day, they set out across the fields towards Cotehele House, and although dogs are welcome in the estate grounds, Pippa decides to leave the spaniels at home as she wants to show her guests around the main house. She asks Jake to keep an eye on them.

'No problem,' he says in his broad Cornish accent. 'The doggies are no trouble and as long as I make a fuss of them whenever I enter the house, they're happy to stay in the kitchen.'

It's another clear spring day and the mist that hung low earlier over the river has now cleared, leaving an unencumbered view of the peaceful landscape. As Simon and Ian fall behind, engrossed in discussing marketing ideas for the farm, Ellinor keeps pace with Pippa's longer stride. Coming into view in the middle of an adjacent field is an unusual three-sided, castellated stone structure.

'What's that?' she asks.

'The Prospect Tower,' Pippa says. 'A fairy-tale building, don't you think? It's easy to imagine Rapunzel singing from an upper room while dangling her long plait out of the window to attract the attention of her prince.'

Ellinor laughs. 'Your imagination is something else! But I agree . . . It's easy to visualise. But what's its purpose?'

'It's a folly, built in the mid-eighteenth century,' Pippa replies. 'Possibly it was built as an eye-catching landmark or a signalling tower, if the need arose, although it has been suggested it was erected to commemorate the visit of George III to Cotehele in 1789.'

'Folly or not, it's an intriguing building,' Ellinor observes. 'Is it on your farm?'

'No. That land belongs to the Cotehele Estate. We won't climb the tower today as there's so much to pack in, but the view from the top makes the effort worthwhile. The panoramic vista over the Tamar Valley is quite heart-stopping, and the view of the Calstock Viaduct is a photo opportunity not to be missed.'

'We will just have to come back,' Ellinor says with conviction.

'Do,' Pippa responds heartily. 'At the first opportunity. You know you're always welcome here, Elli. In fact, if you haven't got anything pressing to return to and you don't mind Jake being around, you could always stay on . . . for as long as you like.'

Taken aback at the generosity of her cousin's wife, Ellinor feels a lump form in her throat. Visiting someone for a weekend is very different to staying for an extended length of time.

'That's very kind of you, Pippa.'

'Not kind! It's great having you around.' Pippa looks over her shoulder at the men still deep in conversation. 'And it's good for Ian to have someone other than me to talk to about his visions for the farm.'

Ellinor glances back at her husband. He seems different somehow, as if some of Ian's enthusiasm has transferred itself onto him. Perhaps this short break is doing them both good and will ease the unspoken tension between them.

'Come on, let's continue on and leave the boys to their money-making schemes,' Pippa says, linking arms with Ellinor.

Turning away, they walk down the hill and across the sloping field towards the trees on the far boundary.

'This is a magical wood,' Pippa says in a stage whisper.

Ellinor raises an eyebrow.

'It is,' Pippa asserts. 'You'll see! Follow me.'

Unlinking her arm, Pippa climbs over a stile. Ellinor follows and finds herself on a path running parallel to the woodland, its verges full of primroses, celandine and daffodils.

'This footpath connects with the tracks around Cotehele,' Pippa explains, 'but we're taking this route.'

As they enter the woodland and take a narrow path more accustomed to the paws and hooves of wild animals than the soles of walking boots, Ellinor is immediately aware of a deep, lingering stillness, and she has the strongest impression they're being observed. An ancient air pervades, and dappled light filtering through the freshly unfurling pale green buds of the tree canopy plays milky colours across the leaf litter on the forest floor. It's soft underfoot and as Ellinor follows Pippa, she glances around the mixed woodland covering the sloping valley – oaks and ash, sweet chestnut, sycamore and beech, with an understorey of hazel and holly. It seems to her that Pippa is right – it *is* a magical place! She can easily imagine little animals and mythical creatures peering out from behind the trunks of trees and through the foliage, quietly observing the intruders' progress through *their* wood. Neither woman speaks; each instinctively knows her voice would be unwelcome in this tranquil, undisturbed place.

Presently, they come to the edge of a clearing where the grass grows long and early wildflowers turn their faces up to the sun. In the centre of the hidden glade, bathed in shafts of sunlight, are the ruins of a small stone cottage. A largely intact chimney stack stands proudly at one end, but all the windows, doors and roof are long-gone, and only the front wall reaches, in part, to the first floor. Defiantly resisting the march of time, the cottage refuses to allow nature to wholly consume it, and as Ellinor gazes at its remains, it seems to her that they adamantly announce, 'I once stood here!'

You did, a soft voice says in her head.

'What?' Ellinor says out loud.

'Sorry, what was that?' Pippa asks, turning to her.

Ellinor shakes her head. 'Nothing of importance.'

A tingle tiptoes up her spine as the internal voice returns: *You know that's not true.*

She glances around, but other than Pippa there is no one else in the glade.

'What is this place?' she asks, taking a step towards the ruined building.

'This is the cottage you glimpsed yesterday,' Pippa replies. 'We don't know much about it. Until 1947, the Cotehele Estate owned our farmhouse and lands, and – as Ian said – these ruins sit at the periphery of our acreage. They were included in the deal when the Estate sold off the farm.'

Approaching the front wall, where young saplings and ivy have taken root in the crevices as nature does its best to cover the tracks of man, Ellinor runs her fingers over the smooth stonework. She wonders whose hands built these sturdy walls and who has occupied the cottage over the years. And when was it last inhabited? As she feels the warmth emanating from the stones, inexplicably she feels comforted, as if rediscovering a dear friend. One not seen for a very long time.

'Is it OK to enter?' she asks.

'Yes, although there's not much to see,' Pippa replies.

Ellinor approaches the entrance. The doorframe has all but rotted away, although two rusty hinges clinging to what remains, fly free, as if seeking the wooden door they once embraced. She steps over the threshold into the open space that had been someone's home and glances around at the ruined walls. The east and north elevations have mostly disappeared; a few large base stones remain in place. The only window openings are in the front wall – two on the ground floor, with corresponding impressions a few feet above – but there's nothing else of obvious interest, apart from the chimney breast with its open fireplace at the far end. Crossing over to it now, she gazes at the granite rubbing post that someone has inserted to act as a mantel and notices the markings inscribed into it. Momentarily, her hand hovers over them before her fingers track the various score marks and swirls.

'I've always thought they were rather unusual,' Pippa says, joining her.

'Do you know what they mean?'

'Not a clue. I think they're witch marks. You know, to ward off evil.'

Ellinor glances down at the twigs and leaves scattered in the hearth and notices amongst them the remains of a nest. Leaning forward, she peers up inside the chimney breast. It's obvious the cottage has been lived in at some point, as the stones are blackened from many fires. At the top she can see a square of daylight infiltrating the dark interior.

'It's sweet, isn't it?' Pippa says, moving away to the centre of the dirt floor open to the elements.

Ellinor withdraws her head and turns to Pippa. 'I bet it was cosy when the fire was lit. I imagine there were no more than two rooms on each floor.'

'If that! I expect it was originally a single-storey dwelling.'

'I wonder who lived here,' Ellinor quietly ponders.

Pippa pulls a vacant face. 'Maybe a farm or estate worker, or perhaps someone employed in the main house. Cotehele isn't far from here.'

'Do you know how recently it was inhabited?'

'No. As I said, we don't know much about it. There's a stream running at the back that feeds into the Tamar, but there's no electricity. I suppose whoever lived here used a generator. If we ever get around to developing it we may have to do the same, although I suppose we could install solar panels. The cost of connecting to the grid would be astronomical!'

A sudden movement at the entrance makes both women turn.

'Ah, there you are!' Ian exclaims, stepping into the ruins and closely followed by Simon. 'We wondered if you'd given up on us and continued on to the house.'

'No. Just waiting for you to catch up,' Pippa says with a grin.

As Simon looks around the space, Ellinor points out the markings on the mantelpiece. But with very little else to see, after a further ten minutes the party exits the cottage and makes its way towards a track on the far side of the clearing. However, Ellinor hangs back, oddly reluctant to leave, and something makes her turn. The silence is impenetrable – as if time is held in suspension – and she's certain she's being observed. The hairs on the back of her neck prick and a feeling of unease settles upon her. Cautiously she looks around.

'This way,' Pippa calls over from the edge of the trees.

Ellinor is about to follow the fast-disappearing figures, when an imperceptible movement amongst the trees on the edge of the clearing makes her pause and focus on an area of woodland to the right of the ruined cottage. She catches her breath, certain that two round amber eyes at approximately waist-height watch her through the dense foliage. What manner of beast is that? A deer? Suddenly, way off, she hears the hollow hoot of an owl calling for its mate. In an instant, the eyes disappear, but not before she catches sight of a long snout and a flash of shaggy grey hair, which leave only a tremble of foliage in their wake.

Do wolves roam freely in Cornwall? She's heard accounts of big-cat sightings on Dartmoor and Bodmin Moor.

'Elli, you'll get left behind,' Simon calls out, having backtracked to the clearing.

'Coming.'

Ellinor scrutinises the bushes one last time, but whatever was there has gone. Turning on her heels, she hurries to catch up with the rest of her group.

Ten

The friends follow a winding path through the ancient woodland with the stream chattering companionably alongside, tumbling unhurriedly around moss-covered boulders, as it makes its way to the river.

'This is the Danescombe Valley,' Pippa explains. 'It's full of reminders of its mining heritage. When you next pay us a visit it's worth visiting the ruins of the sawmill, and the papermill at the top of the valley.'

Elli turns to Simon with shining eyes. 'We must come back soon.'

'I agree,' he says enthusiastically. 'There's a lot to discover.'

She smiles with relief. For the first time since *the incident* she detects a relaxation in their responses to each other, as if a promise of their former relationship returns.

The track has turned to mud in places, and as Ellinor carefully picks her way around a particularly boggy area of ground she spies an old mine chimney visible through the treeline.

'It's not much further,' Pippa calls out from the front of the procession. She navigates a short, steep slope. 'If you take that path,' she says, indicating a fork to the left, 'it eventually leads to the quay where you get a good idea of the course of the river.'

'There's a tearoom on the quay,' Ian adds. 'It's a pleasant place to stop for a coffee and pasty, and there are also lime kilns and an interesting museum, plus a Victorian Tamar sailing barge is moored up – the *Shamrock*. The river is inter-tidal, and in the nineteenth century the quay would have been bustling with vessels loading and unloading cargo that was shipped to and from Plymouth, and small boats would have carried market-garden produce to sell at Devonport Market. But you'd have no idea of that today! It's a tranquil setting where people canoe, kayak and paddleboard from the slipway.'

'Has the area always been a paradise for market gardeners?' Ellinor asks.

'Yes. It was a day out for many,' Ian continues, 'and people travelled upriver in crowded paddle steamers to see the blossoming orchards. Also, during the Second World War, the Tamar Valley produced an enormous quantity of fruit and vegetables to help feed the nation. Growers were encouraged to *Dig for Victory*, and many acres of daffodil bulbs were dug up and replanted on banks and hedgerows, leaving the land free for the cultivation of food products.'

'So, when your old farmer planted that first orchard he was continuing an age-old tradition,' Simon comments.

'He was,' Ian responds. 'Although he was probably one of the first farmers to *diversify*. That's only become a thing in recent years . . . sadly out of necessity.'

As they follow the path through the trees, Pippa provides a running commentary. 'Did you know that Cotehele means wood-on-estuary? It derives from the old Cornish *cote* for "wood" and *hele* for "estuary". . . This path that we're on runs along the edge of a beautiful garden known as Valley Garden, which has charming terraces, a medieval stew pond and a dovecote.'

Glancing through the trees, Ellinor catches sight of swathes of lush foliage and splashes of colour, and it occurs to her that they are entering yet *another* magical, fairy tale world. As she walks along the pathway through exotic plantings she becomes aware of a presence in the air, and for the second time in less than an hour the hairs on the back of her neck tingle. Warily, she glances around. It's early in the season – the house only recently re-opening to the public – and there are very few visitors about. All is peaceful. Ellinor tells herself that there's nothing out of the ordinary to cause alarm, and to calm down.

Presently, they arrive at the courtyard in front of the Visitors Reception. As Ian holds open the door, Ellinor follows Pippa and Simon into the building.

'Age before beauty!' Ian says, giving her a wink.

'Pearls before swine,' she counters with a grin.

'Good morning. Have you visited Cotehele before?' an assistant asks, as they approach the reception desk to present their National Trust membership cards.

Ellinor shakes her head. 'We haven't, but my cousin and his wife live locally and they have.' She indicates Ian and Pippa.

The woman smiles warmly. 'You've come at a good time for your first visit. The daffodils are glorious this year and I'm sure you'll enjoy looking around the house. Cotehele was the ancestral home of the Edgcumbes and it remained in the family for nearly six-hundred years.'

'A cherished home,' comments Simon.

'Actually, no,' the woman corrects him. 'The Edgcumbes preserved Cotehele as a historic talking point rather than a comfortable family home, but I'll let my colleagues in the house tell you all about that. Would you like a guidebook?'

Ellinor purchases one and follows the rest of her party towards a door at the far end of the reception area. As she steps out onto a gravelled pathway, her face breaks into a broad smile. Swathes of yellow daffodils nod at her in welcome.

'It's quite a sight, isn't it?' Pippa says, turning to her.

'Yes. They seem so happy and uplifting!' Ellinor responds with a chuckle.

'I like that.' Pippa smiles. 'Happy daffs!'

Ellinor turns towards a handsome, castellated gatehouse tower with attractive granite and slate-stone buildings extending on either side. Two tall chimneys rise from a low roofline, and dormer windows break up the catslide roof of an adjacent charming cottage. The property sits well in its setting, and the rambling buildings give the impression of it materialising out of the mists of legend. Ellinor glances around, wondering what else will further this notion.

Having gone on ahead, Ian and Simon reach the tower's granite mullioned archway that leads to the inner courtyard of Cotehele House. Before entering, they turn to check on their wives' progress. Ellinor and Pippa are not far behind and they follow the men through the tunnelled archway, feeling the small cobblestones beneath the soles of their walking shoes. Suddenly, Ellinor draws in a sharp breath. Laid out before her is a perfect quadrangle of attractive low buildings adorned with numerous diamond-paned mullioned windows.

'This is perfection.' She breathes out softly.

Pippa looks across at her and smiles. 'I rather agree with you.'

'It's not at all austere. In fact, I could imagine living here.'

Pippa's smile broadens. 'It does have that air about it.'

Ellinor gazes around in wonder. The property seems familiar, as if she knows its hidden nooks and crannies, and yet she's never visited before. She'd expected an inanimate building, austere and remote, but this feels homely, and she hadn't thought it would evoke such strong emotions. She shakes her head.

Ellinor and Pippa continue across the courtyard towards an open door, where a petite older woman wearing a fleece jacket displaying the Cotehele logo greets them.

'Hello,' Pippa responds.

Ellinor smiles politely.

'Do you know the history of Cotehele?' the room guide enquires.

'No,' Ellinor says.

'Cotehele was built by the Edgcumbe family, and from 1353 it became their ancestral home,' the woman informs her audience. 'Sir Richard Edgcumbe started remodelling the original thirteenth-century property in 1485, with later works carried out by his son, Piers. For nearly six centuries it remained in the family's ownership until Kenelm, the sixth Earl of Mount Edgcumbe, passed it to the National Trust in 1947.'

'Goodness, that's a long time,' observes Ellinor.

The woman's stature perceptibly grows, as if she had something to do with the longevity of the family's ownership.

'What a fascinating job you have, guiding people around,' Ellinor adds with a smile.

The room guide beams. 'Not only do we have original furniture and armour at Cotehele, but also remarkable tapestries.'

As the woman stands back from the doorway, Ellinor and Pippa enter the Great Tudor Hall. Inexplicably, nostalgia consumes Ellinor as she scans the room. Massive flagstones cover the floor, heraldic stained-glass panels adorn the windows, and suspended from the impressive and intricate timber-roof trusses are three brass chandeliers. Displayed on the lime-washed walls are numerous antlers and weaponry – amongst them, swords and shields, pikes, guns and pistols, body armour and helmets. And beneath them, with their backrests against the wall, are several ornately carved oak chairs.

Ellinor notices Simon and Ian examining a pair of long bones flanking a doorway at the far end of the hall.

'Impressive, aren't they?' the guide says, noting Ellinor's focus.

'What are they?' she asks.

'The jawbone of a whale, as they measure over two-and-a-half metres long.'

Ellinor raises her eyebrows.

'It's unusual to find one intact, and this is the only example in the National Trust's entire collection,' continues the woman. 'Until recently its origins were a mystery, but research and DNA testing have revealed it belonged to a common Rorqual whale that washed up at nearby Colona Beach in Mevagissey, in 1875. I believe it was recorded as eighteen metres long.'

'Goodness!' Ellinor exclaims.

'Shall we catch up with the boys?' Pippa suggests, motioning towards Ian and Simon, who are exiting the hall.

'Through there is the kitchen.' The room guide points after the disappearing men. 'And we currently have an exhibition about Henry Tudor's bid to overthrow Richard III, and Sir Richard Edgcumbe's support of the Buckingham Rebellion. His involvement caused quite a stir and put all at Cotehele in danger.'

Eleven

Pippa walks towards the door and follows Simon and Ian out of the Great Hall.

'Thank you for the interesting information,' Ellinor says to the assistant.

'That's what we're here for,' the woman replies with a polite smile.

Turning, Ellinor hurries to catch up with her party and enters a dimly lit passage. She's surprised not to see the others in the hallway and presumes they must have gone on ahead, eager to view the exhibition. Making her way carefully along the uneven flagstones, she observes the rough finish to the walls and the candle sconces that give off a flickering light. The National Trust has gone to great efforts to give visitors an immersive experience, she thinks. The smell of roasting pork wafts along the passageway, and on reaching an open door at the far end, Ellinor peers in.

Rustic wooden shelves line the walls, on which are displayed a variety of different-sized pewter plates, jugs and tankards, glazed terracotta pots, an old iron oil lamp, plus a number of implements she's unable to name. Bunches of drying herbs and flowers hang from hooks, and in the centre of the room is a large wooden table, around which four women of varying ages prepare food, their hair tucked neatly beneath white caps. Each wears an apron tied around the waist of a muted-coloured dress with a tightly laced bodice, over a long-sleeved, white cotton underdress. Behind them is an enormous blackened inglenook with a glowing fire in its hearth, above which several cast-iron kettles and pots are suspended on large hooks, and turning slowly on a spit is a whole pig. The air is hot and filled with delicious, mouth-watering scents, and although it's not long since breakfast, Ellinor's stomach rumbles.

All at once, a door on the far side of the kitchen opens a few inches and a man's voice carries on the air. The three younger women immediately turn and break into giggles, which quickly reduce to muffled whispers behind flour-covered hands as the older woman scolds them. Ellinor wonders if they're actors, although she hasn't noticed any posters mentioning theatre at Cotehele today, but has she unwittingly walked in on a dramatic one-act play that requires visitor participation? If so, should she comment on it? She shifts uncertainly. The movement causes the older woman to glance in her direction and a look of shock sweeps across her face as her eyes open wide. Taking a hurried step back, she mumbles something and makes the sign of the cross.

Ellinor frowns and glances over her shoulder, but she's alone. She turns back to the kitchen.

The door on the far side opens wider and suddenly Simon enters. Ellinor's jaw drops. What's he doing? Has her husband been cajoled into taking part in this cameo piece? If so, it's totally out of character!

Simon's dark hair falls freely onto his shoulders. It's obviously a wig, although it looks authentic. A tight crimson-velvet doublet with slits on the chest and sleeves, allowing him room to move and show off the fine shirt beneath, reaches to his waist. On his legs are hose tied to the waist with laces. Ellinor's right eyebrow lifts at the sight of the obvious cod piece. His short, loose gown has long-hanging sleeves that fall open to show the contrasting facings, and in his left hand is a flat hat with a jewelled rim. Despite her surprise, Ellinor can't help but think her husband cuts a dashing figure.

As Simon strides across the room, he makes a comment to the young women who immediately turn pink and start giggling again.

Ellinor's left eyebrow joins her right.

'Be off with you!' the older woman says in a thick Cornish accent, flapping her hands at him. 'Don't you be mischief-making and flummoxing my girls.'

Simon gives an exaggerated low bow, sweeping the floor with his hat. Straightening up, he winks at the three young women. 'A pleasant day to you, fair maidens.'

And with that, he turns and strides towards the open doorway.

Hastily gathering her senses, Ellinor steps away deeper into the gloom, but as Simon passes by, the air ripples in his wake, distorting the view of the passageway into an unstable watery realm. She shakes her head, as if to dislodge the vision and steady the scene. Suddenly his footsteps falter, and slowly he turns.

'And what have we here?' he asks, observing her pressed up against the wall. Taking a step towards her, he scans her face. 'Pray, what is your name?'

Ellinor gives a small, embarrassed laugh. 'Simon, what on earth are you doing?'

'Simon?' His forehead creases. 'You are mistaken, pretty lady. My name is William.'

Ellinor snorts. 'OK, you can stop play-acting now.'

His frown deepens.

'Play-acting?'

Ellinor gazes into her husband's eyes and a tremor of anxiety lodges in her throat. She glances back into the kitchen where the women are now busy at their chores once again, kneading bread and mixing ingredients in bowls with large wooden spoons.

'Where are Ian and Pippa?' she asks. 'Or was it only you who was persuaded to take part?'

'Take part? To what do you allude?'

Now Ellinor frowns. Peering over his shoulder along the passageway, she notices the scene has stabilised once more, and she takes in the flickering candlelight, the deep shadows and the rough finish to the walls.

'Stop it, Simon. You're frightening me.'

'Do not be alarmed, there is nothing to fear.' His gaze is quizzical. 'Are you a friend of Philippa's?'

Ellinor swallows rising panic. This has gone on long enough. 'You know very well who she is to me.'

Observing her clothes, he gives a perplexed frown and eyes her curiously. 'What strange attire, more fitting of a man. But you are *no* man!'

She expects him to break into laughter and tell her it's all been a bit of a joke, but he doesn't.

'Simon, this is *not* funny.'

He turns the palms of his hands up to the ceiling. 'I know not of this Simon.'

'OK, *William* . . . whatever!' she says, attempting to keep the anxiety from her voice.

Suddenly a figure blocks the light from the doorway, and Ellinor shrinks back further into the darkness.

'You still here, William?' the cook asks, her tone brisk.

'I am, Mistress Tindle,' he replies, without taking his eyes from Ellinor.

'Well, then, kindly remove your cur. The kitchen is no place for the likes of it!'

'At your command,' Simon says, turning to face the woman.

Ellinor watches as the woman peers into the gloom. Spying her, the cook crosses herself again and quickly disappears back into the kitchen.

'Branok,' Simon calls.

A flurry of grey appears in the doorway and Ellinor's hand flies to her throat. Another wolf? she thinks, recalling what she thought she'd seen at the cottage ruins. Surely not! Her heart starts to pound.

'I must take my leave of you, fair maiden,' Simon says, turning back to her. 'But before I depart, pray tell me your name.'

Ellinor gazes into her husband's bright blue eyes, which

twinkle with boyish mischief. *That* spirit had totally disarmed her when they first met, but then work demands and responsibilities had infiltrated their relationship and she hasn't seen this level of rascally gaiety in him for a long time. OK . . . If this is how he wants to play it, she'll go along with it.

'Ellinor,' she replies. 'My name is Ellinor.'

He holds her gaze, and the warmth interweaving the playfulness in his eyes mesmerises her. This is what had made her fall in love with him so quickly – that special look, saved only for her.

He bows deeply. Then, with a flourish of his gown, he turns away and walks swiftly along the passage with the grey shadow at his side. But as he approaches the far end, he half turns and regards her again.

'A beautiful name, befitting the Lady Ellinor.'

She tuts, even as a smile tugs at her lips. Since when has her husband spoken in such poetic language? Obviously, he's still in character and taking his role *very* seriously!

Without further ado, he disappears through the doorway. The grey shadow, however, remains and gazes back at the woman hiding in the gloom, its amber eyes aglow.

Since *the incident*, Ellinor has become a dab hand at dealing with anxiety attacks, and now she concentrates on refusing to succumb to another one. Steadying her nerves, she closes her eyes and takes a deep breath as she wills away the sudden onset of dizziness and nausea. And there's something else, too . . . an inexplicable longing for home and a yearning for something lost.

'Ah, there you are!' Ian's voice rings out loud and clear.

Ellinor opens her eyes and blinks in surprise. Once again, the passageway is bright and welcoming. Gone are the animal and the candlelit wall sconces, and the flagstone floor once again gleams beneath shafts of sunlight streaming in through a diamond-paned window. Spooked, and aware of her trembling hands and rapid heartbeat, she peers into the kitchen. There's not a soul about. In disbelief, Ellinor enters the room. The wooden table is bare, apart from a couple of bowls and a rolling pin strategically placed; and where the pig had been roasting, the iron spit is now clean and the hearth cold, with no signs of a fire.

'Where's Simon?' she asks urgently.

'With Pippa, checking out the exhibition,' Ian says, curiously observing her from the doorway. He stands back abruptly as she hurriedly exits the kitchen and peers along the passageway.

'Which way is it?' Ellinor demands.

Ian points to his left.

Without hesitation she sets off, desperate to see her husband and banish the mad hallucination from her mind.

'Everything OK, cuz?' Ian asks, as he rushes to catch up with her fast-disappearing figure.

Twelve

'So let me get this straight,' Simon says, sitting up in bed and plumping the pillows into a comfortable backrest. 'You followed us out of the Great Hall into the passage, but we weren't there, and the kitchen was full of women preparing food. And roast pork was on the menu.'

She pulls a wry face at his last remark. 'Yes, there was a whole pig turning on a spit.'

'Well, there was no one there when we looked in, more's the pity. I'd have fancied a bit of crackling.'

'You do believe me, don't you?'

Simon runs his fingers through his hair. 'To be perfectly honest, I'm not sure what to believe.'

She sighs in exasperation.

'I don't think you're lying, Elli,' he adds quickly, 'it's just that . . . maybe you imagined it. I mean, the place is overloaded with atmosphere and it's easy to get a strong sense of the past as you wander around.'

She sits down heavily on the edge of the bed. 'Simon, it was *much* more than imagination! While I watched the women at work in the kitchen the cook caught sight of me. She made the sign of the cross.'

Simon frowns.

Ellinor hesitates before delivering the next piece of information. Will it prompt her husband to suggest she book an appointment with the shrink the minute they get home?

She glances at him uncertainly. 'And then a door on the far side of the room opened and you walked in.'

His eyes widen. 'What do you mean, *I* walked in?'

'It was you . . . in medieval costume.'

Simon stares at her, incredulously. 'I can assure you, I've never worn medieval clothing, not even to a fancy dress party.' Reaching out, he lays a hand gently on her arm. 'Maybe *the incident* has caused your emotions to go into overdrive, and in an attempt to forewarn you of any perceived dangers they manifest all sorts of possible scenarios.'

She shakes her head. 'You spoke to me, and you had a dog.'

'But we don't have a dog.'

'I know!' she exclaims. Rising from the bed, she paces the room and wonders if she's going mad.

Simon considers his wife carefully. 'Elli, the brain is capable of miraculous things. This is the first time you've been away from home and out of your comfort zone since . . .' His voice peters out. Taking a deep breath, he continues, 'It's not surprising that you're reacting to this new environment. Your senses are on full alert.'

Ellinor stops and turns to him. 'But it was so real. I could even smell the roast pork.'

Simon gives a small laugh. 'You were probably hungry, and your mind conjured it up.' He pats the bed beside him. 'A good night's sleep is what you need . . .' He pauses. 'Also, there's something I want to discuss with you.'

She contemplates him for a long moment before giving a brief smile and slipping beneath the duvet. 'What do you want to discuss?'

'Well, as you know, Ian and Pippa are desperate to inject more funds into the farm and move the business on to the next level.'

She nods.

'Ian and I have been playing around with several ideas as how best to do that. I think they have the bare bones of a good business model and I'd like to invest.'

Ellinor turns to her husband. He's on a good salary and their savings are at a healthy level, but . . . 'How much are you talking about?'

'We've still got to crunch numbers, but I'm considering a fairly substantial amount.'

She frowns.

'With your cousin and Pippa's enthusiasm,' he continues, 'combined with the farm's location, it could develop into an exciting business. There's plenty of room for expansion and it's in such a secluded and tranquil setting, it's just crying out for a wild campsite. We've discussed diversifying to provide eco-glamping with bell tents, yurts and shepherds huts – and a couple of communal fire pits and wood burning barbeques, et cetera . . .'

Ellinor gazes at Simon and catches a glimpse of the once unencumbered and enthusiastic young man who had so entranced her.

'And, as it's a Dark Skies area, we could invest in a few telescopes and set up an observatory.'

'Are you considering a hands-on role?' she asks.

'Initially I'll simply inject capital into the business, but who knows what the future may bring? London currently provides us with a good living, and with Heathrow not too far away it's convenient for your work.'

Ellinor winces at the thought of returning to airline duties.

'But I can't imagine being in the rat race into my dotage,' Simon concludes.

She snorts. 'Simon, you've just turned thirty!'

'Exactly, Elli. So now is the time to look to the future, and if that means radical changes, then why not? At the moment we have relative youth and health on our side, but the one thing cast in stone is that we're not getting any younger.'

'You may have health,' she says quietly.

He reaches for her hand. 'And so will you, my beautiful Ellinor. Have you looked in the mirror this weekend? I haven't seen you looking so rosy-cheeked for ages. This place seems to agree with you. It's doing you the world of good.'

'It's obvious why you're in marketing!' she says, giving him a lopsided grin. 'Do you think this is a sound investment?

Obviously, it goes without saying that I want Ian and Pippa to succeed, but I'd hate you to lose money.'

'I do.' Simon squeezes her hand. 'Both Ian and Pippa possess good business heads. With their boundless energy and desire to make this corner of England work for them, I believe they're on the cusp of creating a sustainable and flourishing enterprise.'

'I suspect I already know what you're going to do,' Ellinor says, not wishing to dampen her husband's enthusiasm.

Smiling broadly, he pulls her into a hug. But as his mouth seeks hers, she clenches her jaw and averts her face.

'I'm so tired,' she says lamely. 'Let's get some sleep. We've a long drive ahead of us tomorrow.'

Ellinor forces a smile and turns away. Burrowing under the duvet, she tries to ignore the waves of confusion and disappointment emanating from her husband. But however much she'd like to, she can't force her emotions. She's not ready . . .

'Goodnight, Si.' Reaching for the bedside light, she switches it off.

'Goodnight.' His voice is flat, and after a long moment he rolls away.

All is silent but Ellinor can't sleep. Gazing through the gap in the curtains at the night sky, she casts her mind back over the day's events and a pair of twinkling, bright blue eyes, full of boyish mischief, invades her thoughts. If her mind has conjured it all up, as Simon suggests, it's a fascinating place to inhabit. After a while, she drifts off, but less than an hour later, her eyes flicker rapidly beneath closed lids, and her breath comes ever quicker as the corners of her mouth turn up in a smile . . .

It's a cool day and she wraps her shawl tightly around her shoulders, as she wanders through a thick forest alongside a slow-flowing river. Soon she reaches the clearing with the hidden dwelling. Stepping from the trees into the glade, Ellinor stares in awe at the single-storey thatched stone cottage, as a warm feeling and the words *love nest* whisper in her ear.

He's already here . . . waiting. Wood smoke rising from the chimney quickly disperses into an ice-blue sky, and behind the partly shuttered windows she sees flickering candlelight casting light into the shadows. Lying across the threshold of the door and blocking entry is a large, rough-coated grey dog. As Ellinor walks towards the cottage, the wolfhound raises its head and observes her with an all-knowing gaze.

In the still of the night, Ellinor mutters, 'Branok . . .'

Simon sleeps on, undisturbed. Only the barn owl gliding across the courtyard on silent wings hears her musings, and it inclines its head in the direction of the open window.

Thirteen

'The weekend is over far too quickly!' Pippa exclaims, pulling a sad face and giving Ellinor a hug.

'I know. It seems only five minutes since you welcomed us into your home.'

'You must visit again soon.' Pippa squeezes Ellinor's arm. 'And remember, if you want to stay for however long, you're welcome any time.'

'That's really generous, Pippa.' Briefly succumbing to an unfamiliar pull, Ellinor considers not returning to Surrey with Simon.

'Not at all! I'd be grateful of the company and another female about the place. There's way too much testosterone around here, what with that hunk, Jake, distracting me at every turn!' She winks.

Ellinor snorts. 'I must admit, the man has grown on me since my initial reaction to him.'

Pippa smiles. Stepping away, she bids Simon goodbye.

'Well, cuz.' Ian kisses Ellinor on her cheek. 'Lovely to see you, but don't leave it too long before your next visit.'

'If Si has his way, we'll be back next Saturday!' Ellinor smiles into her cousin's kind eyes. 'Then, you'll be complaining to Pippa that you don't have any private time anymore!'

'Rubbish! You'd both be welcomed with open arms,' Ian confirms.

'Ready?' Simon asks.

Ellinor nods.

Picking up their weekend bag, he follows his wife to the car and presses the key fob. As the doors of the Audi unlock, he places the holdall in the boot before turning back to Ian and Pippa standing on the porch step.

'Once again, guys, thanks for a wonderful stay. I'll phone in the next couple of days with an update, once I've gone through the figures.'

'Looking forward to it,' Ian responds with a smile.

'And don't forget,' Pippa calls out, 'turn left at the end of the drive, follow the lane for approximately a quarter of a mile, and then take the stone track on the right with the footpath sign. You'll find the ruins down there after about three hundred yards.'

'Will do.' Simon climbs into the driver's seat.

'Bye,' Ellinor says, as she opens the passenger door. She's about to get in when she glances towards the barn situated at right angles to the farmhouse and shields her eyes from the sun. 'Oh, look, the owl has come to say goodbye!'

Ian and Pippa turn towards the old threshing barn. Standing motionless in the hayloft entrance, the barn owl observes the comings and goings in the courtyard below.

'You're honoured,' Pippa says. 'We don't often see him about in broad daylight. He's normally active at dusk or during the night.'

Ellinor stares at the heart-shaped face and the beady button-black eyes, and it seems to her there's deep wisdom in his gaze. 'He's a beauty!'

'That he is,' Pippa responds.

'Well, bye again.' With one last look at the owl, Ellinor slides into the passenger seat and fastens her seatbelt.

As Simon puts the car into a three-point turn and heads off down the drive, Ellinor opens her side window. Extending her arm, she waves until Ian and Pippa are out of sight.

'OK, remind me why we're visiting the ruined cottage again before heading home,' Simon asks, peering both ways along the quiet lane before turning left.

'Humour me, Si. There's something I want to check.'

Within minutes they reach the footpath sign, part-buried in the hedge, and as Simon carefully navigates along the track, the grass growing freely down its centre tickles the underside of the Audi. Soon they come to a padlocked five-bar wooden gate preventing vehicular access to the woodland beyond.

'Looks like this is as far as we go,' Simon says, pulling on the handbrake. 'Hope we're not blocking the track for anyone.'

'Don't worry. We'll hear if another car approaches,' Ellinor says, undoing her seatbelt and opening the car door.

'How do you know that?' Simon asks. 'We don't know how far the ruins are from here.'

She smiles. 'They're just over there.' She points vaguely into the forest.

Simon is unconvinced. 'How can you possibly know that? Yesterday, we approached from across the fields.'

'It's OK, Si. Trust me.'

With a frown, he gets out of the car and watches in surprise as his wife climbs confidently over the gate and heads off down the track.

'Hey, Elli. Wait up.'

Pressing the key fob, he follows her over the gate and lengthens his strides after her fast-disappearing figure. As he catches her up, she turns, and her face is energised and flushed, and her eyes are sparkling.

Suddenly Ellinor veers off the track into what appears to be dense foliage. 'It's this way.'

'Seriously, Elli. How do you know that?'

'I just do.'

He glances at his watch and when he looks up again, his wife is some way ahead. Striding out, he calls out, 'Are you following a path?'

She looks back at him in surprise. 'Yes. Don't you see it?'

'No, I don't.'

He gazes around. The waist-high ferns and brambles grow unhindered in this part of the woodland and he rolls down his sleeves, frowning as he scan's his wife's arms. She's shorter than him and standing in the middle of a patch of brambles, and yet her bare skin is scratch-free.

'Just stick with me,' Ellinor says. 'The clearing's over there, beyond that oak tree.' She points deeper into the woodland.

Simon peers into the trees, but there's no sign of the ruined dwelling. However, within minutes they reach the glade and as they hover at the edge of the forest, shafts of sunlight stream into the dell, bathing the grey stones of the ruins in a golden hue. The only sound permeating the peace and quiet is the babbling brook and Ellinor gazes around with a beatific smile on her face.

'Elli.'

'Hmm?' she says distractedly. Glancing at her husband, she's surprised to see him there.

'Why have we come here?' he asks softly, as if fearful of breaking whatever spell she appears to be under.

'Come with me.' Her eyes shine as she takes hold of his hand and guides him towards the remains of the cottage. 'Imagine this.' She turns in a circle and beams up at him. 'A wildflower cottage garden with a fence and a gate leading out to the lane; and over there by the stream, a summerhouse with decking.'

He looks at her askance.

'And here.' She drags him towards the entrance of the dwelling. 'A rambling honeysuckle wending its way around the door and then . . .' she steps over the threshold '. . . wooden floors and exposed beams, a country kitchen with an Aga, or a range cooker – I haven't worked out the finer details yet!' She pulls her husband towards the far wall. 'And over here, an oak turning staircase leading up to two bedrooms and a bathroom.' She gazes at him in delight.

'For us?' Simon asks hesitantly.

'Yes!' says Ellinor, almost jumping with excitement. 'I thought that as you're keen to get involved with Ian and Pippa's enterprise we'd need a base down here, and if we decide to follow in their footsteps and put down roots in Cornwall, well then, we'd already have a home to transition into smoothly.'

'Elli,' Simon says carefully, 'Ian and Pippa already have plans for these . . . well . . . ruins. They've already told us they've been through the planning process.'

She pulls a face. 'But what if we make them an offer they can't refuse? Once Jake finishes the holiday let at the farm, we could ask him to develop this. For us!'

Simon smiles affectionately at his wife. 'You've thought everything through, haven't you?'

'Not everything. But if you're intent on backing my cousin's enterprise, then maybe the way to go about it is to buy into his and Pippa's dream and inject money into the project by purchasing these ruins.'

She gazes around the quiet sun-kissed clearing, which, as yesterday, seems to possess a magical quality. In fact, a thick haze lingers in the air and as she glances towards the edge of the forest, she's certain a pair of round, amber eyes keenly observes her from amongst the foliage. But on taking a closer look, she sees it's just a sunbeam striking the leaves and turning them a glorious russet colour.

'In that way,' she continues, turning back to her husband, 'not only will we have helped them financially, but we will also gain something of our own.'

'For use as a holiday home?'

'Ye–es,' she says uncertainly, 'although I'm sure there'll be a time when we may want to move in permanently. Just think, wouldn't it be the most wonderful place to raise a family?'

Caught unaware by the direction the conversation has taken, a hopeful smile tugs at Simon's lips. 'But what about your career? You love being a flight attendant! I suppose you could join an airline flying out of Exeter or Newquay.'

'Oh *that*,' she says dismissively, 'I've been giving it a lot of thought, and I don't ever want to step inside a plane again.'

As Ellinor gazes around the quiet glade, something tells her that the essence of this special place is in her bones.

'Well, you've certainly given me a lot to consider,' Simon says, checking his watch. 'But for the moment, we'd better be going.'

She nods. 'I guess so.'

Turning away, they head through the trees towards the track where they'd left the car. But before the ruins are once again hidden from view, Ellinor gazes back at the remains of the stone cottage sitting peacefully and undisturbed in the setting. She can't explain it, but it feels like *home*. And as soon as she allows the thought to form, a keen sense of both longing and loss assaults her.

Fourteen

Later that week, back in Surrey, Ellinor sits cross-legged on the couch with her laptop balanced on her knees. It's a still afternoon and the house is quiet . . . just as she likes it. She enters 'Cornish names and meanings' into the search box and scans the various pages appearing on the screen.

The names are listed alphabetically, and it doesn't take long to scroll down to 'B' and find the one she's looking for. A shiver of excitement courses through her as she realises the name is relevant to the area where she'd had the vision.

Branok – Cornish name derived from the Celtic word *brano*, which means raven, crow.

'Spooky,' she says under her breath.

Ellinor types in 'what do ravens and crows symbolise?' and waits patiently for the results to display. She reads through the listings and opens one that looks hopeful – ancient animal wisdom and observations of an intuitive wildlife artist. Avidly, she devours the information.

Different wild species of animal and their unique wisdom create certain vibrations, energy and power in the world, which resonates and vibrates within each of us. These animals are our best teachers and if you are prepared to connect deeply and learn from them, it is possible to change yourself and lead a more evolved and conscious life.

Looking up from the screen, Ellinor gazes unseeing into the distance. The artist's words resonate with her. Carefully, she reviews her life, which until *the incident* has been a series of goals and achievements – lifestyle and career choices that have left little room for anything beyond the demands of instant gratification. She considers that to many people this may seem privileged and self-centred; living in life's shallows. Pressing her lips together, as her immediate surroundings come back into focus, she glances around at the designer trappings of a wealthy existence and raises a sardonic eyebrow. Ellinor returns her attention to the screen.

Ravens (Corvus corax): part of the Corvid family. This special group of birds has a unique purpose and reason for being here in the world. Incorrectly, some people label them harbingers of doom, resonant of death, darkness and all unpleasant things, and they are persecuted and blamed for much. Ravens have a strongly feminine energy, receptive and intuitive, and people who are frightened of that intuitive knowing will naturally project negativity onto such beings. With a palpable gift of foreseeing future events, and possessing a universal intelligence, they have a high level of intuitive power and wisdom, which most humans are unable to reach. They are worthy of our reverence and deep respect at the highest levels.

Ravens are also prophetic and connected with not only this world but also the other worlds. Proficient in flying between the veils – between the worlds – they engage and communicate with ancestral wisdom just as easily as they do in this world, here in their physical bodies. Humans have forgotten how to reconnect through the veils and working with raven energy will open the gateway to that connection.

Ellinor bites her lip. How many of her friends and work colleagues would think that *the incident* had fried her brain if she discussed this with any of them? Even though Simon was indulgent when she recounted her experience at Cotehele, she knows he was only humouring her.

Ravens are keen to show true independence, which is tightly linked to interdependence; they engage in a situation independently, or work with others to help them. These birds are very good at teaching us about the power of true freedom, which is the willingness to walk alone when required, but also to walk with others and to help and support, and be helped and supported by others, and this idea of self-governing. They can effectively help us to look at how we can sidestep all the lower energies and vibrations of chaos and suffering, and twisted patriarchy and matriarchy that is very prevalent in today's mixed-up human world. It's not that we don't acknowledge it and see it, but we don't live in it. Instead, we live in our own self-governance, connected with nature and giving of service, so that we can bring good into the world from as balanced a place as we can possibly manage, as much as we can.

Part of the ravens' purpose for living on Earth is to assist in the evolution of consciousness; to move beyond the imbalances that humanity creates. Other species don't create the imbalance that humans do, so by holding the consciousness within themselves they call out vibrationally to those who are out of alignment, to support their shift.

Ellinor pauses. She had no idea there were people who had the ability to tap into wildlife and interpret their wisdom! This is a lot of information to take in . . .

Ravens are shapeshifters. They can morph between the worlds, and if you're lucky enough to see them in the wild, sit quietly and observe their behaviour; you may experience some interesting things. It's all about the level of frequency at which they operate. They are amazing allies if you respectfully approach and ask for their help and support. They're also very much associated with the life-death-life eternal cycle. All animals know this is natural and that it's a part of our experience. Death is not to be feared; it is simply another door opening and a beautiful transition. The perception of humans is very different, and we become fearful and untrusting of the thought of death and what it means, and that it's somehow a bad and awful thing. Ravens can help us with transitions in our lifetime, whether that's from life to death, or if it's key transitions in our life – the changing of the seasons; the changing of our roles; or the changing of geographical locations. This isn't about turning up and demanding. It's about mutually reciprocating, giving and receiving, asking them how you may serve and be of service to the ravens, and to nature and Mother Earth, without expectation of instant miracles, and very respectfully building an ongoing relationship through loving, compassionate communication.

Leaving the laptop open, Ellinor rises off the couch and makes her way to the kitchen, in need of an injection of caffeine. Her head swims with the understandings and different ideas that this intuitive wildlife artist has introduced into her consciousness, and she can't wait to discover further revelations. Quickly making herself an instant coffee, she returns to the couch and immediately picks up from where she'd left off.

Ravens can also help us with developing our psychic abilities. From the third eye, or the brow Chakra, we are able to tune in and quieten down our busy-ness and listen, see, and feel inwardly what is coming and what is naturally evolving for us, as we move forward in our lives, and being able to do that in a balanced and emotionally mature way, thinking of the greater good rather than our own selfish needs. We put ourselves into that, as we are equal, but we don't do it from a narcissistic place of 'I want this' and 'I must have it now'. They can help us to re-sensitise and re-engage with our intuitive psychic capabilities – this is so valuable to those of us who seek to serve the Earth and the cosmos, in the best and highest ways.

Ravens will also guide us when there are toxic situations that we need to move away from, or remove from our experience, and that can be helpful. Sometimes we believe that situations in our life are fixed and can't be changed, but the teachings of the animals are that everything changes and shifts – it's only the resistance that we put in the way that causes a lot of the difficulties that we experience. They are versatile, highly adaptive and are constantly morphing. They're mystical and super-intelligent, with a real and deep kenning of truth; not just reading information (as in our definition) and saying they know something. Knowing is different from kenning. Kenning is that deep truth that we really need to learn to access more fully in today's human world.

These birds are multi-dimensional and truly magical. They're also magnificent healers, helping us to become whole and remember all that we are, and are part of – the cosmic cycles of life-death-life, and the ability to walk, or fly forward in that wholeness, no matter what this is, whether it's a transition through to death and beyond, or whether it's coming back from that into life. It's being able to work fluidly with that, which is one of the raven's major gifts, wisdoms and medicines. Take some time connecting and tuning in to raven energy.

Puffing out her cheeks, Ellinor expels a long breath and closes the laptop. Raven wisdom has blown her mind! She doesn't admit to understanding it all, but certain key points stand out.

'So, Branok, you're a magnificent healer. Is that why you've appeared? You want to help me become whole and remember all that I am and am part of.'

Is that why she feels inexplicably comforted whenever she thinks of the derelict cottage, and why a keen yearning besieged her when she had to leave?

Rising to her feet, Ellinor crosses over to the French

windows. There's no sign of the foxes – she hadn't expected there to be – but her attention is drawn to the flowerbed on the right-hand side of the garden. Perched on a branch in the red maple, a large black bird eyes her intently. She inhales sharply. Surely not? Perhaps it's a crow, because she's never witnessed a raven in the garden before. There again, she probably wouldn't have noticed even if it had stood right in front of her. Opening her phone, she navigates to a page of birds and opens an image. She stares at the detail in disbelief and then incredulously back at the tree. It's definitely a raven! What did she just read? That ravens have a palpable sense of knowing of future events and a high level of intuitive power, which most humans are unable to reach.

Ellinor gazes at the bird, expecting it to fly away, but it remains on the branch and cocks its head, eyeing her through the window. All at once she feels exposed. Thinking of Alfred Hitchcock's film, *The Birds*, she snorts, embarrassed to have instantly considered the bird in an unfavourable light, as a harbinger of doom, death, darkness and all unpleasant things. Maybe, she is frightened of the raven's innate knowing of the feminine, receptive, intuitive space. Is that what's going on here? Has she ignored who she truly is and foolishly filled her life with fripperies and shallowness? Ellinor frowns. She should suspend her beliefs and wipe the slate clean of all the things she's previously heard about Corvids. And hadn't the article reported that ravens are worthy of our reverence and deep respect at the highest levels?

All at once, a deep sense of calm encompasses Ellinor.

'I have the deepest respect and reverence for you,' she whispers. 'Is there something you wish to disclose to me?'

Extending its wings, the black bird swoops down from the branch and hops across the lawn towards the house. As it reaches the closed French doors, it taps on the glass with its powerful beak.

Close up, the raven is huge, and in the afternoon sunshine its glossy ebony plumage shimmers hues of purple and blue. Ellinor studies the bird through the window, observing the elongated, loose, erectile throat feathers, which give it a scruffy appearance, the nasal bristles that cover almost half of the upper ridge of its bill, and the unusual pale grey feather extending obliquely down its chest. Cocking its head again, the bird observes her with intelligent, dark-brown eyes.

Ellinor softens her gaze and tilts her head, mirroring its stance. 'Tell me what you see,' she says quietly.

Opening its beak, the bird lets out a soft bark . . .'Prruk-prruk'. Suddenly it turns its head and stares at something deep in the garden. Ellinor looks, but there's nothing disturbing the peace of the afternoon. Glancing down again, she sees the bird once more holds her in its sight. Is it trying to convey something? The raven repeats its bark, and then in one smooth movement flies off into the afternoon sky.

Ellinor stands at the French doors for a while longer, and as she curiously examines this first connection with a wild animal, she experiences an unfamiliar resonation and vibration stirring within her.

Fifteen

That evening, the phone loudly ringing disrupts the calm of the house. Quickly, Simon snatches up the handset and listens to the person on the other end. He motions to his wife.

'Ian, I'll put you on loudspeaker so that Elli can hear.'

'Good idea.' Ian's voice carries across the room. 'Hi, cuz.'

'Hi yourself,' Ellinor responds.

'Pippa and I have discussed your proposals to buy the ruins and an area of surrounding woodland as a buffer,' Ian explains.

Ellinor's heart leaps into her mouth and she crosses her fingers tightly.

'And although we'd considered developing the site ourselves at some point in the future,' he continues, 'we've decided we'd love to have you guys as close neighbours. So, it's all systems go as far as we're concerned.'

Ellinor lets out a sigh of relief. She's still not sure why it's so important to her to buy the plot, but the thought of having a toe in that part of the country is immensely comforting.

'That's terrific news!' Simon says enthusiastically, giving Ellinor the thumbs up.

'We'll contact our solicitors first thing tomorrow and instruct them to draw up the necessary paperwork,' Ian advises. 'Who do you use?'

Simon provides him with the name of the solicitor he's used for years.

'We've also sounded out Jake on your behalf,' Ian adds. 'After he's finished our holiday let he has a small job to do in Saltash, which he says shouldn't take more than a couple of weeks. Then he can commit to you.'

'That's fantastic!' Ellinor exclaims. 'Please thank him very much. And, Ian, we noticed on the plans you emailed earlier in the week that it was a Graham Haynes who drew them up. Do you think he'd be prepared to tweak them slightly?'

'I don't see why not. Depends on what you want. It's not what you know but who you know, and he managed to push our ideas through planning for a simple redevelopment without a hiccup. Graham lives locally, so he can always pop over if there are any issues. I'll email you his contact details, if you like.'

'Yes please. We don't intend to build anything eyebrow-raising, maybe just add an extension to the cottage.'

'Sounds good. Well, I'll leave you to enjoy your evening. Catch up later in the week.'

Finishing the call, Simon replaces the handset and looks across at Ellinor. 'So, we're really going to do this?'

'Yes!' she replies without hesitation. A fizz of excitement takes hold and she tries to recall when she last felt so energised. 'It'll be such fun!'

He smiles at her enthusiasm. 'I take it you'll hand in your notice now.'

Ellinor colours. 'I've already written it out.'

He gives an amused laugh. 'No one can accuse you of procrastination once you've got the bit between your teeth, Ellinor Forrester!'

She smiles sheepishly. 'I *so* need this, Si.'

'I know.'

'Thank you for making it possible.'

Walking across the room, he gives her a careful hug, as if anything more robust would shatter his fragile wife into a thousand pieces.

For once, Ellinor doesn't automatically freeze, and with relief she returns his hug.

'Perhaps we will find a way back,' Simon says softly, dropping a light kiss on her lips. He lingers for a moment.

Her husband is good at kissing, and they've indulged in a

lot of that over the course of their relationship, but Ellinor stiffens. It's still too much . . .

'It's OK, Elli. I'll not force things.'

She knows he's disappointed at her rejection. Resting her head against his chest, she mumbles, 'Thank you for not piling on the pressure.'

Simon strokes her long, glossy hair. 'Come to me when you're ready. As I've said before, I'll be here.'

Silently, they stand holding each other for a while longer.

'Tell you what,' Simon says, suddenly drawing away. 'I'll fix us a drink before supper. Can I tempt you with a glass of wine?'

'You can,' she says with a small, wobbly smile.

As he walks from the room, Ellinor wanders over to the couch and reaches for her laptop, and by the time her husband returns with the drinks, she's navigated to a page of characterful house designs.

'Here you go,' Simon says, handing her a glass.

'Thanks.' She takes a sip of wine and places the glass on the coffee table. 'Look, Si. What do you think of these?'

Sitting down beside her, he peers at the images on the screen. 'I like the look of that one. Contemporary, but with a nod to yesteryear.'

'It caught my eye, too.'

'We don't have to build anything large-scale,' he says. 'It can be our cosy weekend love nest.'

She glances sharply at him. *Love nest!* She's heard those words recently . . . she's sure of it.

'If Ian and Pippa's business goes the way we expect it to,' he continues, 'I want to be there, and as hands-on as possible.'

'It'll be good for you to get out of London,' Ellinor says, still mulling over where she's heard those words. 'And the plot's large enough to add further extensions to the cottage in the future, if we need to.'

Simon gazes lovingly at his wife.

'What?' she asks, catching his look.

'You,' he says, gently squeezing her arm. 'I love it when you're all fired up!'

'It's been a long time since I felt like this. And it's true, I can't wait to get started on the project.'

For the next twenty minutes they pore over the different house designs, and as they discuss the merits of each, a sense of purpose takes hold.

'Several layouts would suit us,' Ellinor says, happily. 'I hope the architect will be able to incorporate them into the current plans.'

Simon drains his glass and gets to his feet. 'Why don't you send enquiries to the companies while I make supper? Spag bol OK?'

'Hmm . . .' She glances up distractedly.

'Spaghetti bolognaise?'

'Oh, yes.' She smiles, but as soon as he turns away her attention is once more on the screen. Filling out half a dozen housebuilders' enquiry forms, she sends her requests and then sits back in contentment. It's good to get the ball rolling.

Ellinor gazes towards the French doors. It's growing increasingly dark outside. Rising from the couch, she crosses the room and peers through the glass into the garden. Shadows lengthen across the lawn. Will the dog fox and vixen make an appearance this evening? They may even have young by now, and it would be good to see the cubs. Suddenly a shape shifts amongst the far flowerbed, and she holds her breath. But it's not the vulpines paying her a visit. It's a raven, and she wonders if it's the same one.

Hopping out from beneath the protection of the bushes onto the lawn, momentarily the bird stands motionless. Then, turning towards the house, it strides purposefully across the grass and hops up onto the stone terrace. Confidently, it approaches the French doors, and its beady eyes immediately lock onto Ellinor standing at the windows. The unusual grey feather, slanting across its chest, confirms it's the same bird that had visited her before, and once again Ellinor has the strongest impression that it's trying to convey something to her. If only she knew how to unlock the pathway of communication. What had that article said? *This isn't about turning up and asking and demanding. It's about mutually reciprocating, giving and receiving, asking them how you may serve, and be of service to the ravens, to nature, to Mother Earth, without expectation of instant miracles.*

She's never considered anything so mystical before, but perhaps it's time . . .

'Thought you might like a top-up.' Simon's voice breaks the spell.

Glancing over her shoulder, she watches him approach with an open bottle in hand.

'What's that bird?' he asks, halting abruptly and pointing at the window.

'A raven,' she answers simply.

As she turns back to the French doors, the bird flies away in a blur of ebony feathers. Straining her eyes, she peers into the depths of the garden and attempts to follow its flight, but it soon merges with the deepening gloom and disappears into the night. She sighs, and taking hold of the curtains, she draws them to and blocks out the night.

Sixteen

Next morning, Ellinor sits at the breakfast bar nursing a cup of coffee, as Simon pokes his head around the kitchen door.

'It's Stuart's last day today,' he announces. 'Some of the team are meeting up after work to give him a good send-off. I have no idea what time it will finish, but I'll try not to be too late.'

'Shall I prepare supper for you?'

'No. I'll grab something while I'm out.' He smiles at his wife. 'And don't forget, I'll book a table for Friday evening at that new restaurant in the village, if you feel up to it.'

She nods. 'Yes, do.'

'That's a step in the right direction,' Simon says, entering the room and kissing his wife on the cheek. 'Good luck today, honey.'

'Thanks. I know it's the right thing for me, but I can't help feeling anxious.'

He squeezes her shoulder. 'Remember, Elli, it's your life. You have every right to choose how you live it.'

She smiles up at him. 'Thanks for the reminder.'

'And anyway, you won't have time to fly around the world soon. Our Cornish adventure awaits!' He gives her a wink.

A delighted chuckle springs from her throat and Simon grins.

'It's months since I've heard that enchanting sound.' He glances at the large clock on the kitchen wall. 'Hell, is that the time already? Must dash.'

'See you when I see you,' Ellinor calls out after his rapidly disappearing figure.

She listens to the sound of his footsteps diminishing along

the hall and the front door closing. A moment later, the Audi's engine roars into life and its tyres crunch across gravel as her husband drives away. Finishing her coffee, Ellinor opens her notebook. It's filled with reminders as to why she's doing this, and she takes a deep breath. Briefly, her hand hovers hesitantly over her mobile lying on the breakfast bar, but steeling herself, determinedly she picks it up.

Her psychotherapist expresses surprise when Ellinor calmly explains her plans and her belief that she no longer needs counselling.

'Anyway,' Ellinor concludes, 'the long and the short of it is that I want to discontinue our appointments.'

'How did you cope with the visit to your cousin's?' Sarah enquires.

Ellinor envisages the woman reaching for her notebook and recording a few observations.

'All went well, thanks,' she says, without missing a beat.

She chooses to omit the strange experience at Cotehele, and doesn't mention her kneejerk reaction to Jake. After all, she tells herself, anyone would have responded in that way at his sudden, unexpected, larger-than-life appearance.

'I need to see you again for a final assessment before I can sign you off,' Sarah advises.

They arrange an appointment for later in the week.

Next, Ellinor phones the airline's Human Resources Management team. After being put through to her handler, Helen Matthews, she announces her decision to leave their employment with immediate effect.

'Under the circumstances, I fully understand your decision,' Helen says. 'I'll arrange for your P45 to be sent to you, and I'll formally contact the psychotherapist assigned to you and close the case. You may also be entitled to compensation, following a psychiatric report.' The woman pauses. 'For your information, Captain Andrews resigned immediately after the incident, and he has no intention of ever flying again. However, I'm sorry to report that the attacker has been found to have mental-health issues and no charges will be brought against him.'

Ellinor closes her eyes and concentrates on even breathing. 'So be it.'

'And, Ellinor, please know that you have our support.' Her handler's voice is sympathetic. 'No one should ever have to go through what you did. We wish you all the very best.'

They speak for a short while longer and when Ellinor finishes the call and puts down the phone, she lets out a long breath, allowing the tension to leave her body. It's only taken half an hour, but now the deed is done. Climbing off the stool, she walks over to the American fridge/freezer and pours herself a glass of orange juice before returning to the breakfast bar. Ellinor opens her laptop and checks the inbox for messages. There are several replies to her house-building enquiries, and she sorts through them, opening pages and scanning the various options on offer. There's a wide selection – from rustic cottages; off-the-shelf family homes; oak-framed farmhouses; eco-friendly log cabins; chalet-style German kit homes; and contemporary, carbon-positive box houses. The possibilities are mind-boggling! Closing her eyes, Ellinor imagines the single-storey thatched cottage with wood smoke drifting from its chimney that had come to her in a vision, and as warmth squeezes her heart, she smiles.

Love nest . . .

Her eyes fly open. Those words again! Only this time they weren't just in her head. She'd heard the man's voice as clear as day, as if he were sitting with her in the kitchen, chatting over a cup of coffee. She glances around and laughs at herself. But she knows whose voice it belongs to. It's the man who had caused such a commotion with the kitchen maids at the National Trust property.

Opening Google, she types 'History of Cotehele' into the search box and waits for the results. A nervous, anticipatory excitement takes hold, but suddenly the screen is filled with entries and she impatiently scans the information for details of past ownership. So engrossed is Ellinor by the history of the property that she doesn't notice the hours flying by.

The medieval manor house originated circa 1300, with alterations made in the early fifteenth century by Sir Richard Edgcumbe. The main phase of development was undertaken between 1485 and 1489, and was continued by his son, Sir Piers Edgcumbe, between 1489 and 1520.

She recalls the reception assistant informing her that the family had owned the property for centuries, and it's interesting to learn that it was the first house accepted by the Treasury in payment of death duty.

Next, Ellinor researches the Edgcumbe family's ancient lineage.

'William . . .' she mutters under her breath. 'That was your name. Could you have been an Edgcumbe?'

The man's garments were of fine quality and richly coloured, suggesting he was a nobleman, but although she searches several sites and discovers several records for William Edgcumbe, none of the men referred to are of the era his clothes suggest.

Ellinor frowns in frustration. Then she remembers that William had asked if she was a friend of Philippa's, and she scans the various pages for that name. But she can't find any mention.

'So, it was a moment of madness!' she exclaims in exasperation. 'Mind games and pure hallucination.'

But the scene is vividly etched in her brain. It had felt so real – the noises, the scents, the textures – as if she were living it . . .

Suddenly her tummy rumbles. Ellinor glances up at the clock and is astonished to find that it's past three. She's been sitting at the breakfast bar, searching for imaginary people since Simon departed for the office earlier that morning. No wonder she's hungry! She walks over to the fridge, opens the door and scrutinises the contents for inspiration, but interrupted by the ringing phone, she crosses the room and lifts the handset.

'Mrs Forrester?' enquires a man's voice.

'Yes.'

'Good afternoon. My name is John Steadman. You recently enquired about one of our rustic cottages and I emailed the relevant information to you. Is this a convenient time to talk?'

Ellinor's stomach rumbles again.

'Absolutely,' she replies.

Lunch will just have to wait.

Seventeen

It's late Saturday morning and as Ellinor enters the room, she observes that Simon is still in bed.

'Here you go, sleepyhead,' she says, approaching him with a mug of tea in her hand.

Her husband stirs. 'What time is it?' he asks, pushing himself up into a sitting position.

'Ten fifteen. I thought you'd appreciate a lie-in after your hard week.'

'Tell me about it!' He grimaces and takes the mug from her. 'One meeting after another.'

Ellinor crosses over to the window and draws back the curtains. A sullen sky threatens rain. Glancing down into the garden, she observes the gardener enlarging the pond that he'd started digging earlier in the week. They've already had a catch-up this morning and he's assured her that the rudimentary, gaping hole at the edge of the decking will swiftly take shape, and the mounds of excavated earth will transform into a beautiful rockery.

'Tim's here,' she comments. 'He says the pond should be ready for me to plant up very soon.'

'That'll be good for you,' Simon says.

Turning away from the window, she gives her husband a questioning look. 'What? You mean the exercise?'

He laughs. 'Well, yes, that . . . but I was thinking more of giving you something to do.'

'Simon!' she exclaims, ruffled by the implication.

'Don't get me wrong, Elli. It's not that I think you sit around all day scratching your head. I just mean it will give you focus.'

She decides to accept his explanation and wonders if this

is the right time to put forward her proposal. Walking over to the bed, Ellinor perches on the edge of the mattress and composes herself.

'Si, I've been thinking . . .'

'Uh-oh! Now what's coming?' he says, in a teasing voice.

'My *focus* is to get the cottage built sooner rather than later, and I wondered if . . .' She trails off nervously.

'Go on,' he encourages, blowing robustly on the surface of his tea.

'Well.' She shifts position. 'What would you say if I accepted Ian and Pippa's offer to stay with them? That way, I'll be able to project-manage and push things forward.'

Simon straightens up. 'Wouldn't you rather employ someone to do that?'

She shakes her head. 'This is important to me, Simon, and I don't think I want anyone else involved. I mean, they wouldn't understand my passion for the build.'

Passion . . . The word resonates comfortably, nestling alongside *love nest*.

Ellinor's brow creases in confusion. She loves her husband dearly, but Simon and she have been together for several years, and although they respect and trust each other implicitly, the heady honeymoon period is a thing of the past.

'Hmm . . .' Simon elevates one eyebrow. 'Do you seriously expect me to fend for myself? You know how useless men are at that!'

She chuckles. 'You know damn well you're more than capable. And, anyway, you can come down at weekends, so it would only be from Monday to Friday. I'm sure you'll cope admirably.'

'Thank you, dear wife, for clarifying my visitation rights,' he teases.

'It also means that you can test out living in Cornwall until you decide to move down full-time.'

She glances at him and senses his quick brain mulling over everything she suggests.

'Well, I certainly want to be hands-on as much as possible.' He looks her straight in the eye. 'But, Elli, will you be OK there on your own without me? I mean, do you think you've recovered sufficiently from . . . well, you know what?'

'But I won't be on my own, will I? I'll be with Ian and Pippa, and Jake. And when we left Comfort Wood Farm, Pippa said I'd be welcome anytime for as long as I'd like. Obviously, I'll pay rent.'

Simon makes a sound at the back of his throat. 'If I know your cousin and his wife, they won't hear of that.'

'Then I'll contribute towards the food bill.' Ellinor scrutinises her husband's open face. He's rarely able to hide his feelings. 'So does that mean you're happy for me to speak to Ian and Pippa about this?'

'If that's what you want then of course I'm happy.'

'It is, Simon.' She gives him a heartfelt hug. 'You have no idea what this means to me.'

'If this is the reaction I get in agreeing to your whims, then I've just learned something of great importance.'

She punches him playfully on the arm. 'It's not as though it will be forever. I'll come home some weekends, but I really want to get this project off the ground as quickly as possible.'

'I hope you *will* want to come home!' Simon's eyes dance in amusement. 'But I suggest you book the Mini in for a service before you embark on your Cornish adventure.'

'I'll phone the garage this morning,' she agrees.

Leaning forward, Simon tentatively kisses her on the mouth. But Eleanor's mind is already on her plans for the forthcoming weeks, and she responds with a perfunctory kiss. Rising from the bed, she heads towards the door.

'Do you want breakfast, or shall we have brunch as it's late?' she asks from the doorway.

'Brunch,' Simon replies, masking his feelings with a stretch. 'But, first, I'll grab a shower.'

* * *

Over the following week, Ellinor visits the local garden centre and purchases a variety of plants for the newly created pond. She follows the aquatic assistant's advice and chooses flowers and marginals attractive to damsels and dragonflies, and carefully loads a selection of Ragged-Robin, Mare's-tail, Greater Reedmace, Greater Spearwort, Soft Rush, Cuckoo-flower, Arrowhead, Meadowsweet, Marsh Marigold and Amphibious Bistort into the boot of her car. Hurrying home, she and Tim waste no time in planting up, and as the minutes pass, a curious sense of fulfilment infuses Ellinor. It's as if she's reconnected with a part of her soul that she barely knew existed. A couple of hours later, she stands back and admires their handiwork and is surprised at how much she's enjoyed getting her hands dirty.

Although the edges of the pond look bare, Tim assures her the plants will soon establish and the landscaped area will appear natural. 'By mid-summer you won't recognise it. It'll be a haven for frogs and toads once they've discovered the pond, which won't take long.'

On the Friday evening, Ellinor and Simon dine at the newly opened local restaurant. It's a bit of a landmark as it's the first time she's eaten out since *the incident*, and throughout the evening the therapist's voice resounds in her head. *Baby steps*. Much to Ellinor's relief, the occasion passes without anything untoward occurring and she senses the return of some of her previous strength of character. As Simon drives the two miles home, she smiles to herself, realising that she feels confident in tackling the Cornish plan she's put into action.

Sunday morning arrives quickly, and as Simon carries her suitcase to the Mini, she follows him out of the house. The day is fair, and light cloud cover drifts across a baby-blue sky, and the hint of spring in the air only increases Ellinor's sense of purpose and optimism.

Simon places her suitcase in the boot of the car and turns to her. 'Now, are you sure about this? You know, it's not too late to change your mind.'

'Simon, I'm absolutely sure.' She gives his arm a squeeze. 'I'll phone you as soon as I get there.'

'Well, OK, then.' Fleetingly, her confident, self-assured husband appears at a loss.

It's unusual for him to show signs of vulnerability, and rising onto her tiptoes she plants a kiss on his mouth. 'I've made sure there's plenty of food in the freezer, although I'm sure you'll probably dine out most evenings.'

Guiltily, his eyes meet hers.

'Ha! Caught you out,' Ellinor says triumphantly. 'I know you only too well.'

'I admit, some of the guys at work suggested we try out a new wine bar close to the office this week,' he says awkwardly.

'And I hope you have a wonderful time,' she responds, without missing a beat. 'But, Si, it's only five days until we see each other again.'

He pulls a sad face. 'Five long days.'

Opening the driver's door, she climbs in and looks up at him. 'They will go by in a flash, you'll see.'

'Drive safely, Elli.'

'I will.'

'I'll miss you,' he adds.

'You, too.'

Ellinor turns on the engine and eases the car into gear. As she drives towards the open entrance gates she glances in the rear-view mirror and catches a hint of a frown puckering her husband's forehead. Opening the side window, she gives him an enthusiastic wave. She's about to turn onto the private road when she notices a lone raven sitting on the hedge observing her, the grey feather slanting across its chest declaring it as her recent visitor. Suddenly her senses tingle. Feeling foolish, she gives it a smile and wonders if it will still be here when she next comes back to Surrey.

Pulling out into the quiet road, Ellinor sets off for Cornwall, and several hours of a non-eventful journey later, she crosses the Tamar Bridge. Tension immediately lifts from her shoulders and she follows the sat nav's directions through the twisting country lanes. It's not long before she turns up the track leading to Comfort Wood Farm, and as she drives into the courtyard it seems to her that the farmhouse smiles in welcome.

Eighteen

'So, Elli,' Ian says, as he sets a plate of bacon and eggs on the table in front of her. 'What do you have planned for today?'

Ellinor glances up at her cousin. Having arrived late afternoon the previous day, and after unpacking her suitcase and settling into her room, she, Ian and Pippa had met up with Jake and his partner, Jessica, for supper at a local pub. She'd been surprised to witness the big bear of a man acting so gently and considerately towards his significant other, and often heart-warmingly deferring to the diminutive woman at his side. Everything about the man was large – his thatch of red hair, the appropriately bushy beard, the wide, generous mouth and big teeth, hands at least twice the size of Ellinor's, the bulging biceps straining his shirt . . . and his height. Six feet, four inches, Jessica proudly informed her when she'd enquired. Being a Sunday night, the inn wasn't too busy, and thankfully she'd coped well with the general noise and commotion.

Now, this morning, at the start of a brand-new week, she feels a growing excitement at the prospect of embracing the first day of her new Cornish life.

'I thought I'd ring Graham Haynes and arrange to meet up with him one day this week. I also want to revisit the site,' she says.

Ian pulls out a chair opposite her at the dining table. 'It's great that you're going to develop the old cottage, and I can't think of a better couple to take it on.' He helps himself to a slice of toast. 'Do you think Simon will permanently decamp to Cornwall at some point?'

Ellinor swallows a mouthful of bacon. 'I think he might!

He's eager to be involved with your enterprise and talks about how he wants to shape his future away from London. The delights of the capital seem to have dimmed for him a little, although, apparently, he and some colleagues are checking out a new wine bar this week!' She pulls a wry face.

Ian laughs. 'When this farm became a reality, I didn't think twice about leaving the city. Don't get me wrong, we enjoyed our life in Hertfordshire and London, but sometimes you need more of a challenge than a routine commute to a nine-to-five job with the occasional weekend jolly. Not for one moment have we looked back, however many sleepless nights we've had since setting all this up.' He gazes thoughtfully at Ellinor across the table. 'I just know you're going to thrive here, Elli. I feel it in my bones.'

'Thank you, Ian. I do feel stronger each day. The horror of *the incident* is diminishing, although I still have nightmares, but not so many these days. I truly believe I'm on the road to healing.'

He smiles at her. 'Of course you are, Elli. The tranquil air of the Tamar Valley and a completely different way of life will help you regain your equilibrium.'

'You always were the voice of reason and wisdom, Ian,' she says sincerely. 'How is that? I mean, our families don't exactly have an exceptional track record where rational and savvy thinking is concerned, do they?'

He snorts.

Ellinor thinks back to the days when her dad and his brother, Trevor – Ian's father – had attempted several joint business ventures without success. Throughout her childhood, money was always tight, and she and her sister had often gone without, surrounded by friends who paraded an endless supply of trendy clothes and the latest gadgets, and were regularly whisked off to exotic locations by their well-heeled parents. She and Chloe had had to be content with 'second-hand' and cheap copies of the latest brands at best, and holidays were usually at caravan parks along the south coast. Interrupting her stream of consciousness, Ellinor considers whether that was why she'd chosen to become a flight attendant – treating herself to a lifestyle she thought her school friends had enjoyed. Ian's childhood had been much the same, with the two families often taking caravanning holidays together. Eventually, their fathers gave up on their dreams of running their own business together and found jobs that provided a steady income, albeit not a particularly inspired work life. She wonders now if that's why Ian has taken the plunge and struck out on his own . . . with Pippa, of course.

'Our poor old mums and dads,' Ian comments. 'Still enduring the daily commute.'

'Yes,' she says thoughtfully.

'Maybe they'll retire down here,' Ian adds, helping himself to another slice of toast.

Ellinor can't imagine her mother leaving the Hertfordshire village where she's lived all her life and giving up her circle of friends.

'Who knows what the future has in store,' she responds.

Suddenly, a draught springs up out of nowhere, and Ellinor rubs her arms and glances at the door. It's closed, and she gives a small frown.

'I think I'll go and call Graham now.' Rising to her feet, she picks up her empty plate and mug.

'Don't worry about clearing the table,' Ian says between mouthfuls. 'I'll do that. You go and make that phone call.'

A couple of hours later, having exchanged trainers for walking shoes, Ellinor sets off along the lane. Reaching the footpath sign, she turns down the rough track that accesses the woods. The line of grass down its centre has grown since she was last here, and keeping to the outer edge, she gazes over the hedgerows and observes the three-sided castellated stone structure a couple of fields away. If she listens hard enough, will she hear Rapunzel singing from a room high up in the tower? Ellinor snorts. What nonsense! Suddenly a burst of birdsong reverberates through the woodland.

That's the only singing I'm likely to hear.

Presently, she comes to the five-bar wooden gate, which today stands open, and she wonders if Ian is working in the area. He hadn't said anything at breakfast. She glances around but there's no sign of his Land Rover.

Diverting off the footpath, Ellinor walks among the trees and follows the narrow track. Mounting excitement consumes her as she picks her way across the soft leaf litter and clambers over fallen branches. Again, she's aware of a deep and ancient stillness. It's as if a different world exists here amongst the mixed woodland; one undisturbed by the march of time.

Dappled light filters through the tree canopy and milky colours drift across the forest floor, and way off to her right, deep in the woodland, she hears the muffled sound of a chainsaw.

Is that where Ian is? She decides to seek him out after she's visited the ruins.

As on her previous visits, the forest seems a magical place to Ellinor, and she looks around for any signs of animals or mythical beings that may be hiding amongst the hazel and holly, inquisitively watching. But all is still, and if there are any creatures observing the intruder, they keep well out of sight.

It's not long before Ellinor reaches the clearing, and pausing at the edge of the trees, she gazes at the ruined remains of the cottage. In her mind's eye, she can clearly envisage the homestead that she plans to create. The forest encroaches in on the glade, but it doesn't feel menacing, even when a sudden blinding light appears through the trees, completely encircling the clearing and making the tree trunks stand out darkly against its brilliance. It reminds her of an alien spaceship's searchlights flooding the area from above and she glances up, but the sky is comfortingly blue with no signs of a UFO. She lets out an embarrassed chuckle.

I've been watching far too many sci-fi films, and I blame my husband for that!

Intrigued, she watches as a yellow haze emanates out from the white luminescence, swirling and growing in density to a beautiful, warm golden glow. The mist weaves its way through the woodland towards the glade, and as if in response, the ruined walls of the cottage glint gold in the morning sunlight. All at once, Ellinor detects the sweet scent of honeysuckle and she looks around, but there's no sign of the plant growing wild in the immediate vicinity.

'That's odd,' she mutters.

It's what she intends to train around the front door, once there is one . . .

Keeping to the edge of the clearing, she walks over to a fallen log and perches on its gnarly bark. From the back pocket of her jeans, she extracts a housebuilder's brochure and flicks through the pages until she reaches the design she's interested in. Holding the booklet open in front of her, she squints and visualises the style of rustic cottage that will replace the current ruins.

'Perfect,' she says, in little more than a whisper.

Nineteen

The sound of a snapping twig rudely breaches the peace and tranquillity. Immediately, Ellinor is on high alert and she scans the trees in the direction of the noise.

Are those shadows shifting in the golden light?

With pounding heart, her fingers automatically fly to the scar on her neck as she relives the nightmare moment her attacker had pressed the blade into her skin. Springing to her feet, she readies herself to flee.

The mellow hoot of an owl carries on the breeze and suddenly she realises she can no longer hear the muffled noise of the chainsaw. The forest has fallen silent. She glances at her watch – twelve noon. Perhaps Ian, or whoever, has stopped for lunch.

Quivering leaves on a holly tree at the far edge of the clearing catch her attention, and with laser-like precision, Ellinor focuses on an area of woodland to the right of the ruined cottage – the exact spot where she'd previously seen an animal observing her. Is it her imagination or do two amber eyes stare back? Catching her breath, she suppresses rising panic and peers into the undergrowth.

No way! This cannot be happening again . . .

Unwaveringly, the round eyes observe her.

The owl hoots once more, and as the animal turns its head she catches sight of a long snout and rough, wiry grey hair. It's exactly what happened before. Only this time, the creature abandons the cover of the dense foliage and steps out into the clearing.

Branok!

The large hound is surprisingly quick and light on its

feet as it trots across the glade towards her. Ellinor takes a step back and glances anxiously into the woodland. She'll have no chance of outrunning it if the animal comes for her. She'll have to climb a tree. But the dog doesn't seem threatening as it closes the distance between them – more curious. Behind it, a shadow takes shape in the trees and she stares in disbelief as her husband emerges into the glade, with a brace of pheasants dangling from one hand.

How can Simon be in Cornwall? He has meetings and appointments all week. And anyway, apart from his disapproval of game shooting, it's the wrong season!

A whooshing sound fills Ellinor's head and as her legs threaten to buckle, she staggers.

'Why, if it isn't the fair Lady Ellinor!' Simon exclaims, with a disarming smile.

The breath stalls in her throat. She's obviously slipped into that dreamlike world of her imagination, as she had before at Cotehele. Perhaps she's not as far into recovery as she'd thought. Was it rash to have cancelled her appointments with the therapist? Ellinor remains rooted to the spot. What should she do? Run? She glances at the hound, now only a couple of yards away from her, and notices a curious dark grey feather-shaped mark slanting across its chest. Cocking its head, the dog's amber eyes observe her with interest.

With superhuman effort, Ellinor sucks air into her lungs. 'What are you doing here?'

Simon laughs. 'I could ask the same of you.'

Reaching the wolfhound, he places a reassuring hand on its neck.

'But, Simon, I don't understand.'

'That name again!' Quizzically, he considers her. 'Who *is* this Simon?'

Ellinor's mind focuses on the man before her, and as the panic briefly lifts, she observes his leather boots, breeches and tunic. Even in her heightened state, the rational portion of her brain registers how *very* attractive he looks in this style of outfit. But then she notices the crossbow slung across his back and fear closes in on her once more.

'What brings you to my humble abode?'

'Your abode?' she croaks.

He grins. 'Yes. My abode.'

Confused, she scans the glade, and her eyes widen. In the centre of the clearing is a single-storey stone cottage, the reeds of its thatched roof gleaming burnished gold in the sunlight, and around its wooden door is a tangle of pink-and-gold honeysuckle in full bloom.

'So, I ask again. What brings you here?'

Slowly, Ellinor turns back to the man. This isn't real! Surely she will snap out of this wild fantasy before too long.

'I . . .' She hesitates. How can she possibly answer?

Raising his eyebrows, he waits patiently.

She tries again. 'I was going for a walk and stumbled across it.'

Is that a good enough explanation?

She glances down and notices that the housebuilding brochure she was holding has vanished.

'Ah, that would explain your unusual garments,' he says, casting his eyes down her denim-clad legs to her walking shoes. 'I recall that this was your attire on the last occasion we had the good fortune to meet. Maybe you were out walking then?'

As his eyes lock on hers, she notices the twinkle of amusement in his gaze.

'Well, fair Ellinor,' he continues, 'I welcome you to my home. Come, you must be thirsty. We shall take spiced ale together.'

As if caught in a fairy tale, unable to control the outcome of events, Ellinor finds herself accompanying him across the clearing towards the cottage. Suddenly, the harsh, metallic call of a pheasant and the sound of flapping wings erupt from the trees and the wolfhound's head snaps around.

'Calm, Branok,' the man says in a soothing voice. 'No more hunting today.'

Ellinor shakes her head. *What is going on?*

Pushing open the door, he enters the cottage and Ellinor nervously follows. Standing just inside the room, she glances around. It's simply furnished, with an open fire at one end, and in a corner is a large sack cloth draped over a branch wedged into the space between the roof and the top of the walls. Behind it, she glimpses a simple low bed. A scrubbed table and a bench seat nestle against the front wall, and next to this are a couple of rustic planks balanced on wooden boxes providing storage for a selection of earthenware bowls and jugs.

Ellinor watches as the man places the crossbow against the wall and hangs the brace of pheasants on a hook. She glances back at the open door where the dog has now settled across the threshold with its head on its paws. There's no other means of escape.

'Please excuse the simplicity of my home, which is ill-prepared to entertain such a fine lady,' he says, crossing over to the wooden boxes.

He takes out a couple of wooden drinking vessels. Keeping one eye on Ellinor, he removes the stopper from one of the earthenware jugs and pours golden liquid into the cups.

'Sit,' he says, replacing the stopper.

Hesitantly, Ellinor crosses over to the table and sits down on the very edge of the bench seat. Accepting the offered cup, she takes a sip. The clear honey-coloured nectar is warm and full of spices and herbs. She composes her face as she swallows. It's like nothing she's ever tasted before and it's not unpleasant . . . just *different*.

'I thought I may have seen you during these past three months,' the man says, sitting down on the bench seat next to her. 'But when I asked after you, Phillipa informed me that you had returned to Surrey and your family.'

Three months? More like three weeks! And Phillipa . . . does he mean Pippa? Why hasn't Pippa mentioned him to me if she's spoken to him, too?

'I did return to Surrey,' she confirms.

He nods. 'But Phillipa tells me you visit her often?'

Ellinor frowns. It's too complicated to go into detail and she simply replies, 'I do.'

'She's a good woman, and one who I'm proud to call *cousin*,' he says sincerely.

'Phillipa is your cousin?'

Her mind is seriously playing games with her! In this dreamlike state, everything is slightly altered. Keeping her hand steady, Ellinor places the cup on the table. She can't listen to him and drink at the same time, and if she's not careful she will choke.

'She is. My mother's sister's child. Of course, Phillipa has siblings in Kent, but her marriage has brought her to this part of the country.' His gaze rests upon her. 'But you know this.'

Ellinor simply nods, incapable of understanding why she has conjured up this hallucination.

'Tell me, Ellinor, what brings you here?'

Her mouth has turned dry. 'To Comfort Wood Farm?'

He frowns. 'Of what do you speak? I know not of this Comfort Wood Farm . . . or Simon.'

Ellinor lets out a silent sigh. It's all very well her brain messing with her, but it could at least give her some guidance and perhaps a helpful heads-up.

'I meant to say, Phillipa's farm.'

His frown eases.

'I haven't been well,' she continues. 'I've come here to recover.'

His gaze softens. 'I trust that whatever ails you will be gone soon enough.'

She wonders what he'd say if she told him about the flight and the passenger that threatened her. He'd think she was mad and probably pronounce her a witch, and at best, throw her out, or worst . . . God only knows! She shudders. Glancing down at her watch, she's surprised not to see it around her wrist. The tongue of the buckle had worked loose, and she'd meant to have it repaired, but she'd never got around to it. She was wearing it when she sat on the log and she can't lose it! It was a present from Simon . . . an expensive one at that. Once this madness is over, she will carefully retrace her steps from the door of the cottage to the log and search for it.

Ellinor takes a large gulp of ale to try and steady her nerves and replaces the wooden cup on the table.

'More ale?' he asks.

She glances at him. It's odd sitting here with this man who is her husband, behaving as if they're little more than strangers. But if her brain isn't going to save her from this alternative world it's conjured up, she will just have to take control.

'No. I must be on my way.' Ellinor gets to her feet, surprised to see the flicker of disappointment in his eyes. 'Thank you for the drink. It was very kind of you.'

'My pleasure, Ellinor.' He gives her a disarmingly attractive smile.

Quickly, she turns towards the door to hide the smile tugging at her own mouth, while inwardly mocking herself for her reaction to his.

'Branok,' he commands. 'Move.'

The wolfhound raises its head and surveys them for a moment before lumbering to its feet and moving out of the way.

As Ellinor steps over the threshold and out into the warm sunlight, she scans the surrounding area for her watch and glances over towards the log where she'd been sitting. But the log is no longer there.

'Ellinor.'

She turns at the sound of his familiar voice.

'I hope our paths cross again before too long.' Taking her hand in his, he lightly grazes her knuckles with his lips.

'Simon . . .' she starts, before his raised eyebrow stops her.

'William.' He smiles.

A sudden thrill rips through her body at his touch, and she stares wide-eyed at this version of her husband standing in the doorway. This dream – or flight of fancy – is certainly putting her through a maelstrom of emotions.

'I hope so too . . . William,' she whispers, amazed that her voice has taken on such a silky tone.

'Farewell, lovely maiden.' There's a sparkle in his bright blue eyes. 'Until we meet again.'

Concentrating on putting one foot in front of the other, Ellinor takes an unsteady step into the clearing. She hears William call to his dog, but it seems as though his voice comes from somewhere far away. And there's another sound too, increasing in volume – the whine of a chainsaw. Shielding her eyes from the sun, she looks across towards the edge of the glade and experiences a sudden rush of relief as she spots the fallen log. Abruptly, she turns back to the cottage, but it's no longer there, and only the ruined walls bask peacefully in the afternoon sunshine in the centre of this undisturbed oasis. All at once she's besieged by nausea and deep disappointment, and an inexplicable longing for home, and a yearning for something lost consumes her.

'Oh, for goodness' sake!' she says out loud. 'You wanted to get back to reality.'

Feeling foolish, she looks around. But no one is eavesdropping, and glancing over towards the log again, she notices the pages of the housebuilding brochure fluttering in a gentle breeze, and lying beside it is her watch, its glass face glinting in the sunlight. Walking over, she stoops to pick it up and quickly secures it around her wrist. The second hand moves around the clockface but suddenly she freezes, and a puzzled frown settles on her face.

'What the . . .?'

She's been in that dreamworld for what seems like hours, so why are the hands only pointing to two minutes past twelve?

Twenty

On Thursday afternoon, Ellinor helps Ian and Pippa prepare for the farmers' market taking place the following day. Organisation is a well-oiled machine and she happily throws herself into the work. Ian fills sterilised bottles with apple juice and Ellinor then sticks on Comfort Wood Farm labels, ensuring they're straight, before passing the bottles to Pippa who carefully packs them into crates.

'A fine production line we've got going here,' Ian says, giving Ellinor a wink. 'A third pair of hands makes all the difference, doesn't it, Pippa?'

'Sure does!' agrees his wife.

Ellinor smiles, thankful she's being useful. 'Is the new cider equipment operated manually?'

'No, it's mechanised,' Ian replies. 'We'd be slaves to spending time in this barn otherwise, and the rest of the farm would go to rack and ruin!'

'Thank goodness we live in the twenty-first century and we have the choice,' Pippa comments, as she starts filling a new crate. 'It must have been tough in former times.'

Remembering that William said he'd spoken with Philippa, Ellinor scrutinises the woman, wondering if she, too, inhabits that dreamlike world. But as Pippa glances up and gives her a genuine smile, no secrets show in her open face.

The next morning, Pippa brings the van to a stop at the mini roundabout and indicates left, as she waits for a gap in the flow of traffic.

'Is Tavistock always this busy?' Ellinor asks.

'Not always. We've hit commuter time and the school

run,' Pippa replies. A fine rain descends, and she switches on the wipers, which clear the windscreen with a sweeping hypnotic effect.

'I know Sir Francis Drake is linked to Plymouth,' Ellinor says, observing the proud figure standing on a stone plinth in the centre of the roundabout. 'But why is there a statue of him here?'

'He was born near here,' explains Pippa, turning left and joining the stream of vehicles heading towards Tavistock. 'Apparently, in 1882 plans were put into action by Plymouth dignitaries to raise funds for a statue of Drake on the Hoe, to commemorate the three-hundredth anniversary of the defeat of the Spanish Armada. But, incensed at the idea that Plymothians had the cheek to attempt to steal their famous son' – Pippa lifts an amused eyebrow – 'the good people of Tavistock decided to raise funds for their own bronze statue. As it turned out, they didn't have to. The Ninth Duke of Bedford paid for it and gifted the statue to the town.'

'How very generous of him!'

Pippa laughs. 'Yes. Over the years several Dukes of Bedford have been generous to Tavistock. Philanthropy must be a strong trait in that family.'

Ellinor takes in the surroundings as the traffic makes its way slowly towards the charming market town nestled on the western edge of Dartmoor. To her right is a pleasant tree-lined area of open land with a sensory garden, bowling and tennis clubs.

'The town's inhabitants are very well catered for,' Ellinor observes, before suddenly exclaiming, 'Wow! They're hardy souls.' She gestures towards half-a-dozen people ignoring the weather and continuing to play on the tennis courts.

'Obviously determined to make the most of their membership,' Pippa remarks drily.

Turning in the opposite direction, Ellinor gazes out of the passenger window at a line of substantial, stylish Victorian townhouses set back from the road. Many are private properties with neat, landscaped front gardens enclosed by trimmed box hedges and natural stone walling, but a few signs announce hotels, nurseries, solicitors' offices and alternative healthcare businesses.

'Tavistock is an ancient stannary town,' Pippa says, continuing in her role as tour guide. 'It has a recorded history dating back to at least 961 when Tavistock Abbey was founded, now sadly in ruins, as it fell foul to King Henry VIII's Dissolution of the Monasteries. Though today, the town is thriving. There's a popular arts centre with regular live music events and a cinema, a couple of swimming-pool complexes – and not only does the town have the picturesque River Tavy running through it, but also a four-mile-long canal that stretches from Abbey Weir to Morwellham Quay.'

'Full of history,' Ellinor remarks.

'Yes. Even the Vikings created havoc in Tavistock!' Pippa says, as they pass the stone-built, castellated Bedford Hotel. At the mini roundabout, she indicates left. 'The Seventh Duke of Bedford,' she announces, before Ellinor has a chance to ask who the second statue represents. 'He was responsible for many of the town's public buildings. However, these days he spends his time eyeballing Drake at the far end of the road.'

Ellinor laughs.

Pippa drives into the town centre and takes a narrow turning to the right, following a lane that runs alongside the river. Most of the allocated parking is already taken, but there are a couple of spaces, and she quickly and efficiently manoeuvres the van into a bay and pulls on the handbrake.

'The Pannier Market is through there,' she says, pointing to an open gateway. 'We'll load the crates onto the sack truck . . . and then let the fun begin!'

Several hours later, Ellinor places three bottles of apple juice in a sturdy carrier bag, along with a business flyer, and hands it over to an elderly gentleman standing on the other side of the table.

'Thank you,' he says politely.

Ellinor smiles. 'I hope you enjoy your purchases.'

'Oh, I will, young lady. I like to stock up whenever Pippa is in the market. It's the first stall I visit, because I wouldn't want her to run out before I get to her.'

'Her apple juice is very special,' Ellinor says.

'It is! I can't abide the rubbish supermarkets pass off for juice these days. Full of preservatives.'

He gives her a cheeky wink before walking away to inspect the goods for sale on the opposite stall. Ellinor smiles to herself as she watches him engage in conversation with the stallholder. It's obviously as much a social event for the man as a shopping spree. Sitting down on a chair, she realises she's been on her feet all morning and her back aches. She glances at her watch – still two hours to go until the market closes, although they've sold out of most of the stock. She turns her head at the sound of Pippa's voice.

'Here you go.' Her cousin's wife approaches, holding aloft two large polystyrene cups and a paper bag. 'Spicy butternut-squash soup and baguettes. I thought that would keep us going.'

'Thanks.' Ellinor relieves her of a cup.

'I see you've sold more bottles,' Pippa says, as she sits down on the chair next to Ellinor. Placing her cup on the table, she tears open the paper bag.

'There was a flurry as soon as you left,' Ellinor replies.

'Typical!' Pippa says, picking up a baguette and taking a bite.

'That gentleman over there says he always comes to you first, as he doesn't want you to run out before he has a chance to buy anything from you.'

Pippa gazes across the market to the elderly man, who is now examining medals and badges on a stall selling military memorabilia.

'That's Wilf,' she says. 'He was my very first customer and he's been buying regularly from me ever since.'

'He seems a sweet old soul,' Ellinor comments.

'He is.' Pippa nods. 'He lost his wife last year and I think he visits the market most days when it's open.'

'It would be nice if he visited the farm one day,' Ellinor suggests, removing the lid of her polystyrene cup and blowing on the soup.

'That's a good idea. We could offer visits to the orchards and, if there was enough interest, organise a minibus to pick up people from the town. We could provide cream teas and sell juice, and apples when they're harvested.'

'Just a thought,' Ellinor says with a smile. Pippa's enthusiasm is *so* infectious.

'Well, thank you, Elli. It's a terrific thought!'

Fortunately, a lull in the day allows the two women to enjoy their lunch relatively undisturbed.

'What time is Simon expected to arrive today?' Pippa asks, draining the last drop of her soup.

'He said he'd try to get away early and drive straight down. If not, I doubt we'll see him much before nine.'

'I'll leave supper in the warming oven for him, if he doesn't make it in time to eat with us.' Pippa places her empty cup in the bag allocated for rubbish.

'I can't wait to tell him what the architect said,' Ellinor enthuses. 'He'll be thrilled with the changes he's suggested. It's going to be a wonderful home.'

Pippa nods. 'Graham does have good ideas. When I first proposed the holiday let, he came up with some innovative solutions regarding the outhouses that I hadn't considered. It was his idea to knock through to the coal shed and include the old dairy to create a second bedroom with a bathroom en suite. Initially, we'd designed it as a cosy, bijou cottage with just one bedroom and a shower room, which, of course, would be fine if we only wanted to rent it to one couple, or a single person. Now, we'll be able to offer it to two couples or a family.'

'That's good,' Ellinor says. 'I didn't feel at all uncomfortable discussing my ideas with him. In fact, Graham encouraged me to think outside the box and Simon will be surprised at what we've come up with.'

'Judging by what you described the other day, I think he will be very surprised!'

'Hopefully, in a good way.'

'Well, if not, just remember . . . it's wise to keep our respective significant others on their toes!' Pippa laughs.

As two women with a young child approach the stall, Pippa gets to her feet and soon she's describing the farm and the orchards to a spellbound audience. The interaction pays off, culminating in the sale of four bottles of apple juice and the promise that the women and their families will visit the farm for a day out during the summer. Lifting the lid off the moneybox, Pippa slips their payment into it before sitting down again.

'Pippa . . .' Ellinor ventures.

'Yes?'

'I know you were living in London at the time you met Ian, but where did you grow up?'

'Kent. My family have a small farm near Rye.' Pippa gives her an inquisitive look. 'Why do you ask?'

'It's obvious you love the countryside, and I wondered what your background was. All I knew was that you worked in IT.'

Pippa snorts. 'Out of necessity . . . although I'm eternally grateful that it brought Ian into my life. London was expensive and IT work paid the bills. My parents spend their lives trying to make thirty acres work for them.' She pauses thoughtfully. 'What with the contrary British weather and the dependence on healthy animals, it's always been tough, although it was a brilliantly unencumbered upbringing. My folks are total optimists and real troupers, and they instilled in us kids that you never get anywhere without putting in a bit of hard graft.'

'I think they've passed on more than that,' Ellinor says. 'Boundless enthusiasm and a passion for nature and the environment.'

'What do they say? The apple doesn't fall far from the tree.' Pippa gives a deep-bellied laugh. 'Pun intended!'

Ellinor smiles, hesitating briefly before asking the burning question. 'So, do you have other family living in Kent?'

'My sister didn't go far. She settled in Canterbury with her solicitor husband. My brother is in Edinburgh with his partner.'

'What about cousins?' Ellinor strives for a casual tone.

'Cousins? A few, although Dad's sister's offspring are all high-flyers and work in finance, in some form or other. They all gravitated to London at the earliest opportunity, but most are now dispersed around the globe.'

Ellinor cuts to the chase. 'Do you have a cousin called William?'

Pippa pulls a bemused face. 'Why do you think I have a cousin called William?'

Concentrating on the floor, Ellinor says feebly, 'I thought I'd heard you mention a cousin by that name, that's all.'

'No.' Pippa frowns. 'How odd! I wonder why you thought that.'

'I must have misheard.'

'As far as I'm aware, there are no members of the wider family called William. Oh, heads up!' she says in a loud whisper. 'Customers incoming.'

Ellinor looks up and smiles at the approaching group, but as she rises to her feet, discontent niggles. William is simply a figment of her crazy, mixed-up imagination.

She *must* be going mad!

Twenty-One

It's Sunday afternoon and Ellinor and Simon relax in the snug, sitting together on the familiar, battered leather sofa that Ian had originally bought for his flat. The thick walls of the old farmhouse keep the inside temperature cool, and the wood burner is lit. Laid out on the coffee table are the architect's amended drawings for the cottage's new layout.

'What do you think of the design?' Ellinor asks her husband.

'Terrific,' he replies. 'I like the glass extension.'

Ellinor smiles. It's good having Simon with her again, and feeling unusually at peace with the world, she automatically snuggles up to him. 'It sits well with the stone cottage, doesn't it? Light will flood in through the floor-to-ceiling windows in those rooms.'

Delighted by her gesture of closeness, Simon places his arm around Ellinor's shoulders.

'Hopefully, there'll be light flooding into our marriage again as well.' He turns to face her. 'And I can't wait for that, Elli.'

She wishes he hadn't drawn attention to the difficult emotional waters they currently navigate, and despondently she fights the urge to pull away. Since her husband's arrival thirty-six hours before, their time together at Comfort Wood Farm has passed easily enough and she has *almost* forgotten her hesitation whenever he wraps her in his arms. But any physical contact not initiated by her still triggers the horror of being trapped and held against her will.

'I hope so, too,' Ellinor says, quietly extricating herself from his hold and hoping he won't be offended.

'I know so, Elli.'

She smiles uncertainly. How can he be so sure? She can't promise anything.

All at once a cool draught swirls around her legs and Ellinor glances up. Strange . . . the temperature has dropped, but there's no obvious reason why. The window is closed, but she notices the orange flames suddenly flicker and leap behind the glass door of the wood burner, as if they, too, sense the unusual current of air. The room has grown hazy, as if cloaked in a heavy veil, and suddenly the door opens. Ellinor watches in astonishment as shadowy figures enter – a middle-aged woman and a girl, both wearing long skirts and aprons, and a young man in loose trousers. Their features are indistinct, and all their garments are dull, muted colours.

'Simon. Who are those people?'

He obviously hasn't heard her as he continues to inspect the plans on the table. She turns her attention back to the scene playing out in the room.

The figures walk silently towards rustic shelves lining the far wall, that Ellinor hasn't noticed before. Picking up a platter of fish from them, the woman turns and speaks to the girl, but although her lips move, there is no sound. The girl nods and takes down a couple of loaves from a shelf while the young man lifts a couple of heavy jugs, which are obviously full. But before Ellinor can make sense of what she's witnessing, as quickly as the figures had appeared, they suddenly disperse into the shadows and disappear.

Simon rises to his feet. Crossing over to the wood burner, he opens the door and throws on another log and immediately the snug returns to its previously warm temperature. He turns back to the sofa.

'Did you see them?' Ellinor whispers.

His look is uncomprehending. 'What?'

'The people.'

Glancing towards the window, he peers out.

'Not out there, Si. In here!'

Simon's eyes widen. 'Elli, there's been no one in here apart from us.'

Her gaze focuses on the bare stone wall where the shelves had been. 'Oh God, I'm going mad!' Letting out a groan, she buries her head in her hands.

'What exactly did you see?' Simon asks, sitting down beside her again. When she doesn't answer, he carefully prises open her hands.

Ellinor's stricken eyes meet her husband's curious gaze. 'I felt a draught and then the door opened, and a woman, a girl and a young man entered. They took down plates of food and jugs from wooden shelves on that wall over there.'

She points to the exposed stone wall opposite. Apart from a tasteful watercolour of the meandering River Tamar in a wooden frame, nothing else adorns it.

Simon frowns.

'I know it sounds crazy,' she says, alarmed by the shrill in her voice. 'But I tell you, that's what I saw!'

Simon contemplates his wife with a puzzled gaze. Slowly, he says, 'If that's what you saw, then that's what you saw.'

Suddenly the door opens, making them both jump.

'Nice and cosy in here,' Pippa says, as she enters the room carrying a tray laden with mugs and a plate of biscuits and cakes. 'I thought you might like afternoon tea.'

'That's kind.' Simon folds up the architect's plans and makes space on the coffee table.

'It's a wonderful design,' Pippa says, nodding to the drawings as she places down the tray.

'Yes,' he replies. 'We're very happy with the large glass extension.'

'Wonderful!' Pippa enthuses, handing them each a mug of tea. 'A marriage of old and new.'

A shiver snakes its way up Ellinor's spine and she rubs her arms.

'If you're cold, Elli, put another log on the fire,' Pippa

says. 'Although I must say it feels very warm in here at the moment.'

'I'm not cold.' Ellinor smiles weakly. 'It's just what you said, *a marriage of old and new*.'

'Well, that's what it is, isn't it?' Pippa says, sitting in the opposite armchair. 'I'm not sure why, but I find it peculiarly satisfying when what's gone before is incorporated into current-day living. Of course, in your case, you'll be replicating the old with a new-build masquerading as ancient. Still, if anyone can pull it off, it's Graham, and Jake and his men. You're in safe hands there.' Picking up the plate of biscuits and cakes, she offers them around.

Ellinor declines.

Helping himself to a blueberry muffin and glancing at his wife, Simon asks, 'Was this room ever used as something other than a snug?'

Pippa takes a moment to consider his question. 'Well, the farmhouse has changed quite a bit over the centuries, so we understand. This is the oldest part of the house, circa fifteenth century. I'm not sure but I believe the kitchen was where the dining room is now, and as this leads directly off' – she indicates the snug with a sweep of her hand – 'it wouldn't surprise me if this was once a dairy or a pantry.' She selects a chocolate biscuit from the plate and takes a bite. 'Why do you ask?'

Ellinor turns to her husband with a triumphant look.

Simon's eyebrows knit together in a troubled frown. 'Elli thought she saw some people in here.' His eyes meet Pippa's.

'Oh, I expect they were the ghosts of Comfort Wood Farm,' Pippa says nonchalantly.

Simon's eyes widen.

'You know about them?' Ellinor exclaims.

Pippa glances at her. 'We've never experienced anything ourselves, but old houses are bound to have the odd ghost or two, aren't they? I mean, over the past five centuries this farmhouse has seen a lot of change and no doubt weathered many a storm.'

'So, you don't know of any specific ghosts?' Ellinor persists.

Pippa gives her a guarded look. 'This was the main farmhouse for Cotehele House in the fifteenth century, and I'm sure there must have been occasions when the Edgcumbe family visited. Of course, that was during the time of the Wars of the Roses when many folk from different walks of life took up arms to fight for whatever side they were on. As we learned at the exhibition, Richard Edgcumbe played a major part.' She glances around the room. 'I'm sure if these walls could talk, they'd have many a tale to tell.'

Ellinor's gaze slides across to the charming watercolour gracing the far wall, where she'd seen the rustic shelves full of all manner of wooden, pewter and brass kitchen paraphernalia and crockery.

Am I simply making up these visions from the snippets of information I hear?

What else could it be . . .?

Twenty-Two

'Is it that time already?' Ellinor asks, as she watches her husband getting dressed by the dim glow of the bedside lamp.

''Fraid so!' Simon glances at his watch. 'If the roads are clear, hopefully I should be at work by eight.'

'I'll come down with you and say goodbye.'

'No need to do that, Elli. You stay nice and warm under the duvet.'

He walks over to the wardrobe and opens the doors quietly. Taking out his weekend bag, he removes a pair of jeans and a couple of sweatshirts from their hangers and places them in it, grabs a few items of underwear from the chest of drawers and gives the room a final check.

'I'll give you a ring tonight,' he says, zipping up the bag and approaching the bed.

Ellinor sits up and holds out her hand to him. 'Drive safely, Simon.'

Taking hold of her fingers, he drops a gentle kiss on her lips, and when she doesn't recoil, he smiles tenderly.

'It's been a great weekend, Elli. I just wish we had longer together.'

'Me, too,' she responds.

Ellinor observes as *professional* Simon takes over, his mind already focused on the next few hours. It never fails to amaze her how easily he switches from playful to professional in the blink of an eye.

Grabbing the handles of the bag, he heads towards the door. 'See you in five days,' he says softly, before silently exiting from the room.

Ellinor listens to the sound of creaking floorboards as

Simon makes his way along the landing of the slumbering household. It's dark, but then at three in the morning what else would it be? Slipping out of bed, she crosses over to the window and draws back the curtains. A moon rides high in the night sky, casting an eerie silver light over the landscape. She opens the old casement and gazes down, as her husband steps out from beneath the covered porch, located immediately below the window. Like a burglar, stealthily he crosses the stone-chipped courtyard to his vehicle. The click of the car doors as they unlock is shockingly loud in the quiet of the night and Simon glances back at the house. Seeing his wife standing at the open window, he blows her a kiss before opening the driver's door and climbing in. As the car's powerful engine starts up and the vehicle edges its way across the yard, Ellinor wonders how many other people over the centuries have left the farmhouse in the dead of night, and what were their reasons for doing so?

As the Audi's taillights disappear down the drive, she casts her eyes around the courtyard. The farm buildings are silhouetted by the strange, eerie light and dark shapes play amongst the shadows, and tease the senses. Her gaze comes to rest on the nearest barn and there, perched at the edge of the hayloft, is the barn owl silently observing her. Ellinor holds her breath. Unhurriedly, it spreads its wings before launching to glide between the buildings across the courtyard.

Beautiful . . . If not a somewhat ghostly apparition against the gloaming!

Closing the window, Ellinor quickly returns to the warmth of her bed and blessed sleep.

Some while later, a sharp knocking sound brutally jolts Ellinor into wakefulness and as the door flies opens, incomprehension and disorientation swamp her.

'Eleanora, get dressed!'

She stares in bewilderment at the figure in the doorway.

Why is Pippa calling me Eleanora and why is she wearing a long dress? It is Pippa . . . isn't it? She peers at the woman through the gloom and sees the face of her cousin's wife, though she is dressed very unlike Pippa.

'What time is it?' Ellinor asks.

'Daybreak.'

When has Pippa ever demanded that she get up at daybreak? Since arriving at Comfort Wood Farm, she's been encouraged to keep her own time and come and go as she pleases.

'What's wrong?' she asks, suddenly gripped with the notion that something may have happened to Simon.

The woman enters the room. 'Richard Edgcumbe and his men are on their way here. We must attend to them.'

Ellinor's eyes widen. Richard Edgcumbe? Pippa has never referred to a friend or acquaintance by that name. In fact, the only time she's heard it mentioned was when they visited Cotehele and again, yesterday, when they'd sat in the snug having tea. But *that* Richard Edgcumbe existed in the fifteenth century.

This has got to be a dream . . . Or a nightmare!

Ellinor doesn't move.

Letting out an impatient sigh, Pippa crosses to a wooden chest at the side of the room and gathers up several garments draped across it. Unceremoniously, she dumps them on the bed.

'Get dressed, Eleanora, and be quick about it. We must be ready and not keep them waiting.'

As Pippa hurries from the room, Ellinor casts her eyes wildly around. The bedroom seems familiar . . . and yet not. As her eyes grow accustomed to the gloom, she becomes aware that the matching oak wardrobe and chest of drawers no longer dominate one wall. Instead, a heavily carved wooden chest and a chair are in their place. Throwing back the covers, she's shocked to find that not only is she naked – where's the T-shirt gone that she usually wears? – but also the duvet has turned into a linen sheet, a blanket, and a reversible coverlet. And as Ellinor swings her legs over the edge of the mattress, she's surprised to find that the floor is further away than expected. Turning back, she stares open-mouthed.

What's happened to the king-size bed that matches the other furniture in the room?

This bed is no more than a small double with a tall wooden headrest, beneath which a bolster supports a pillow covered by a small, crumpled sheet. Ellinor's gaze swings over to the window where sunlight seeps around the edges of a closed wooden shutter.

And where are the curtains?

Crossing over to the window, she opens the shutter and stands back, aghast. Gone is the diamond-paned leaded window. In fact, there's no glass in the frame at all, just several misshapen wooden uprights . . . like the bars of a cell.

'What the f—?' she exclaims with a shudder.

If she closes her eyes, she's sure the room will return to normal once she opens them again. Squeezing her eyes tightly shut, she wills the familiar surroundings to re-emerge.

'Breathe, Elli. Don't panic,' she soothes.

But on tentatively opening one eyelid, she quickly closes it again.

'Don't you dare have a panic attack,' she growls. 'Not now!'

Opening her eyes fully, she forces herself to take deep breaths.

Footsteps thunder along the landing and Ellinor frowns. There's no one else in the house other than Ian and Pippa, and she can't imagine either of them making that racket. A cool breath of air enters the room through the open window, and she shivers. As goosebumps form on her skin, she glances around for her clothes, but they are nowhere in sight, and as she eyes the bundle of clothing on the bed, with a sinking feeling she realises there is no other option.

How do I wear these clothes? Do I wear them all, or pick and choose?

But, as if well practised, she slips the white-linen chemise over her head, dislodging a cap in the process.

Why the hell am I wearing a head covering?

Impatiently, she casts it aside and rolls on a pair of fine woollen hose, securing them in place with braids just beneath her knees. Next, spying a pair of leather shoes with pointy toes, she slips her feet into them.

I'd never wear a pair like this. They're ridiculous!

Ellinor gazes down at the verdant green, flat-fronted kirtle lying on the bedcover and runs her hands over the silk damask. Slipping the garment over her head, she dexterously tightens the front laces, shakes out the skirt and smooths down the material. Next, she picks up the dark blue damask kirtle with the rabbit-fur trim and puts this on. To her surprise, the garments fit perfectly.

Walking over to the carved chest, she lifts the heavy lid and takes out a wide red leather belt with a small pouch attached, and secures it high around her body, just below the bust. Lastly, extracting a jewelled silk band from the pouch, she secures the hairpiece around her head and leaves her hair to fall loosely over her shoulders. The actions seem completely familiar to her and she frowns. It's obvious she's done this before.

Sudden noises from outside pique her interest and making sure she keeps well out of sight, she crosses over to the open window as several men walk up the track. Seeing their outfits, she shrinks back. This is definitely a very strange dream. How long will she be caught in its throes? As the group of men cross the yard towards the house, a lone figure enters the farmyard behind them, whistling as if he hasn't a care in the world. Taking a cautious step towards the window, Ellinor's eyes open wide.

Simon?

But observing his leather boots, woollen hose, long doublet, cloak and felt hat, with sudden shocking clarity she realises that this is none other than the alternative version of her husband.

William!

As William strides across the farmyard, he glances up and his eyes lock with hers. Immediately, the whistling stops and a smile spreads across his face. Even at this distance the twinkle in his eyes is evident and without warning, warmth floods Ellinor's heart. Removing his hat, with a dramatic flourish he bows low, sweeping the ground, and despite her anxiety, Ellinor momentarily forgets her predicament.

Straightening up, William continues across the yard and gives her a wink before entering the farmhouse beneath her window.

Twenty-Three

Men's voices drift up from below, as Ellinor makes her way cautiously along the upper passage. At the head of the stairs she pauses.

'Eleanora, there you are!' Pippa says, looking up from the ground floor with a plate of meat in her hands. 'The men are here.'

Ellinor takes a tentative step, even though every sinew in her body screams for her to turn tail and run.

'Bring the jugs of ale from the buttery,' Pippa instructs, as she continues walking towards an open doorway.

Ellinor is about to ask where that is, but the woman has already disappeared. A sudden burst of laughter erupts as she descends the stairs, and she hovers uncertainly on the bottom step as the young man she'd seen previously in the snug approaches.

'Good day to you, Mistress Eleanora,' he says, passing her by.

'Good day,' she mumbles. 'The buttery?' She points to the doorway he's just emerged from.

His expression is quizzical as he gives her a nod.

Ellinor heads towards the door. Instantly, she recognises the room as the one in her vision that replaced the snug where she and Simon had been sitting. It's nothing like the kitchen at Comfort Wood Farm, but then she recalls Pippa referring to it as the pantry. The room is dimly lit. Wooden barred windows along one wall provide only a modicum of light to the surroundings, and lined along the opposite wall are the rustic shelves filled with an assortment of crockery, cups and bowls. On the far side of the room is an open archway. She's about to cross over to it when the middle-aged woman and the girl she'd seen before suddenly emerge, carrying plates and pewter tankards. With a look of shock, the woman comes to a sudden halt, and the girl hurtles into her.

'Goodness, mistress, you afeared me!' the woman says in a broad Cornish accent.

'I'm sorry,' Ellinor mumbles.

'Well, we haven't the time to worry about such things. Fetch the jugs of ale.'

Ellinor glances around, but she can't see any jugs, or ale.

The woman gives her a strange look. 'Are you ailing, Mistress Eleanora?'

Ellinor shakes her head. 'The buttery?' She points towards the archway.

The woman frowns, but says in a kindly voice, 'We'll wait for you here.'

As Ellinor crosses the room, the young girl gives her a shy smile. Pausing briefly in the entrance, she peers into the buttery. This room, too, is dark and cool. Along one wall are several oak caskets, and opposite them is a shelf filled with a selection of earthenware jugs. Behind her, in the pantry, she hears the woman clear her throat meaningfully, and propelled into action, Ellinor takes down a couple of jugs and fills them with ale from one of the caskets. Mindful not to spill a drop, she joins the woman and girl and follows them from the room.

Passing the simple wooden staircase, they walk through the doorway that Pippa and the young man had used, and as she enters the room Ellinor tries not to gasp. This is an open hall; nothing like anything in the present-day farmhouse. Spanning opposite walls, with their shutters open, is a line of tall windows with roughly sawn wooden bars that seem prevalent throughout the building. The floor area is not overly large, but it's the height of the room and the massive timbers and trusses rising to the roof space that are so surprising and create a sense of grandeur. In the centre Ellinor notices an open fire, over which is suspended a cauldron hanging from a metal A-frame, and at the far end of the room is a group of men sitting on bench seats around a long table.

'Eleanora, don't just stand there,' Pippa hisses. 'Offer the ale.'

Jumping to attention, she starts walking towards the table. As she draws closer, with a sudden shock she sees Ian, and beside him sits Jake, his thatch of red hair unmistakable. Her gaze moves to the man sitting next to him and her heart misses a beat . . . William. The others are strangers, but at the head of the table she recognises the man from the portrait she'd seen displayed in Cotehele House – Richard Edgcumbe.

Ellinor wills her legs not to buckle as she forces one foot in front of the other.

'And here comes my cousin, Eleanora,' says Ian, raising his tankard to her.

So . . . I'm still his cousin in this alternative world.

As several faces turn in her direction, suddenly the room feels hot and airless, and it occurs to Ellinor that if she faints, it will be a welcome escape.

'Eleanora,' Richard Edgcumbe says, observing her with shrewd eyes. 'From where have you come?'

Hysteria threatens. She's tempted to say the twenty-first century, but then concludes this may not be the wisest admission.

'Surrey,' Ian says, before she's had the chance to consider a suitable response.

'I've always found it a very pleasant county,' Richard says. 'Although, of course, the new king has conferred the title of Earl of Surrey on Thomas Howard.' He raises a sardonic eyebrow. 'And his father, John, is now Duke of Norfolk! The *generous* king has granted the family additional lands.'

Ellinor wonders why the conversation around the table has suddenly diminished. Is it because the Lord of the Manor speaks, or is there some other reason the assembled men hang on to his every word?

'I trust you don't find the company of us country folk too dull,' Richard adds with a smile.

'Not at all,' she responds. 'I enjoy it here.' Colouring at the little white lie, she quickly tops up the nearest man's tankard.

Avoiding eye contact with anyone, Ellinor works her way around the table with the jug, noting that Richard, having spoken to her, immediately diverts his attention to Ian, and soon the two men are deep in conversation. As she approaches William, she can't help but register the broadness of his shoulders and the way his dark hair curls down his back. All at once, heat consumes her. This is a harder, more muscled version of Simon – one she's only seen when her husband puts himself through punishing workouts at the gym when preparing to run the Marathon. City living has softened Simon's physique. This man's, however, is honed and ready for battle.

Ready for battle? Why did I think of that?

'Why, if it isn't the fair Lady Ellinor!' William exclaims, turning to her with mischief glinting in his bright blue eyes. 'We meet again.'

'Indeed, we do, sir,' she replies, raising one eyebrow. 'Ale?'

His joyful laugh makes her heart leap, and wisely she tells herself to keep a rational head. As William holds out his tankard, she concentrates on tipping the jug and pouring ale without spilling a drop.

'I trust you are healing well,' he says, lowering his voice to an intimate tone.

'I am. Thank you.'

Well, I was . . . before plunging into this strange adventure.

He gazes at her with something bordering on affection and Ellinor feels herself involuntarily blush.

He smiles with delight. 'So, tell me, fair maiden. How long are we graced with your company on this occasion?'

Good question!

'I'm here for as long as I am.'

William takes a sip of ale, and his eyes narrow as he

contemplates her. 'Mistress Ellinor, you are a tease! But perhaps you will care to visit my humble abode again while you are here?' The mischievous twinkle returns to his eyes. 'Branok and I enjoy your company so.'

She chuckles. 'Well, now, if Branok enjoys my company, how can I possibly refuse?'

Ellinor checks herself. Why is she flirting with her husband's alter ego; a man conjured up by her crazy brain? Admittedly, he's subtly altered in this weird and wondrous dream-state, but, nevertheless, she believes William *is* Simon. After all, this is how they'd been with each other when she and her husband first met. His teasing, sunny nature and playfulness had immediately caught her attention, and here he is again – in the guise of William – displaying the exact same traits that had so wholly enchanted her. It's a heady realisation; a chance to revisit the time when she and Simon had fallen in love so swiftly and completely.

Jake leans forward. 'Do you intend keeping Eleanora all to yourself, Will?' he asks, with a grin.

Catching Ellinor's eye, William mutters under his breath, 'Now that would be a fine thing.'

Her cheeks flame.

'A man could die of thirst,' Jake adds, holding out his tankard.

Moving towards the big man, Ellinor refills his drinking vessel. 'Sorry to keep you waiting, Jake.'

'Is that what they call men in Surrey going by the name of John?' he asks, good-naturedly.

'Think yourself lucky.' William's eyes glitter with mirth. 'She will insist on calling me Simon!'

She shakes her head. 'Jake, John . . . what is in a name?'

This really is complicated! If Jake is John in this dreamland I find myself in, what is my cousin called? Is he still Ian, or is he known by another name?

Moving to him now, she tops up his ale and looks enquiringly at Richard, who places a hand over his tankard.

'No more. I must be in full possession of my wits.' He turns to her cousin. 'Ian, it is time to attend to important matters.'

So, Ian has retained his name!

Rising to his feet, Richard clears his throat, and immediately a hush descends around the table.

From out of the corner of her eye, Ellinor notices Pippa frantically trying to catch her attention. Gesturing dramatically, she instructs her to put the jugs on the table and join her and the servants at the back of the room. Ellinor does as directed, thinking that the woman is definitely a Philippa in this fantasy land; she's far bossier than Pippa in the real world.

The real world . . .

Ellinor shakes her head.

OK. This is a bizarre and interesting dream, but it's time to wake up!

As she walks over to the small group at the back of the hall, she hears Richard talking to the men.

'It is rumoured that Edward V and his brother, Richard of Shrewsbury, are no longer in the Tower of London. The princes have not been seen for some weeks and it is widely believed that the usurper, Richard of Gloucester, has ordered them murdered.'

Exclamations resound around the table.

Ellinor's eyes widen. She wasn't interested in history at school, but even she knows about the Princes in the Tower. Why, and from where, has her brain dredged this up?

'There is a conspiracy arising amongst a number of disaffected gentry,' Richard continues, 'and Harry Stafford, Duke of Buckingham, has proposed that Henry Tudor, Earl of Richmond, return from exile in Brittany to take the throne and marry the Princes' elder sister, Elizabeth of York.'

The man pauses, allowing his words to sink in with those assembled at the table, before speaking again.

'We are all supporters of, and believers in, Henry Tudor's legitimate claim to the throne, and there are plans afoot for forces to assemble in Kent, Surrey and Essex to march on London. Other forces will gather at Newbury and Salisbury. The Bishop of Exeter will lead a revolt in Devon, and Buckingham will lead an army from Wales and the Marches to join them. Henry Tudor intends to sail from France with three thousand five hundred men and join forces with Buckingham and Exeter.'

Silence hangs heavily in the air and when the young man standing next to Ellinor coughs, several men turn and stare at him, making him flush crimson to the roots of his hair.

Ian glances meaningfully across the hall in their direction, and Ellinor watches as an unspoken communication passes between him and Phillipa.

'Come, let us leave the men to discuss their business in private,' Philippa says sharply.

Ellinor's head swims. What madness is this? What has made her conjure up the Wars of the Roses? As she follows Philippa and the servants from the hall, she hears Richard telling Henry Tudor's group of loyal supporters that timings for the uprisings have still to be finalised, but that he expects them to take place within the next few weeks.

Feeling faint, Ellinor catches hold of Philippa's arm. 'I'm just stepping out for some fresh air.'

The woman eyes her with a look verging on suspicion. 'Be quick. There's plenty of work to do.'

Twenty-Four

As Ellinor steps through the doorway and out into the early morning sunshine, the bright light makes her feel dizzy. Supporting herself with one hand, she leans heavily against the wall of the farmhouse and forces herself to take deep breaths.

What the hell is going on?

A pricking sensation at the back of her neck alerts her to being observed, and she glances up. On the opposite side of the yard is Branok, waiting patiently for his master, and shielding her eyes from the glare of the sun, she watches as the dog curiously observes her. His inquisitive amber eyes never waver, not even when several of the men spill out of the door. William is amongst them and she smiles at him as he passes by, but he doesn't acknowledge her. Setting off across the yard, he calls to his dog. The wolfhound doesn't immediately join his master; instead, it continues to stare in Ellinor's direction. As William walks further down the track, he turns back and scans the yard, and she raises a hand in farewell. But, again, he doesn't respond.

'Branok!' he calls.

The dog gives her one last look before turning away and trotting after the fast-disappearing men.

She frowns.

How could William not have seen me? I'm standing here in plain sight.

All at once a heavy veil descends and the scene before her turns to an unstable, watery realm. Waves of dizziness and nausea claim her and Ellinor closes her eyes, but this only brings on a keen sense of longing for something lost. Opening her eyes again, she sees that the air has cleared and the courtyard is steady once more. Glancing across to where the Irish wolfhound had been standing, a raven now watches her keenly. She catches her breath.

Surely not?

But as she focuses on the bird, she notices the telltale grey feather on its chest.

No way! It's too much of a coincidence. How can it be the same raven that visits me in Surrey?

'Oh, there you are!'

Distractedly, Ellinor turns towards the voice.

Pippa steps out into the courtyard and joins her. 'Did Simon get off OK last night?'

'Yes,' she says, quickly pulling herself together. 'I don't envy him leaving at such an unearthly hour, but he doesn't seem to mind.'

'Good man,' Pippa says with a smile. She looks around the courtyard. 'What are you doing out here?'

Ellinor glances down. She's no longer wearing the many layers of clothing; she's in her staple outfit of jeans and sweatshirt. But try as she might, she cannot recall waking, dressing and walking outside.

'Just getting some fresh air,' she says, for want of a better answer.

'Well, come in for some breakfast.'

'Thanks.'

As Pippa turns away, Ellinor scans the courtyard. It's empty. Has the raven flown away, or did she simply imagine it? Frowning, she turns and enters the farmhouse. As she makes her way to the dining room she takes in the building's architecture, but there are no obvious features hinting at the layout as it had appeared to her only minutes before.

Ian is already at the table when she enters, and Ellinor slides into the seat opposite him.

'Good morning.' He gives her a smile. 'What time did Simon leave?'

'Around three,' she replies. 'I hope the car didn't disturb you.'

'Didn't hear a sound,' he says. 'Our bedroom's at the back of the house, so we rarely hear anything out front.'

'Elli, do you want full English?' Pippa asks, from the kitchen doorway.

Ellinor shakes her head. Nausea still lingers. 'Just toast please.'

'Right you are.' Pippa turns away.

She smiles to herself. The *Phillipa* of the most recent adventure wouldn't have asked that. She'd have expected her to make her own breakfast, and no doubt provide for everyone else at the same time.

'Ian, do you know what the layout of the farmhouse was during the fifteenth century?' Ellinor asks casually.

'Now, there's a question,' he says, raising his eyebrows. 'Not sure that I do. There were several plans with the deeds, but I don't recall anything dating back that far. If any were ever drawn up, they're probably lost in the mists of time. Why? What's your interest?'

Ellinor glances around at the dining room's panelled walls and diamond-paned windows. Pippa had told her this was once the kitchen, but there was only a pantry and buttery here earlier. Perhaps this was the kitchen during a later period.

'I find it intriguing,' Ellinor replies. 'The house must have changed a lot over the centuries.'

Ian nods. 'I would think so, but I doubt we'll ever know for certain. A lot of these old houses started life as open halls, with cross passageways added later.'

'And you haven't witnessed anything here?' she asks cautiously. Even though Pippa said neither she nor Ian had seen anything spooky at the farm, Ellinor wants to hear it from Ian himself.

'Do you mean ghosts haunting the corridors?' he asks with an amused expression.

Ellinor blushes. 'Well, yes.'

'No. We've slept like babes since we arrived. Probably something to do with being totally knackered at the end of each day.' Thoughtfully, he assesses his cousin. 'Pippa mentioned you imagined you'd seen something in the snug, but this house is full of shadows and no doubt it was just that. A trick of the light.'

'Pippa said they were probably the ghosts of Comfort Wood Farm.' Ellinor purses her lips.

Ian laughs. 'She was just teasing! We've never picked up on any odd atmosphere, Elli. But if anything does disturb you or cause you to worry, just let me know,' he adds with a kindly smile.

'Thanks,' she says, wondering what he'd say if she told him she'd overheard him discussing plans with Richard Edgcumbe for Henry Tudor to take the throne from Richard III.

'Here you go,' Pippa says, entering the room, holding two plates.

'Elli wants to know if we have any documents that show the original layout of the farmhouse,' Ian says. 'There was nothing with the deeds dating to the fifteenth century, was there?'

Pippa places the plates on the table – eggs, bacon, sausages, baked beans, fried mushrooms and tomatoes for her husband; toast for Ellinor.

'No there wasn't. When we first purchased the farm I looked quite extensively before becoming entrenched in building the business.' She considers Ellinor. 'There may be something in the public library about the history of the place, but I doubt there would be plans of the house.'

'Not to worry. It just interested me, that's all.' Ellinor thinly butters a slice of toast. 'Perhaps I'll visit the library. Where's the local one for this area?'

'There's one in Saltash,' Pippa says.

'Or Tavistock,' adds Ian. 'Richard Edgcumbe was twice MP for Tavistock. He was also appointed sheriff of Devonshire, so the library there is sure to have some information about the man.'

Twenty-Five

Throughout the week the weather improves, and though it's only mid-April it feels more like summer. As the temperatures continue to rise, one afternoon Pippa and Ellinor decide to take the spaniels for a walk. It's a beautiful day with very little cloud in the sky and the dogs scamper excitedly ahead across the fields in the direction of the river.

'What a treat this weather is,' Pippa says, negotiating a stile. 'I hope it lingers for a while. The orchards will be alive with pollinators.'

Following her, Ellinor stands with one foot on either side of the wooden stile, taking in the scenery. 'It's a great view from up here.'

'It *is* a good viewpoint,' agrees Pippa.

Shielding her eyes, Ellinor follows the river as it snakes its way south through the landscape. 'You'd never know Plymouth was just over there.' She points in the general direction of the city.

'We're in a good position, that's for sure. Occasionally we manage to muster the energy to venture into the city for the theatre or cinema, but for the most part we're happy being busy little recluses in our own small corner of Cornwall!'

Ellinor smiles. 'I don't blame you. Comfort Wood Farm is heaven.'

Pippa glances up at her. 'I'm so glad you and Simon *get* it, Elli. Some of our friends back in the South-East think we've gone completely nuts!'

'Well, we don't. I know Simon thinks you're living the dream.'

In the mid-distance, the spaniels stop and look back at the two women.

'Better catch them up,' says Pippa. 'They're usually good boys and come to call, but occasionally they only selectively remember their training.'

Ellinor laughs. Stepping down from the stile, she lengthens her stride to catch up with Pippa. A gentle breeze ruffles her hair, and she gazes around at the unspoilt landscape with delight. Only that morning, the architect had phoned with the exciting news that amendments to the original planning application had been approved. Soon – once his other project is finished – Jake and his men will start work on rebuilding the cottage, and then it will be full steam ahead. Ellinor smiles as a bubble of excitement rises. It won't be long before she, too, will call this area *home*.

High above, a kestrel circles on invisible thermals as it keeps a lookout for any unsuspecting small mammals rooting amongst the grass. It's a beautiful sight – wild and free. Shockingly, Ellinor realises that she's only noticed these birds before hovering over the verges of the M25 as she'd journeyed to and from Heathrow. Her life then – wrapped up as it was with travel to exotic locations and far-flung cities – didn't encompass nature. She'd always been too pre-occupied with flight timings, airports and hotels, and there wasn't room to consider anything else. But now . . . a suggestion of what it must feel like to be wild and free nudges her, and she glances across at the woman striding across the fields. Pippa knows what it is to be just that. No one has ever made her feel small or intimidated . . . or *terrorised*. Ellinor checks her thoughts, refusing to allow the memories to resurface. She will only look to the future from now on. She and Simon have so much to look forward to, and maybe in this environment she will finally relax enough to resume trying for a family. God knows, she and her husband have been trying to conceive from the first moment they met, but her mind and body have always been too wired and stressed out.

As soon as Pippa and Ellinor catch up with the dogs, the spaniels rush down the sloping field towards the edge of the woods.

'Those rascals had better not disappear in the trees,' Pippa mutters.

Fortunately, the dogs choose to respond to their mistress's command, and they wait patiently for the humans to catch up. Having entered the woodland, it's not long before Pippa diverts off the main path and follows a narrow track, seemingly little more than a route animals would take. As the spaniels scamper off down the hillside towards the river, Ellinor follows. Suddenly, they emerge from the trees onto an old stone quay covered in grass, and the dogs immediately trot down an adjacent slipway, pausing only briefly at the sparkling water's edge, before wading straight in.

'This is well hidden,' Ellinor says, glancing around the secluded spot.

'Not many people bother to divert off the main path,' Pippa replies, 'but they don't know what they're missing. It's great for picnics, and there's nothing better than an evening's swim here after a hard day's work.'

Ellinor sits on the grass and watches the dogs venture into deeper water. On the opposite bank, an area of reeds gives way to a plateau of grass bordered by a thin line of trees. Behind it, fields sweep uphill to a further area of woodland.

'It's so picturesque,' she says appreciatively.

Pippa smiles. 'When tourists visit Cornwall they mostly head west and completely bypass the Tamar Valley. But we don't mind, because it means having the area to ourselves.'

A movement amongst the reed beds on the Devon bank catches Ellinor's attention and she notices a pied flycatcher gripping on to a gently swaying reed. Suddenly, two mallard ducks emerge, and immediately both spaniels alter course mid-stream to paddle after them.

'Rufus, Rusty!' Pippa calls out. 'Come here!'

But the dogs choose deafness at that moment and continue to chase after the ducks, which have now picked up speed.

'Honestly . . . those two scoundrels!' Pippa hurries down the slipway and calls to the dogs again.

Lazily, Ellinor watches the dogs pursue the waterfowl. Sunlight shimmers on the water . . . and suddenly the scene slides and her vision grows hazy. Feeling lightheaded, she closes her eyes, but the next minute a shower of cold water sends her scrambling to her feet.

'Yikes!' she exclaims.

Standing square in front of her is Branok, the Irish wolfhound. Shaking again, he sends a further cascade in her direction.

Her eyes widen as she takes in the stone quay, now little more than an area of rough grass with a small wooden landing stage and a ladder that descends into the water. In the centre is a bare patch of ground where a flat stone balances on a couple of charred logs. Looking across to the opposite bank, Ellinor is shocked to see dense vegetation, and how narrow and overgrown the river is. A large reed bed takes up a fair proportion of the waterway, and behind it, a heavily wooded area stretches uphill. The adjacent fields, she notices, are full of sheep.

Distracted by a loud splashing sound, she turns towards the noise and her jaw drops. Powering through the water towards her is Simon, although she realises that with Branok present it must be William. As he draws nearer, he stops swimming.

'Why, fair Ellinor, you have discovered my secret place!' he says, smiling broadly.

Uncertainty overwhelms her, and she looks wildly around for Pippa and the spaniels. But the river is empty, and her cousin's wife no longer stands at the slipway calling to them. The next minute, however, her confusion turns to something else at the sight of William, standing waist-deep in the river. Rivulets of water stream down his muscular arms and over his chest, as the sunlight accentuates his well-defined physique. Refusing to allow her eyes to open any wider, Ellinor takes in this fine, alternative version of her husband.

He really is spectacular!

'Once again, you surprise me,' William says, appraising her. 'And again, you are dressed in such strange garments?'

Ellinor gazes down at her skimpy T-shirt, her denim shorts – which expose a great deal of leg – and her walking shoes.

'Why?' she says cheekily. 'Don't they wear such things in these parts? It's most fashionable in Surrey, you know.'

He gives her a curious look and then laughs. 'You tease, but you look most becoming indeed.'

She gives a small curtsey. 'Why thank you, sir!'

She notices Branok settle down on the grass, his eyebrows twitching as he quietly watches them. But William remains standing waist-deep in the river.

'Aren't you getting out?' Ellinor asks.

'Ah,' he says. 'I fear that you have me at a disadvantage.'

'Oh, why so?'

William's look turns sheepish. 'I am unclothed.'

He points to a pile of garments on the grass that she hadn't noticed before.

Ellinor gives a hearty laugh. 'Then I suppose I will have to avert my gaze.'

Sitting down once again, she turns her head away, but the next minute she whips it around and gives him a cheeky grin.

He laughs. 'Mistress Ellinor, I plead with you to afford me some small dignity.'

'Very well! If I have to,' she says in mock-exasperation.

Turning away again, she wonders why she automatically falls into intense flirting mode whenever William materialises. Is it because she feels safe, being the instigator of this version of her husband?

With his hands modestly covering himself, William strides out of the water and across the grass to his clothes. Despite her assurances, Ellinor can't help but look. His figure is both familiar and alien – it is Simon's, only *not* – and the number of scars covering his body shocks her. What has caused them?

Suddenly he looks across at her and she quickly turns away, averting her gaze.

'Eyes closed, Lady Ellinor.'

She gives a low laugh. 'I can only imagine what I'm missing!'

No! Even if I have conjured him up from my imagination, I must not be flippant.

Taking another sneaky peek, she finds him staring at her with a look of wonder and disbelief.

'Sorry,' she says, turning away again.

William pulls on his hose and approaches her with something bordering on awe. 'From whence have you manifested?'

She gazes up at him, shielding her eyes from a sun riding high in the sky. But that's not right! It was approaching mid-afternoon when she, Pippa and the dogs had left the farmhouse. The sun would be low and away to the west by now, but it's directly overhead. Obviously, she's yet to master time in this alternative world.

'You know where,' she replies. 'Surrey.'

'I mean . . .' he frowns, 'you are so different to any woman I have known. Not just your garments, but your boldness and speech.'

She skews her mouth sideways. 'You wouldn't believe me if I told you,' she says lightly, 'so I'm not going to.'

William sits down beside her. 'You are a bewitching puzzle, Ellinor.'

'I can assure you I am not the only puzzle here!'

Two small frown lines form between his eyebrows.

'But it's a very pleasant puzzle,' she quickly adds.

His eyes meet hers. Oh, so blue . . .

Suddenly embarrassed, she drops her gaze to his shoulder

and notices the birthmark, in the exact location of her husband's. It's surprising the number of small details her mind has included in this dream-state.

'Have you always had that?' she asks.

He glances down at his shoulder. 'It's a recent wound.'

Ellinor's head snaps up. 'Wound?'

'Yes. I took an arrow.' His fingers feel the puckered area of skin above his armpit. 'The result of a skirmish. We didn't come off well, but neither did we come away in disgrace. We fought strongly and slayed many.'

He's joking, of course! He's got to be . . .

Attempting to keep the shock from her face, Ellinor's eyes meet his quizzical gaze. It's as if he's amused by her reaction, and incomprehension clouds her mind.

'But what of this, Ellinor?' he asks, as he lightly skims his index finger over the raised scar on her neck.

All at once heat consumes her, and instead of automatically flinching away, she finds herself wanting to lean into his touch, despite being embarrassed that he's noticed her disfigurement. She gazes into his eyes: Simon's eyes. Their blueness has darkened to indigo, and she knows what that means. Her husband's eyes always give away heightened emotion. As William's hand gently cups her face, she allows him to draw her towards him. Slowly, his mouth softly covers hers.

Ellinor closes her eyes. If this is her imagination playing mind games, she wholeheartedly welcomes the experience.

A sudden shout causes William to immediately draw back from her. At once, he is on high alert; Branok, too.

Another shout, and William is on his feet.

'Stay hidden, Lady Ellinor,' he commands in a harsh whisper.

As William and Branok set off into the woodland surrounding the secluded landing stage, Ellinor tries to quell her mounting anxiety. Is it the urgency in his voice that causes her heart to race, or the recent, delicious feel of his lips upon hers? She's not sure. She raises her fingers to her mouth where his touch still lingers. It's been so long since she's allowed Simon to kiss her properly. Since *the incident* she's mostly pulled away at any attempt at intimacy, and now it's become an almost impossible obstacle. But this kiss with William happened so naturally. Should she feel guilty at this intimate act? But why should she? Simon *is* William! Her brain has simply altered him in subtle ways, as it has with everything in this *other* world.

A movement at the river's edge catches her attention and her eyes widen as the two spaniels trot up the slipway towards her.

'Good boys, Rusty and Rufus,' Pippa says encouragingly. 'But don't go shaking yourselves over Elli.'

Frantically, Ellinor scans the area for William and Branok, but they are nowhere to be seen. As the familiar dizziness and nausea descend, swiftly followed by keen yearning, Ellinor buries her head in her hands and groans.

'Are you OK?' Pippa asks, stepping onto the quay.

Ellinor glances up.

'Goodness! You look . . .' Pippa casts around for an appropriate word, '. . . bereft!'

Twenty-Six

Shortly after breakfast the next morning, Ellinor drives into Tavistock and visits the library. She's determined to find out more about Richard Edgcumbe and, hopefully, William, although she has very little information to go on where he's concerned.

The weather continues to deceive people into thinking it's summer, and after parking her vehicle in the large, public car park close to the library, she makes a small detour. Stepping through an opening in the high stone wall surrounding the parking area, Ellinor emerges onto a pleasant, leafy walkway running alongside a slow-moving river that meanders around boulders and finds it way over pebbled banks. A dozen ducks paddle downstream. It's so tranquil, and the dappled light playing through the trees and reflecting on the water is calming. It's hard to believe that the busy road into town is only a short distance away, and she takes a moment to enjoy the peace and serenity, aware of people walking along the path on the other side of the shallow river. After a while, she retraces her steps and makes her way across the car park to the library.

Ellinor enters the building through double doors and gazes around the bright, airy room, in which an unruffled air pervades. She's arrived early in the day and only a handful of people are browsing the shelves. Over in the far corner, sitting on small chairs, a group of pre-school children listen attentively to a young woman reading them a story. She's obviously captured their imaginations as there's hardly a peep out of any of the youngsters. Crossing over to the reception desk, Ellinor enquires where the history books are located, and a helpful assistant, whose name badge states *Wendy*, accompanies her to a section over by the windows.

'What period are you interested in?' the woman asks.

'Late fifteenth century,' Ellinor explains, 'around the time of the Princes in the Tower. I'm particularly interested in Richard Edgcumbe's involvement with the revolts that took place following the princes' demise.'

'Ah, the Wars of the Roses,' the library assistant confirms. 'We have several books covering that period. You'll find them on these shelves. If you have difficulty locating what you're after, please don't hesitate to come and find me.'

'Thank you.' Ellinor gives Wendy a smile.

'Take as long as you want. We won't usher you out of the building, unless of course you're still here at closing time!'

'Hopefully I'll find what I'm looking for long before then.'

As Wendy walks away, Ellinor gazes at the rows of books. Somewhere on these shelves there may be answers. Perhaps today she will discover who the mysterious William is.

Three hours later, as she sits in one of the comfortable chairs provided for library users, Ellinor stares at the many tomes open on the table before her. She's discovered plenty about the battles during 1455–1487, which tore England apart in Civil War, and she's learned that at the time this was known as the war between Lancaster and York, more popularly referred to since the nineteenth century as the Wars of the Roses. It hadn't been a period of continual warfare, but rather episodes of conflict interspersed with long periods of peace. During these thirty or so years of struggle and hostility, the moral fibre of some of England's greatest families was sorely tested as motives changed, fortunes waxed and waned, and the nature of kingship was carefully evaluated.

Ellinor rotates her shoulders and stretches her hands high above her head, releasing tension.

'Are you a historian?' Wendy asks from a nearby aisle, where she arranges books on one of the shelves.

'No,' Ellinor responds. 'I'm interested in the period because I'm staying in a house that dates to that time and it's piqued my curiosity.'

'Well, you're certainly very diligent,' the library assistant remarks. 'You've hardly moved from that spot since you arrived.'

Ellinor grimaces as she gets to her feet. 'I do feel a bit stiff. I hadn't realised how fascinating history is, and the time has flown by. Perhaps, I'll wander around the library and stretch my legs.'

The woman nods. 'I'm a bit of a history buff and I feel very fortunate to work here.'

'You're definitely in the right place,' Ellinor says, indicating the many rows of academic accounts and historical novels.

Wendy laughs. 'I dare not pick up a book and start reading, otherwise I'll forget I'm here to work! Did you find what you were looking for?'

'Not really. I'd hoped to find out more about Henry Tudor leaving his exile in France to fight Richard III for the throne.'

The library assistant looks along the shelves and pulls out a book. 'This may help you. It's a straightforward history of the Wars of the Roses and focuses on the main players. It's very readable, not at all dry and academic. More like reading a good novel.'

Ellinor takes the offered book. 'Thank you. I admit I'm a little confused by the number of people who share the same name.'

Wendy chuckles. 'It can be rather complicated keeping track of the names and specific timelines.' She checks her watch. 'I have the book club coming in this afternoon, so I'll leave you to it.'

'Oh, please, don't let me keep you,' Ellinor apologises. 'You've been very helpful.'

The woman makes to turn away, but then hesitates. 'You say you're interested in Henry Tudor's bid to secure the throne. Well, of course, you know his first attempt in October

1483 was unsuccessful. He had to wait until 1485 and the Battle of Bosworth to achieve that.'

Ellinor's ears prick up. 'Why was he unsuccessful on the first occasion?'

'Weather mainly, and premature timing by one of the rebel parties involved. It was known as Buckingham's Rebellion, and although the uprising ultimately failed against Richard III, it was a significant one. Actually, it comprised a number of uprisings in England and parts of Wales.'

A sudden energy possesses Ellinor, and, instinctively, she knows this is important information.

'What happened?'

'Now you're testing my memory,' the woman says, pulling a face.

'Do you mind if I take notes?' Ellinor asks.

'Not at all!'

The two women walk over to the table and sit down. Picking up her pen, Ellinor enthusiastically jots down pointers as the assistant speaks.

'The Princes in the Tower were pronounced illegitimate before Edward V could be crowned king, and many rebels took up arms against Richard of Gloucester who assumed power in the June of that year. Amongst them were loyalists of Edward, and others who had been Yorkist supporters of his father, Edward IV.'

'So much for maintaining sides,' Ellinor mutters.

'History is full of the waxing and waning of loyalties. They were dangerous times, so whether it was from choice or necessity, who knows. Anyway, the plan was for Henry Tudor and his supporters to rise simultaneously with others around the country against Richard III.'

Ellinor scribbles furiously. This was what she'd heard Richard Edgcumbe discussing with the men in the open hall at the farmhouse.

Wendy continues, 'Seven ships sailed from Brittany carrying Breton soldiers in support of Henry Tudor. However, the weather was awful, and it played a large part in the uprising's failure. A gale prevented the ships from landing, and they were forced to return to France, although Henry's ship and two others managed to anchor off Plymouth, where he was confronted by a group of the king's supporters and fled to Brittany.'

'What happened to the other forces?'

'The game was up when Kent launched their rebellion ten days early and announced Harry Stafford, Duke of Buckingham, as their leader, thereby drawing attention to his involvement and sealing his fate. The King acted swiftly and declared bounties on the rebels' heads – one thousand pounds for Buckingham.'

Ellinor's eyes open wide. 'That's a substantial amount in those days!'

'I should say so,' Wendy agrees. 'It's not known for sure whether someone betrayed him or if he was discovered in hiding, but in any event the man was captured, convicted of treason and beheaded in Salisbury.'

A group of chattering women enter the room and the library assistant glances over in their direction. 'That's my book group arriving,' she says, getting to her feet. 'I'd better see to them.'

'Thank you very much,' says Ellinor. 'This is really useful information.'

The woman smiles down at her. 'There's plenty more to learn, but the books you've selected are a good place to start. They should help you to get a more thorough understanding of the Wars of the Roses.'

Twenty-Seven

That evening, Ellinor sits in the snug looking through the various history books she's brought back from the library. The accounts are fascinating, and she makes further notes. Soon her notepad is overflowing with details.

'Fancy a drink?' Ian says, poking his head around the door.

'Sounds like a grand idea. What did you have in mind?'

'Well, I visited a friend today, a producer of plant-based, non-alcoholic drinks, and he gave me a few sample bottles. All are vegan and gluten-free, with no artificial colours or flavours added. I wondered if you'd like to try some.'

'Yes please!'

'They've created a rather wonderful nightcap. I'll bring it through.'

As Ian closes the door, Ellinor gazes around the room, recalling the unusual experience she'd had in here. Along with the wooden shelves filled with all manner of kitchen paraphernalia that had lined the wall where a framed watercolour now hangs, over in the corner by the window there had been a kneading trough and moulding board, and a wooden chest for storing sieved flour. Ellinor shakes her head. How can she possibly know what they were used for? But she does. And she can still conjure up the different floral scents from the bunches of drying herbs and flowers hanging down from hooks. The snug has a timeless atmosphere, and it occurs to her that this *other* room may still be here, simply hidden in a fold of time that prevents her from seeing it.

Voices filter into her musings and she turns towards the door, expecting to see Ian arriving with the drinks. When he doesn't appear, she rises from the sofa and walks towards the door. Urgent, muffled whispers . . . Ellinor stops, and straining her ears, attempts to follow the conversation, but she only catches snippets. However, she's certain one of the voices belongs to William. A sudden hunger consumes her; not one aligned to food.

Drawing closer, she presses her ear to the door and her heart trips in her chest. It's definitely William's voice.

'Henry Tudor has sworn an oath in Rennes Cathedral to marry Edward IV's daughter, Elizabeth of York, once he takes the throne,' William whispers. 'Or one of her sisters, if she dies or marries before he is able to carry out the act.'

Whoever he is talking to replies, but the man's words are inaudible to Ellinor.

William continues, 'The plan is for forces to assemble at Maidstone, Guildford and Essex and march on London in a feint. Our men are primed and ready to act and we will assemble in Exeter. Buckingham has raised a substantial force from his estates in Wales and the Marches and they will join us there.'

Ellinor listens in horror. She must warn him that the uprising will be unsuccessful, and that Buckingham will be captured and executed. What will happen to William? Will he also face the same fate? Fear for his safety engulfs her. With trembling fingers, she lifts the latch and opens the door. Caught off guard, realising they've been overheard, the two men stand back in shock. Disbelief and anxiety register on their faces but as Ellinor opens her mouth to warn them of the disastrous outcome to the plans, William's expression softens and her heart squeezes. All at once the scene loses definition – like an old, faded photograph – and she watches as an approaching figure dominates the scene.

'Look who I found in the hallway,' Ian says, carrying a tray loaded with glasses and bottles.

'Hi Elli,' Simon says, emerging from behind Ian. 'I managed to get away early.'

'That's good,' she replies, as she peers beyond the two men and searches in the shadows for William and the other man.

Entering the room, Simon gives her a hug. 'It's good to see you,' he whispers in her ear.

'You, too,' she says distractedly, sitting down on the sofa. She doesn't want to be here, but in that *other* time.

Ian places the tray on the coffee table. Picking up one of the bottles, he removes the stopper.

'Ice and a slice of orange, cuz?'

She nods, grappling with the keen longing assaulting her.

Ian pours the drink over ice into four glass tumblers, and then adds a dash of Angostura bitters, a slice of orange and a maraschino cherry.

'Pippa's just putting supper on and then she'll join us,' he says, handing Ellinor and Simon each a glass. 'Cheers!'

Clinking glasses, Ellinor takes a sip and she's immediately struck by a strange familiarity. The taste is not dissimilar to the spiced ale that William had given her the day he invited her into his home.

'Do you like it, Elli?' asks Ian.

'Yes. It has a mellow woodiness.'

'You're not wrong there,' he declares. 'It's made with tree saps and aromatic plants.'

'What *are* the ingredients?' Simon asks, sitting down on the sofa next to Ellinor.

Ian picks up the bottle and reads aloud from the label. 'Filtered water, maple syrup, melon hops, botanical extracts of lemon balm, turmeric root, ashwagandha, white willow bark, vanilla, valerian, liquorice root, and ginger . . . among other things.'

'Glad I asked!'

'All these ingredients are good for promoting a sense of calm, relaxation and reducing anxiety,' Ian says. 'And melon hops are part of the cannabis family.'

Simon takes another sip. 'It's seriously good. I suspect that after a couple of glasses of this stuff we'll be relaxed and chilled, and dreamily floating about a foot off the ceiling!'

Ian laughs. 'Yes, but without the usual accompanying hangovers to contend with.' Putting the bottle down, he picks up the remaining glass on the tray. 'I'll go and see how supper's coming along.'

'Can I help?' Ellinor asks.

'No, all's under control, Elli,' Ian assures her. 'You stay here and catch up with your husband. After all, you haven't seen him all week.'

She throws her cousin a smile and takes another sip of the amber nectar.

'So, what's all this?' Simon asks, indicating the books strewn across the table.

'Library books. I wanted to find out about the period when this farmhouse was built.'

Simon raises an eyebrow in surprise. 'You've never been interested in that sort of thing before.'

'No. Anything old and historical always smacked of being a dry subject. But, silly me . . . it's fascinating.'

Simon's eyes widen.

She catches his look. 'It's not like me, is it?'

'Not really.' Simon shakes his head. 'What have you discovered so far that's captured your interest?'

'Nothing specifically about Comfort Wood Farm, but I'm learning about the treacherous and deceitful thirty years that defined the Wars of the Roses and resulted in the downfall of the houses of Lancaster and York; and the emergence of the illustrious Tudor dynasty.'

Incredulously, Simon stares at his wife.

Ellinor continues, 'I'm particularly interested in the uprisings that took place in the late fifteenth century when Henry Tudor attempted to take the throne. He was unsuccessful on his first attempt – that was known as the Buckingham Rebellion – and it wasn't until 1485 and the Battle of Bosworth that he became King when Richard III was killed.'

Silence stretches between them.

Eventually, Simon speaks. 'I've never heard you talk like this before.'

Ellinor glances at her husband. 'I know. It's only now that I think I'm finally waking up to what the important things are in life.'

He regards her for a long moment. 'You're definitely changing.'

'Maybe, Simon. As each day passes, I feel as if I'm finally coming home.' She gives a small, embarrassed laugh. 'Does that sound silly? I mean, Surrey and Hertfordshire have been the only homes I've ever known, so I don't know why Cornwall has this effect on me.'

Simon puts an arm around her shoulders. 'For whatever reason, it suits you, Elli. You look healthier than I've seen you since . . .' he hesitates, not wanting to bring up *the incident* again, '. . . well, for a long time. You seem to be finding inner contentment.'

'I am content.' She smiles warmly. William's twinkling bright blue eyes come to mind, and with a prick of guilt she realises she longs to see them again. Quickly, she adds, 'I can't wait for the day when you join me here.'

He smiles and cautiously strokes her hair. 'Ian has arranged for us to visit a cider farm tomorrow near Truro, so how about we take another look at the cottage site on Sunday?'

Extracting herself from his embrace, Ellinor turns to face him with shining eyes. 'I can't wait to get started on the rebuild. I just know it's going to be the most perfect home.'

'I'm sure it will,' he says softly.

Suddenly the door opens, and Ian appears. 'Guys, supper's ready.'

Simon gets to his feet and walks to the door. Hanging back, Ellinor glances around the snug, feeling the strong pull of that *other* world. Oh, if only she could slip back . . .

Twenty-Eight

Ellinor wakes early, and not wishing to disturb Simon who sleeps soundly beside her, she lies perfectly still and listens to the slowly awakening world outside the window. As she tunes in to the emerging dawn chorus drifting in on a gentle breeze, she hears chickens clucking in the yard and sheep bleating in the fields. From some distance away a dog barks and she wonders if it's one of the spaniels . . . Or could it be Branok? Slipping out of bed and crossing over to the window, she quietly draws back one of the curtains. A murky light fills the courtyard and it takes a while for her eyes to adjust. Shadows tease. Lifting her gaze to the ridge tiles of the opposite barn, she spies the large black bird with its distinctive grey feather.

'Still watching over me,' she whispers.

For several minutes Ellinor stands at the window gazing out at the scene. She longs for that older farmyard to materialise and to see William striding across it, and chivalrously bowing when he spots her. But, realising he's not going to arrive, crashing disappointment replaces her mounting expectation. The mind plays such tricks! Turning, she gazes at her sleeping husband. How can that *other* man appear when he's already in her bed? She glances back at the raven perched statue-like on the roof of the barn and graces it with a smile; one she would gift a dear friend. Cocking its head, the bird keeps one beady eye on her and she's certain there's acknowledgement in its gaze.

'Madness!' Ellinor mutters, shaking her head.

Simon stirs. 'Hmm . . . What time is it?' he asks sleepily.

'Early,' she says, closing the curtain and slipping back beneath the duvet.

His hand reaches for her. 'You're cold. Let me warm you.'

As Simon pulls Ellinor towards him and wraps her in his arms, she attempts not to resist, and for a moment she relaxes. But as soon as her husband's breathing grows deeper and he falls into undisturbed sleep, she moves carefully away from him.

Ellinor lies awake, mulling over all that has happened to her. Why has her imagination conjured up her husband in that alternative world? Is it because she's having difficulty adapting to the sudden change of area, and a familiar face is the way her subconscious can cope with it? No, that's not it! She feels at home here, and when she'd first considered coming to Cornwall not once did she doubt the idea. In fact, she couldn't wait to arrive. It's as if she were drawn here . . .

Ellinor considers this last observation. If something has drawn her here, then what is it?

You know what it is!

The words are loud and clear, and Ellinor gazes around the darkened room, even though she knows the disembodied voice is not from some other being, but from her very soul.

Your destiny awaits you at the edge of the woods.

As the early dawn light sneaks its way through a gap in the curtains, Ellinor turns and gazes at her sleeping husband again. He looks so peaceful lying there. She knows she's lucky to have his patient, unfaltering support since *the incident*. After all, it can't be easy living with her as she works through the trauma left in the wake of that horrific flight.

But what of that *other* Simon? William . . .

Ellinor frowns. It's all too much to consider, especially at this early hour. Turning over, she closes her eyes and as she drifts towards sleep, she hears the voice again.

Everything is connected. All will be well.

Pippa closes the van door on the last crate of apple juice and turns. Anxiously, she searches Ellinor's face. 'Are you sure you'll be OK here on your own?'

'Of course,' Ellinor assures her.

'If I'd known you wouldn't be going with Ian and Simon on their fact-finding mission, I would have cancelled the market.'

'Don't be silly, Pippa. I wouldn't want you to do that. I'm perfectly fine here. Anyway, I thought I might visit Cotehele again.'

'Well, if you're certain,' Pippa says, with a frown of consternation.

'I'm sure!' Ellinor pulls a face at her cousin's wife. 'Now get on, otherwise you'll be late setting up.'

Pippa gives her a hug and climbs into the driver's seat. 'You can leave the dogs in the house. They'll be perfectly fine until I get back.'

'OK. Hope you sell out.'

'So do I!' Pippa puts the van into gear and lowers the window. 'Help yourself to whatever you want for lunch. There's plenty in the fridge.'

Ellinor waves as Pippa drives out of the courtyard. Glancing up at the sky, she decides that rain could be on the agenda. Quickly making her way to her bedroom, she extracts a lightweight waterproof jacket from the wardrobe and stuffs her purse and mobile into its pockets. As she descends the stairs, she stands in the dining room doorway and glances through to the kitchen where the dogs are happily mooching.

'Be good boys,' she says.

Rusty looks up from his bed, but Rufus continues investigating his bowl without a glance in her direction.

Ellinor exits the house and closes the front door behind her. There's definitely rain in the air, and she slips on her jacket before setting off down the drive.

Taking the footpath that cuts across the fields, she enters the woods on the far edge of the National Trust Estate and hesitates. She turns in the direction of the ruined cottage lying hidden in the forest and considers whether to make a detour to it now, but decides not to. Simon has suggested they visit it together tomorrow. Ellinor sets off along the narrow path that wends its way downhill through the trees, plunging deeper into the woodland, and presently she arrives at the track leading up through the gardens to Cotehele House, having not come across another soul.

A cool wind teases the leaves on the branches as she climbs the steep path, but the rain stays away. Ten minutes later, she stops on a terrace to catch her breath. Drawing air deeply into her lungs, she gazes across a woodland scene filled with a mix of natural and exotic planting. Amongst the rich landscape are not only bamboo and palm trees, but also an explosion of nature's colours. The spring green of unfurling immature ferns; vibrant Flame Azaleas, displaying their large, showy, funnel-shaped flowers; a mix of pale pink Rhododendron flowers, reminding her of the tutus of ballet dancers, through to vibrant red and the more extravagant mauves. Somewhere close by is the sound of trickling water, and on further investigation she discovers a meandering brook tumbling down the hillside, hiding beneath swathes of wild garlic and carpets of the large, heart-shaped leaves of the Butterbur. Taking a step towards the granite stones edging the track, she peers over, and her eyes follow the stream as it drops over a small waterfall and journeys on into the valley below.

After a short while she continues, and walking beneath a heavily flowered Rhododendron arcing over the path, she turns a corner and spies a short flight of granite steps next to an intriguing circular building covered in ivy, its slate roof carpeted in moss. Ellinor climbs the steps and emerges into a secluded garden with a tranquil, clear pond, where five moorhens dabble around a coverlet of white waterlilies.

A gravelled path leads to a stone bench, strategically placed for visitors to enjoy the best view of the hidden garden, and she wanders over to it and sits down, and gazes around at the delightful scene before her. The sumptuous, billowing shrubs and trees cast their colourful reflections in the water and everything appears enhanced – as if she's stepped straight into an oil painting. All at once, two young children dressed in brightly coloured trousers and jackets appear on the far side of the pond. Excitedly, they rush to the water and peer into its mirror-like surface.

'Careful now, Jemima, Tamsin,' says a young woman, following not far behind them. 'I don't want you falling in.'

Ellinor sits for several minutes, absorbing the peace and quiet of the setting, recalling that Pippa said the Valley Garden had a medieval stew pond and dovecote, and these must be them. What different days have they witnessed during their long existence? She's read that throughout history many abbeys had stew ponds, where fish bred, lived and grew, and that with the dissolution of monasteries in the 1500s many were reclaimed by nature. But not this one – the National Trust has carefully maintained it.

What type of fish would have been kept in it? Carp?

Gazing at the pool now, she searches for ripples and any telltale signs of lazily meandering carp below the surface that might have descended from those medieval farmed fish. But the water is still, apart from where the moorhens busily forage amongst the waterlilies and reeds.

Suddenly, from out of the corner of her eye, she's aware of a sudden fluttering of white and her gaze lifts to the circular stone building with its domed slatestone roof, onto which half a dozen doves now descend. She watches in fascination as a couple of the birds enter the building through an open lantern on top of the dome. She's learned that pigeons and doves were an important food source historically, and that the birds were also kept for their eggs and dung, which was used as fertiliser and to tan leather. Hadn't she also read that it was used to make gunpowder?

Was the dovecote here before the stew pond, or were they created at the same time?

'Tamsin, Jemima, come with Mummy.' The young

woman holds out her hands to her daughters. 'Daddy's waiting for us in the restaurant.'

Ellinor glances over at the two young girls who are now poking sticks in the water. They can't be much older than five and seven. Their mother calls to them again, and she watches as the children reluctantly abandon their exploration of the pond, the older girl throwing her stick in the water before skipping off up the path. The younger one takes hold of her mother's hand. It's such a small, innocent act, but Ellinor feels as if she's been punched in the stomach and acute sadness engulfs her. She and Simon don't have a little one to take hold of their hands, however many times they've tried for that longed-for child. And now, with her resistance of close contact with him, the likelihood of that happening is further away than ever.

As the little family wander back up the path, she gives a deep sigh.

'Come on, Ellinor Forrester. You didn't come here to be depressed,' she reprimands.

Rising to her feet, she takes a different path leading up the hillside and away from the garden. Within seconds, a charming, thatched Victorian summerhouse comes into view but she continues and soon reaches the entrance to a stone tunnel. Lichen creeps across the ceiling and walls, and the air is cool and damp and, as she enters, it tickles the back of her throat. She increases her pace and soon emerges out on the other side, where a steep flight of steps leads up to higher ground. On reaching the top, she looks up towards the house, stops dead in her tracks and does a double take.

Twenty-Nine

The property is situated on an elevated plateau, enjoying stunning views down the valley to the imposing viaduct at Calstock, but it's not as Ellinor remembers it from her previous visit. Puzzled, she wonders if she's approached the house from a different angle, but however she views this side, it doesn't make sense. It's way too small! A large portion of the building is missing, as are the elegant windows, gable ends and chimney stacks that graced the house on her visit only three weeks before. Ellinor's small frown intensifies as her gaze moves to the gardens. These, too, are altered. Where are the beautifully maintained formal terraces, the neat, gravelled paths and the elegant granite steps? Sweat pricks her forehead as she takes in the wilderness of tangled plants covering the sloping land leading up to the house, and her heart starts to pound. Anxiously, she glances back at the steps leading down to the tunnel. A milky, swirling mist now shrouds the entrance and the air ripples, distorting the passageway into a watery realm. Blinking rapidly, she attempts to stabilise the scene, but a sudden shout and a burst of laughter make her turn towards the house again, and what she sees makes the breath catch in her throat.

Emerging from around one corner of the house are three young girls in colourful, long dresses, and not far behind them is a boy, no more than fourteen, wearing hose and doublet. The lad chases the girls, veering from side to side as he lunges to catch them, and excited squeals and shrieks fill the air. What madness has overtaken her now? Ellinor's eyes widen as William suddenly appears with Richard Edgcumbe, following in the children's wake. Walking at a sedate pace,

166

the two men seem preoccupied and are obviously discussing something of great importance.

Ellinor squeezes her eyes shut.

This isn't real. I must be having a relapse. Perhaps I should see a doctor. Just breathe deeply.

She wills herself to believe that once she opens her eyes, Cotehele in all its splendour will be on the rise of the hill once again, but when she does, the building is still the diminished version of the house. Anxiety takes hold. As the children race down the slope towards her, panic makes her chest tighten and her heart begins to pound. Ellinor glances down at her modern clothes. She must not be seen. Turning back to the tunnel, ignoring her fear, she walks down the steps towards the rippling air. Her legs feel heavy and her footsteps are leaden, as if some great force holds her back and prevents her from escaping. As the sound of pounding feet draw nearer, she slips into the mist at the tunnel entrance just as the children thunder by. Placing a hand over her racing heart, Ellinor attempts to still its manic beating, but the next minute she hears the deep timbre of William's voice and it trips in her chest.

'Carter is with us, my lord.' His words float secretively on the breeze. 'I spoke with him this past week. He and a further dozen men from the village support the Lancastrian bid.'

'Good news indeed,' Richard replies. 'It won't be long before we see action.'

Ellinor peers anxiously towards the entrance. If they enter the tunnel, she will be discovered. And then how will she explain her presence? Horrified, she watches as the mist suddenly disperses and sweeps up the stone steps, continuing its journey over the wild slopes towards the house. As shadows fall across the entrance of the sunken passageway, Ellinor shrinks back, pressing her spine into the damp, cold wall. All at once, the men appear in the opening and she's certain William's gaze is upon her. Surely she can be seen!

'What is it?' Richard asks.

William shakes his head. 'I thought I saw something, but it's nothing.'

'Likely a wild animal. The deer park is untamed.' Richard peers into the gloom. 'But no man need have an ill-provisioned house if there be but attached to it a dovecote and a stew pond, and I have instructed my men to lay a path directly from this passageway.'

'A sound idea,' William responds.

'A fresh supply of fish and meat for the table is important,' Richard continues.

Shouts and laughter ring out and as all four children rush up to the two men, Ellinor wills herself to merge with the dank stonework.

'Father, may we take the dogs into the park?' the boy asks.

'I don't see any reason to not, but leave Rannigan. If he catches sight of a deer he will take chase and set you a merry dance.'

'Thank you, Father,' the oldest girl says, bestowing a bright smile.

As the children run back towards the house, Richard turns to William. 'Come, let us continue our discourse.'

He walks away. William turns and glances into the tunnel again and frowns. Turning back, he hurries to catch up with the older man.

Ellinor tries to calm her nerves and regulate her breathing. She waits for several minutes before cautiously walking towards the entrance and unsteadily climbing the steps. Reaching the top, she gazes across manicured gardens full of well-tended flowering shrubs rising in a series of neat terraces towards the elegant eastern elevation of the house. With considerable relief, she notices a family in modern-day attire wandering along the upper gravelled pathway. Again, dizziness and nausea descend, but she's getting wise to the after-effects of visiting that *other* time. In resignation, she waits for inevitable longing to assault her.

'Good morning.'

Ellinor jumps at the sound of a man's voice. Approaching her is an elderly couple.

'Looks like the rain has moved on,' he comments.

She glances up at a powder-blue sky dotted with puffball clouds. 'That's a relief.'

'This is our first visit to Cotehele,' his female companion explains. 'We're looking for the medieval stew pond and dovecote. Are they through there?' She points into the tunnel.

'They are,' Ellinor replies. 'There was no one there when I left.'

'Always a bonus,' the man says with a grin.

Bidding her farewell, the couple hold firmly on to the wooden handrail and make their way slowly down the flight of steps.

Ellinor glances at her watch in astonishment. It's only just gone ten thirty, but it seems as if it was hours ago when she first set off across the fields from Comfort Wood Farm. Looking up at the house, she visualises the reduced version she'd witnessed and scans the stonework for any obvious signs of alterations. But the extensions and additional architectural features have been seamlessly added over the years and nothing is visible to her layman's eyes.

Turning in the direction of the restaurant, Ellinor decides to treat herself to a coffee and a slice of cake before making her way back to the farm. She deserves it after what she's just experienced.

Thirty

'There's garlic bread in the oven,' Pippa says over her shoulder, as she carries a large bowl of spaghetti bolognaise from the kitchen.

Grabbing a pair of oven gloves, Ellinor opens the door and extracts the golden baguettes.

'Rusty and Rufus, will you please get out from under my feet!' she says in an affectionately ruffled voice to the two interested spaniels gazing beseechingly up at her. 'Sorry, but these are not for you.'

Placing the bread on a wooden platter, she carries it through to the dining room. The dogs follow, venturing as far as the doorway, and then sit and watch.

'Tuck in, everyone,' Pippa instructs.

Ellinor puts the platter down on the dining table and pulls out a chair.

'There's lager or wine, Elli,' Ian says. 'Help yourself.'

'Thanks.' Picking up a bottle, she pours a large glass of red.

'So, you think you can start work on the cottage around mid-week?' Simon asks Jake.

The big man tears off a chunk of garlic bread and nods. 'Wednesday, unless there's a last-minute glitch with the Saltash job.'

Excitement ripples through Ellinor. At last, the cottage's re-creation is within touching distance.

Re-creation?

She frowns.

'The tree surgeons are booked to clear a route to the site on Monday,' Simon continues. 'They expect to have it done in a couple of days, three at most.'

'Derek and his crew,' Ian advises Jake.

'Good bloke, that Derek,' comments Jake. 'He'll get the job done in no time. We'll bring the digger and make a start on the footings.'

'You must be so excited,' says Jessica, sitting next to Jake on the opposite side of the table.

'I am,' Ellinor replies. 'We can't wait for the build to get under way, can we, Si?'

Simon agrees.

'For as long as I can remember, there's always been a dwelling there.' The young woman twirls strands of spaghetti around the prongs of her fork.

Ellinor's hearing fine-tunes.

'Apparently, in the last century there was an old woodcutter living there,' Jessica continues. 'After he died the cottage remained empty. I don't know why. It's in such a gorgeous location you'd have thought someone would have snapped it up.'

'Have you always lived around here?' Ellinor asks.

'Yes. So has Jake.' She smiles at the man next to her. 'We've known each other forever. My parents still live in the village house where I was born.'

'What about you, Jake? Is your home in the village?'

He shakes his head. 'No. I grew up at Greenbank Farm. It's been in the family for generations. In fact, Jess's great-great-grandmother was the dairymaid during my great-great-grandfather's tenancy. Rumour has it he had a soft-spot for her.' Picking up his glass of beer, he swallows a large mouthful. 'Just think, Jess, they could have hooked up and then neither of us would have been born.'

'Well, luckily they didn't,' she says with a grin. 'And here we are!'

Great-great-grandparents. How many years ago would they have lived? Ellinor makes a quick guestimate. *Not the right era for the episodes she's experiencing.*

'How many generations did your family have the farm's tenancy?' she asks.

'Not sure.' Jake looks at her in surprise. 'Hundreds of years, I think. Why?'

'Elli's gained an interest in history since arriving in Cornwall,' Simon helpfully supplies.

'Actually, I've been trying to find out about Comfort Wood Farm,' Ellinor says. 'Specifically around the time it was built. I visited the library, and the assistant pointed me in the direction of books covering the fifteenth century.'

'That would be about the right time,' Jake comments, loading his fork with spaghetti.

'We only have deeds going back to 1947, when the National Trust took over Cotehele House and grounds, and sold off this farm,' Pippa states.

'The Edgcumbe family probably has whatever historical documents there are,' Jake says. 'They owned Comfort Wood Farm and tenanted it out.'

'Is *your* family farm owned by the Edgcumbes?' Ellinor asks.

'No, it's located further downstream and belonged to a neighbouring estate until the owners sold it. My great-grandfather bought it before the First World War.'

Realising she's asking a lot of probing questions, Ellinor aims at a friendly, light-hearted tone. 'I find genealogy fascinating.'

Simon stares at his wife in amazement.

'For instance, is Jake a family name or a distortion of, say, John?'

'Don't think it's a family name.' Taking another swig of beer, Jake observes Ellinor over the rim of his glass with light bewilderment. 'We're not a particularly devout bunch. Mum just liked the name Jacob. There aren't any John's in the immediate family that I know of, but it's a common enough name and I'm sure there must have been a few in the past.'

'Have you ever done your family tree?' she asks airily.

Jake's eyebrows knit together. 'I think there's a copy

knocking about somewhere, but the best place to find people of yesteryear is in the local graveyard.'

The next morning, Simon and Ellinor walk along the track leading from the lane into the woodland. Gorse bushes proudly display their vibrant yellow flowers and a scent of coconut fills the air. Following the previous day's threat of rain, it remains fresh and Ellinor hunkers down into her fleece jacket. Pleasant birdsong filters through the woods, and she smiles. She can't wait to be woken by that glorious, life-affirming sound, once they're living in the cottage. A sudden 'prruk-prruk' rings out and she turns in the direction of the noise.

'I don't believe it!' she exclaims, stopping mid-track.

'What don't you believe?' Simon asks.

'You see that bird over there?' She points to a tree at the edge of the woodland. 'Third branch up.'

'A raven,' says Simon. 'What of it?'

'It's not just any old raven, Si. It's the one from our garden in Surrey.'

He glances at her. 'Are you sure? It's a long way from its home territory.'

She nods. 'It showed up in the courtyard not long after I arrived at Ian and Pippa's.'

'How do you know it's the same one? You must admit, it's quite a stretch . . .'

'It *is* the same one,' she says vehemently. 'See the grey feather on its chest? That's what makes it so recognisable.'

'Perhaps it's looking out for you. You know, like a guardian angel.'

'Maybe,' she replies thoughtfully. 'I do get the impression it's watching over me.'

Suddenly the raven takes to the air, and sweeping high over the woodland, it soon disappears.

'If it's going to make a point of showing up, I suppose I should give it a name,' Ellinor says, as she continues along the track.

'And what are you going to call it?' Simon asks.

'Branok.'

She stops dead. What section of her brain conjured up that?

'Why have you stopped?' Simon asks, halting again. 'Seen something else that's followed you down from Surrey?'

'It's the name.' She gives a small, uncertain laugh. 'I'm not sure why I chose it.'

'Perhaps you read it somewhere, or heard it mentioned on the radio,' Simon suggests. 'Anyway, it's not something to fret over. Some things just name themselves.'

'I'm sure you're right,' Ellinor says quietly.

But it's a mystery, and as she walks along the path, she ponders why she'd chosen that particular name and what the raven's regular appearances mean. Are William's wolfhound and the bird connected in some way?

Presently they reach an area of woodland where several trees have blue crosses painted on their trunks.

'Looks like the tree surgeons have already marked out the driveway,' Simon remarks.

'It's a shame to remove them,' Ellinor says, walking towards the nearest tree and gently touching its rough bark.

'They won't go to waste,' Simon assures her. 'We can use them for firewood, and if any are suitable they can be planked and turned into benches and windowsills, and such like.'

'I like that idea,' she says, turning to him. 'Recycle and reuse.'

The thought of *recycling and reusing* makes her feel a sudden, keen pining for something, and she attempts to unravel the reason for the unusual emotion. But, infuriatingly, like a mischievous sprite, understanding flits away through the trees as soon as she gives it her focus.

'Come on,' Simon encourages. 'Let's see if the driveway has been marked out as we instructed.' Striding to the opposite marked tree, he checks the width of what eventually will be the access to the cottage.

Still mulling over the odd feeling besieging her, Ellinor counts the number of trees destined to be felled.

'That's OK,' says Simon. 'Only the necessary ones have been marked.'

Ellinor agrees. 'I like the way the drive winds through the trees. It will be the perfect entrance.'

She gazes around at the mixed woodland, interspersed with hazel and holly bushes. How peaceful it is here, with the breeze teasing through the treetops against a soundtrack of gentle birdsong, and she wonders how many small mammals and wild animals make their journeys, unseen, through the undergrowth as she and Simon stand here.

From out of nowhere, a rapier-like yearning bombards her. But for what?

She has no idea . . .

Thirty-One

As Ellinor and Simon make their way towards the clearing, a rhythmic sound echoes in the air.

'Have the tree surgeons started already?' Ellinor asks in surprise.

'No. They're not due to start until tomorrow.'

She frowns. 'What's that then?'

Simon stops at the edge of the trees and listens. 'I can hear a woodpecker in the distance doing its thing.'

She snorts. 'No, Simon, it's not a bird!'

He shakes his head. 'Peace and quiet to me . . . apart from Woody's racket.'

It sounds like someone chopping wood, and Ellinor casts her husband an incredulous look.

How can he not hear it?

Ellinor sets off towards the ruins, following the noise. As she rounds the corner of the wall incorporating the mostly intact chimney stack, she comes to an abrupt stop. Over by the stream – stripped to the waist – is William, wielding an axe. As the blade connects with the log, splitting it neatly in two, his muscles glisten in the sunlight. She watches as he bends over, picks up another log and places it on the tree stump. Then, in one deft movement he raises the axe above his head. Suddenly, he glances over in her direction. The axe is already in motion, and it comes down heavily, slightly askew on the log, and sends splinters flying in various directions.

'Ellinor. You have come!' he exclaims. 'You disappeared so suddenly that day by the river that I feared some harm had befallen you.'

The concern in his voice takes her by surprise, and her emotions confuse her. William places the axe head on the ground and rests his hands on the top of the shaft.

Taking a step back, Ellinor peers around the corner and scans the surrounding area. But there's no sign of Simon. She turns to William.

'I'm sorry if my disappearance caused you concern.'

'That it did.' He pulls a wry face. 'When I heard the shouts, I wondered what mischief was afoot. I searched for you.'

Her eyes meet his, and her heart skips a beat. 'You mustn't worry when I disappear.'

'A fair challenge!' He gives a small self-deprecating laugh. 'You have a habit of doing that.'

'I don't do it on purpose,' she says. 'I have no choice. I'm pulled away.'

His brow furrows. 'What pulls you away?'

Ellinor curses herself for being so honest. Is she now going to have to explain everything? What will he make of that? She can hardly understand it herself! But if he truly is a manifestation of her husband, he will understand.

'It's difficult to explain,' she says.

There's kindness in the bright blue eyes that assess her . . . and something else.

Picking up the axe, William walks towards her. 'Come, let us take refreshment. It's mighty hot under this sun.'

It is indeed hot in her fleece. Glancing up, Ellinor is surprised to see the sun riding high in a cloudless sky. It had yet to make an appearance when she and Simon left the farmhouse a little earlier. Unzipping her jacket, she removes it and walks with William around the corner of the cottage towards the entrance door. Sprawled across the threshold, panting, is the Irish wolfhound. It lumbers to its feet as they approach and William runs an affectionate hand over the dog's head before entering the dwelling.

The cottage is as it was before and Ellinor sits down on the wooden bench, placing the fleece on the seat beside her.

Silently, she watches as William props the axe against the end wall. Mesmerised, she can't drag her eyes away from him.

Opening a substantial wooden chest, William takes out a loose cotton shirt and shrugs it on. Then, crossing over to the rustic storage shelves, he extracts the stopper from an earthenware jug and pours ale into two wooden vessels before carrying them over to join Ellinor at the table. Raising his cup to her, he takes a long swallow.

'Are you now recovered from whatever ailed you, Ellinor?'

'I think so,' she replies.

'That is good.' His eyes search hers. 'But I wish to know, what manner of beast is it that pulls you from me?'

Inwardly, Ellinor groans. She really shouldn't have said anything and he's obviously not going to let it pass. If this alternative world is some weird, hallucinatory episode, maybe she *should* tell him, bring things to a head, and kick herself back into reality. After all, Simon must be wondering what's happened to her. But still she hesitates.

I've only just discovered this fascinatingly hypnotic escape route and it makes me feel so alive. Am I prepared to close the door on it so soon?

She gazes at him uncertainly and takes a deep breath. 'William, what I'm about to tell you will be hard to believe, but I ask you to keep an open mind.'

Curious eyes observe her steadily.

'A traumatic experience made me unwell, and that's why I came from Surrey to stay with Ian and Pippa—' quickly, she corrects herself, 'Philippa.'

He nods slowly.

'But that's not the only reason I came to Cornwall.' Ellinor screws up her nose.

This is really difficult, and he will probably think I'm mad! Still, in for a penny, in for a pound . . .

'I'm also here because where I come from, this is in ruins.' She indicates the room with a sweep of the hand. 'My husband and I have purchased your cottage and we are going to rebuild it.'

'Your words confuse me.' His face is a picture of puzzlement. 'I don't understand.'

She shakes her head. 'No. I don't expect you do.'

Picking up her cup, she takes a sip. The spiced ale reminds her of the nightcap that Ian gave her the other night, and it brings a modicum of normality back to the strangeness of the situation. There are so many similarities between this *other* world and her own, she's certain there's a connection. And if it is all in her imagination, then what further damage can she possibly do by telling him everything? He may not even exist! Only . . . the man sitting beside her seems *very* real. She can feel the heat emanating from the body that is so close to hers.

'You have a husband,' he says slowly.

She wants to laugh. Of all that she's said, this is the one thing he's picked up on!

'I do,' she says carefully. 'And he looks exactly like you.'

William raises an eyebrow. 'He does?'

She nods, watching as something clicks into place in his gaze.

'And by what name is your husband known?'

'Simon.'

'Ah, it is he!' A muscle twinges in William's cheek. 'I envy this Simon.'

Ellinor's stomach muscles tighten.

'Where is he now?' William continues. 'In Cornwall or Surrey?'

'He's here with me now.'

He glances around.

'I mean, he *was*,' she adds hurriedly. 'When I went to investigate the noise of chopping wood, he vanished. I don't know where he is now.'

She searches William's face. Even she's confused, so how on earth can he possibly understand?

'Is he in the woods?'

'I think he's still in the clearing.'

William rises to his feet. 'Then I will meet him.'

She places a hand on his arm. 'He won't be there.'

Baffled, William turns to her and slowly sits down again. 'You said he was in the clearing.'

'He is, but you won't see him. You see, I'm not sure he's here . . .' she pauses, before adding, '*in this time.*'

William frowns. 'Your words are difficult to comprehend, Ellinor.'

'I know.' She pulls an apologetic face. 'I'm not sure I fully understand them, either, but please bear with me. I'll do my best to explain what I think may be happening.' She takes a swig of ale for Dutch courage. 'I believe that somehow I may have slipped back in time.'

He stares at her in disbelief but remains silent.

Taking this as a good sign, Ellinor continues, 'When you see me, don't you always remark on my unusual clothes?'

William gives a sharp nod.

'For instance . . .' she grabs her fleece, 'have you ever felt material like this?'

She holds out the jacket for him to inspect.

William rubs his hands over the fabric and runs his thumb along the teeth of the plastic YKK zip, and a deep frown settles on his face.

'We wear these jackets a lot in my time as they're so light and warm,' she explains. 'And that's called a zip.' Inserting the pin of the zip into its plastic box, she takes hold of the tab and pulls it up.

William's eyes open wide. Taking the jacket from her, he pulls the zip up and down several times, and examines the way the teeth open and close.

'Ha!' he exclaims. 'A useful invention.'

'It is,' she says. 'It does away with having to do up all those fiddly laces!'

He glances down at her denim jeans.

'And I wear these a lot, too,' she says, with a smile. 'They're so comfortable.'

'You wore a kirtle when I saw you at the farmhouse.'

'Ah, yes.' She purses her lips, considering how best

180

to explain *that*. With a sharp thrill, she notices his gaze immediately diverts to her mouth and she suppresses a smile. 'I think that's because while I was asleep I somehow unintentionally slipped through time. When I appear in modern clothes I'm awake and already dressed in *my time*.'

He raises his eyes to meet hers. His gaze is full of confusion, mingled with keen interest and curiosity. 'How do you get here?'

She shakes her head. 'I don't know. I have no control over how or when I arrive.'

William sits quietly and she can tell that he's processing everything she's told him. After a while, he breaks the silence.

'What period do you come from?' He raises an eyebrow.

Ellinor hesitates. This is going to blow his mind . . .

'The twenty-first century.'

As if hit by a great force, William sits back sharply, his backbone ramrod straight. 'Five-hundred years in the future?' he says incredulously.

'Yes,' she says softly. 'What year is it now, William?'

He looks at her askance. 'Fourteen eighty-three.'

'Listen carefully, William. This next bit of information is very important . . .'

Ellinor hesitates again. If this isn't simply her imagination and she really has somehow slipped back in time, isn't there a rule about not interfering with the course of history? What implications would that have if she did? Would it be altered in any way?

'And what is that?' William prompts.

She glances at him. He's so like her husband . . . he *is* her husband! And she can't let anything happen to him. Even though her gut instinct warns her that sharing future knowledge with him may not be advisable, could it ever be that bad if it comes from a place of love? She reaches a decision.

'I know how Buckingham's Rebellion turns out, and I have to warn you.'

Thirty-Two

William's eyes slowly darken, reflecting keen intelligence, and warmth floods Ellinor's heart. She recognises the response. It's the same with Simon whenever his business brain kicks in – darkening of the iris, as he gives his total focus to the challenge before him and a fierce commitment to do whatever it takes to succeed. Once again, she marvels at the way her brain has brought her husband into this world with her. William is *so* familiar – the subtle differences only making the electric energy between them so completely delicious. She wonders what her therapist will make of that, and then suddenly remembers that she no longer has one. Was it really the wisest decision to dismiss her?

'Tell me,' William commands, and his voice is suddenly filled with urgency.

Ellinor observes him steadily. 'This period of history is compelling.' She pauses. 'Your wish to see Henry Tudor replace Richard III as King comes to fruition.'

William's mouth twitches. 'But you say you have a warning to impart.'

She nods. 'He will be crowned, but not until 1485.'

William frowns. 'What of now?'

Taking a deep breath, Ellinor outlines the unsuccessful rebellion of 1483 and explains the major part the weather plays in its failure. She has William's total attention, but his reaction to the information she delivers is hard to decipher as his face gives nothing away.

'Please, William, you must be careful,' Ellinor pleads. 'Buckingham does not come out of this well. The rivers Wye and Severn are in flood and impassable due to bad weather, and after several days of waiting for them to retreat, he flees into Shropshire. The King acts swiftly and declares bounties on the rebels' heads – one thousand pounds for Harry Stafford.'

The only sign of emotion in William is a twitch of one eyebrow.

'It's not known whether someone betrays him but he's discovered in hiding, and history records that he is captured and executed for treason. Please take care. Promise me you will not be captured.'

She's not sure how, but suddenly she's in his arms. Eagerly, she surrenders to his passionate, urgent kisses and as his mouth claims hers, his stubble scratches her face . . . but she's beyond caring. Not only does her body respond and fill with desire, but also she realises that not once has she balked at his invasion of her space.

Perhaps the time to heal has truly arrived.

Eventually – with considerable restraint – William draws back. 'I will take care, lovely Ellinor. There is much to live for.'

As twinkling mischief returns to his eyes, Ellinor thinks that William's capacity to switch moods in a second is another of Simon's traits that has accompanied her into this dreamlike realm.

'If we are married in your time,' William says, with a cheeky grin, 'then be it not right that we are husband and wife in this one?'

Ellinor's eyes open wide, and she is about to reply when suddenly Branok barks and William's attention diverts to the door.

'Maybe your Simon has arrived after all.'

Ellinor's head swims. That's not possible. It's her trauma that has brought her here. And if Simon has arrived in this time, how is this going to play out?

William gets to his feet. 'The day grows old and there is much logging to be done.' Walking over to the wall, he picks up the axe, crosses over to the entrance and steps outside.

Ellinor follows, and as she exits the dwelling she notices Branok standing guard.

William takes a long look around the clearing. 'Your Simon is shy to come forward.'

'I'm sure Branok knows he's here,' she says.

William glances down at the hound. 'Aye, he misses nothing.' He smiles at her. 'Can you stay awhile, fair Ellinor?'

I can stay forever . . .

She nods and accompanies William around the side of the cottage.

'You have captured my heart, Mistress Ellinor,' he says, turning to her.

'You always had mine,' she softly responds. Looking up into those bright blue eyes, she's mesmerised by the lights dancing deeply within them.

With his gaze never once leaving her face, William raises her hand to his mouth and kisses it gently. Then, businesslike once more, he strides towards the log pile.

Ellinor closes her eyes.

What the hell am I doing? I must snap out of this intoxication. It's madness!

'Have you discovered the source of the noise?' Simon's voice cuts through her thoughts.

'Simon!' she exclaims, turning to see him rounding the corner of the cottage.

He stops. 'What?'

She turns back to William. But he's not there, and neither is the log pile. No longer is the clearing filled with the noise of splitting wood. The only sound is from the gently burbling brook as it makes its untroubled way through the clearing and deep into the forest, towards the river.

'Are you OK? Your eyes are bright and you look feverish.' Approaching, Simon cups her face in his hands. 'You feel hot and your cheeks have come up in a rash.'

'I'm fine, Si. It's just the heat of the sun.'

He stares at her in astonishment and then looks up at the sky. 'But there is no sun, Elli.'

She shivers.

I've got to be wiser than this.

Simon frowns. 'I think you should sit down for a bit.' Taking hold of her hand, he leads her around to the entrance of the ruined cottage. 'That's odd,' he says, as they enter the open space. 'Your fleece is on the ground over there, but you were wearing it a moment ago.'

A moment ago . . .

Crossing over to it, Ellinor quickly puts it on, and a vision of William's deep curiosity as he examined the workings of the zip comes to her. She starts to sway, dizzy again, as a deep sense of longing sweeps over her.

'Hey, steady,' Simon says, catching hold of her elbow. 'I really think you're not well, Elli. Let's sit on the wall over there.'

He guides her to a section of the abandoned stonework, when suddenly a soft bark rings out and they both look towards the entrance.

'Prruk-prruk.'

The raven stands at the threshold, staring in through the opening with its beady, dark eyes fixed on the couple sitting on the far side of the empty space.

'Your guardian angel takes this *forever-watching-over-you* very seriously,' Simon says, with a grin.

'Thank you, Branok,' Ellinor silently whispers.

Thirty-Three

Early on Monday morning, Simon departs for Surrey and the start of another working week, and over the next two days the tree surgeons clear an access to the cottage. On the Wednesday – true to his word – Jake and his trusty assistant turn up with the digger and make a start on the footings for the enlarged layout of the cottage.

Ellinor glances at her watch – midday. 'Pippa, I'm off to the cottage to check on progress. If you like, I'll take Rusty and Rufus with me.'

Pippa glances up from a desk strewn with paperwork. 'That's great. I'm overloaded with farm accounts. It's best to keep the dogs on leads at the site, especially Rufus. He loves a hole and will run amok amongst the machinery, given half a chance.'

'Will do.'

As she walks to the front door, Ellinor calls to the dogs and immediately they're at her side, tails wagging. Unhooking the leads from the coat rack and attaching them to the spaniels' collars, she exits the farmhouse and glances up at the sky. The sun refuses to show its face from behind the clouds, but the temperature is mild, and bluebells adorn the verges of the drive. From a nearby field lambs bleat and Ellinor smiles.

'Not much to grumble about is there, boys?' she says, glancing down at the two dogs trotting obediently alongside her.

Rusty glances up with soulful eyes, but Rufus strides out on a mission.

Turning left onto the lane, it's not long before she reaches the path that leads to the cottage. Fresh tyre marks in the mud and telltale caterpillar tracks reveal that vehicles and a digger have recently travelled this way.

Several minutes later, Ellinor arrives at the area of trees marked as the entrance to the property. Progress at last . . . Winding its way through the woodland is a cleared access; the felled trees now stacked at the edges, waiting to be removed. As she turns off the main track and follows the newly formed route towards the clearing, she's suddenly overcome by a strong sense of déjà vu and the certainty that she's done this many times before.

'That's just crazy!' she exclaims out loud.

Startled, the dogs gaze up at her.

'Ignore me, boys. It's just your house guest having a ridiculous notion.'

But is it ridiculous? Her feet know the route so well.

However, the next minute any concern over the unusual feeling deserts her. The spaniels sit as she halts at the edge of the clearing, and together they watch the digger deposit a load of earth onto a growing pile at the far end of the ruined walls. Excitement bubbles. It is *really* happening! She and Simon are recreating what once stood here. Suddenly, Ellinor recalls the loud and clear message she'd received.

Your destiny awaits you at the edge of the woods.

She hears her name being called, and a delicious tingling sensation courses through her as she glances around for William. But it's not him who waves and strides towards her. It's Jake.

'Morning,' he says.

'Hi. Looks like you've made a good start.'

'Pete and I don't hang around!' He bends to ruffle the dogs' heads. 'We're pleased with the progress so far. If all goes according to plan we should have the foundations dug by the end of the day.'

Ellinor's eyes widen. 'So soon? But that's wonderful!'

'I do have a query, though. If you come with me, I'll show you on the architect's drawings.'

Falling into step beside him, Ellinor and the dogs walk towards the ruins as the digger operator looks over in their direction. He nods to her and Ellinor raises a hand in acknowledgement.

'That's Pete, Jess's uncle,' Jake explains. 'We've worked together for several years. Salt of the earth, he is; nothing's too much trouble.'

'It's fortunate to have reliable employees,' Ellinor comments.

'Never given me a headache.'

As they enter the ruined enclosure, the dogs look around expectantly. Observing Rufus and Rusty's behaviour, and aware that many animals have sixth sense, Ellinor wonders if they can sense the dog that once lived here . . . or maybe even see him.

In the centre of the open space is a folding plastic table and laid out on top are the architect's drawings, held in place by two mugs, a Thermos flask and a sandwich box.

'Very Heath Robinson!' she comments with a grin.

'Got to be inventive on site,' Jake responds. 'This is what I wanted to run by you. The plans show an enlarged fireplace and I take it you'd like to retain the granite mantelpiece.'

'Yes,' she answers sharply, surprised at her impassioned response.

'That's what I thought. Unfortunately, the stone isn't wide enough for the new opening.'

'How much longer does it need to be?'

'Well, if we're building the new inglenook to these measurements . . .' Jake jabs a finger at the plan, '. . . another two feet.'

Ellinor frowns. She and Simon both agree it's important to retain what very little remains of the original cottage, if possible.

'So,' Jake continues, 'as I see it, you have two options. Either keep the fireplace the size it is now, or replace the mantelpiece with another that fits the new dimensions.'

Ellinor stares at the granite stone with the witch marks. It's part of the cottage's history and was in that position during those oh-so-precious days of William. Biting her lip, she considers what to do. As she glances around the empty space her gaze comes to rest on the entrance.

'What if we found a replacement for it and moved the granite stone to the front door or the porch? It would work as a lintel, wouldn't it?'

Jake assesses the doorway. 'Don't see why not. The new front-door opening is wider than the current entrance, and the porch will be wider still.'

'Wherever we eventually position it, it's important that the witch marks are on display.'

Jake agrees. 'This old cottage was protected by those marks for centuries. It's only good and proper they continue to protect the new building, and all those who live in it.'

Extracting a tape measure from his back pocket, he walks to the fireplace and checks the length of the stone. Then, crossing over to the entrance, he measures the width of the new doorway.

'That'll work.'

Ellinor beams. 'Good! Then that's what we'll do. Can you suggest any reclamation yards in the area? I'll see if they have anything suitable as a replacement for above the fireplace.'

'There are a few around,' Jake says. 'I'll make a list. But I may have something that will do the trick back home.'

Thirty-Four

Forty minutes later, having worked through Jake's other build queries, Ellinor and the spaniels head off through the woods towards the river. It's silent and still amongst the trees, and they pass only two other dog walkers. As they make their way down towards the water, she lets Rufus and Rusty off their leads, and although the dogs veer off the path to explore the undergrowth and follow enticing scents, thankfully both respond when she calls them back.

Presently, she arrives at the narrow track that leads to the river, which she'd previously taken with Pippa and the dogs. The spaniels rush past her down the hillside, aware of what's waiting for them at the bottom. Ellinor follows and it's not long before she emerges from the trees onto the grass-covered stone quay. She stands and gazes at the slow-moving river, which today is murky grey under the sullen sky, before walking down the slipway towards the water. The spaniels remain on the quay, but it's only a moment before Rufus leaps off the stone wall and rushes to join her.

'Come on, Rusty,' she encourages, turning back to the other dog.

At the sound of its name, the spaniel scampers over the grass and down the slipway.

Ellinor picks up a stick and throws it into the shallows and both dogs wade in, but it's Rufus that gets to it first and brings it back to her. Eagerly, he gazes up at her, tail wagging, as he waits for another game. She laughs, and for the next ten minutes she throws the stick for the dogs, again and again.

'OK, enough! You've worn me out.'

Retracing her steps, she walks up the slipway onto the

quay and sits down on the grass, and it's not long before Rusty joins her and lies down at her side, panting. Rufus, however, continues to investigate the shallows.

Ellinor glances around the hidden quay, remembering how it had looked when she'd found herself here in that *other* time. Gazing across the river, she visualises the reed bed as it was centuries ago. Much larger then, it had narrowed the course of the river, and behind it was a heavily forested area stretching away up the hill. Her gaze wanders to the neatly maintained woodland on the opposite hillside and the adjacent large fields of mixed livestock. Those pastures had been smaller and arranged in strips bordered by overgrown hedgerows and full of sheep, with not a single cow in sight.

And then her mind wanders to William. Raising a hand to her neck, she runs an index finger along the puckered ridge of her scar, reliving the sensation of his finger gently tracing it. She hadn't flinched at his touch, and the corners of Ellinor's mouth turn up in a smile at the memory. But will the jagged scar ever lose its ugliness, or will it be forever a hideous reminder? She shakes herself from her thoughts.

'Not going there, Ellinor,' she says out loud.

'Not going where?'

She whips around at the sound of his voice. 'William!'

'My lady,' he teases, sitting down beside her on the grass.

She notices Branok standing vigilant at the edge of the quay. Wondering what the spaniels will make of the wolfhound, she glances down at her side. But Rusty has vanished . . . and so has Rufus. Panic takes hold. She can't lose Pippa and Ian's dogs! Quickly, she reassures herself that although she's slipped through the veil again, the spaniels will still be there in her time. She just hopes they won't get up to too much mischief in her absence.

William takes hold of her hand, and turning it palm uppermost, he raises it to his lips and plants a tender kiss on the soft skin. For a second her heart stops as his eyes drink her in, but the next minute they dance with devilment.

'Pray tell. Where are you not going?'

Ellinor attempts to make light of her thoughts. 'Oh, I was just remembering how I got this scar and it depressed me. That's all.'

Not wanting to draw attention to her imperfection any more than she has to, she extracts her hand from his and swiftly brings her hair forward over her shoulder to cover the scar.

His smile is sympathetic. 'If I were to consider the manner in which I gained my many wounds, I would never have the courage to face another day.'

She contemplates the mark on his shoulder – the same as Simon's birthmark. He'd said it was an arrow wound and she'd thought he was joking . . . But now she thinks he could well have been telling the truth. And then she recalls the numerous scars on his back. How did he get those?

'Have you been in many fights?' she asks.

He gives a hollow laugh. 'You make it sound as if I had a choice! Battles would be a more appropriate description.'

Ellinor considers his words. 'Battles, then.'

He nods. 'A few more than a man would care to indulge in.'

Like a sledgehammer, sudden understanding hits her. His existence is *so* different to hers. She has none of the life and death choices he must have to consider daily, if not hourly. If she chooses one course of action over another, few, if any, will result in a life-threatening outcome – unless, of course, she's extremely unlucky and in the wrong place at the wrong time. Ellinor grimaces and quickly steers her thoughts away from *that* flight. But William must be acutely aware of the fragility of life. She steals a glance at him. Is that why he's so vigorous and fiercely passionate in all he undertakes, because of his consummate understanding that what is here today may easily be gone tomorrow? And is this why she finds him so mesmerising and overwhelmingly attractive? He lives life in the moment, with honesty and commitment, and he has never disguised his feelings for her, however light-heartedly he hints at their depth. She can't deny it – he's increasingly filling her thoughts and she's always hoping to catch a glimpse of him.

Tenderly, William pushes back a lock of hair from her face. 'Ellinor, what has brought about this serious countenance?' he asks softly.

She blinks, only now aware that he's been studying her.

'I was considering the dangers you face.'

He raises an eyebrow and makes a sound at the back of his throat. 'Do not think about that too deeply or the sweet restorative powers of a night's rest will forever desert you.'

Confidently – without a moment's hesitation – he leans in and kisses her on the lips, and Ellinor closes her eyes, relishing the feel of his mouth upon hers.

Suddenly William jumps to his feet. 'Come, sweet Ellinor.' He holds out his hand. 'Let us check the traps and then I shall cook you a fine meal.'

Accepting his firm grip, she gazes up into twinkling eyes as he draws her to her feet. She's never known anyone change mood so quickly! But as swiftly as the thought occurs, she reminds herself that of course she has. Simon . . .

'Branok, stay,' William commands.

Gazing at his master, the dog obediently sits.

William takes a narrow track skirting the edge of the river and Ellinor follows. Several times they are forced to duck beneath overhanging branches and it seems to her that the landscape has transformed into one more suited to a fairy tale. Verdant and resplendent, the colours of the billowing foliage appear magnificently enhanced. The vegetation along the riverbank is dense, and the trees on both sides of the narrowing waterway reach out to intertwine and form a tunnel, beneath which she notices a dozen mallards paddling unhurriedly upstream. Clouds of flies hover low over the river, and suddenly a fish leaps, its scales glinting in the sun. As it disappears once more into its watery realm, only ripples and a series of ever-expanding rings remain on the surface to give away that it had been there.

'Good,' says William. 'The fish are active today.'

Presently they come to a bend in the river. Stretching from one bank to the other is a wooden frame, on which three rows of conical-shaped woven hazel baskets are set out against the incoming tide.

'Stay here,' William says, as he navigates his way down the steep bank. 'Hopefully, there'll be a plump salmon in one of these traps.'

He looks up at her and grins before stepping into the shallows.

Standing on the riverbank, Ellinor watches as William wades out into the water, which soon reaches up to his waist as his feet sink into the mud.

Checking each basket in turn, he calls out, 'We are in luck! Our bellies will be full today.'

Extracting the fish and bringing them to the shore, he quickly dispatches the salmon and lays them out on the bank. Ellinor stares down at the five blue-silver bodies with their pinkish undersides and wonders how they will taste. She's never had fish so freshly caught.

William snaps off lengths of ivy runners and selecting a thin branch nestling amongst the undergrowth, he ties the salmon in place on the improvised walking stick.

'Hungry?' he asks, glancing at Ellinor.

She gives him a smile and nods. 'I'm interested to see how you'll cook the fish.'

'Over a fire.' He considers her for a long moment. 'Why, how do you cook them?'

She laughs, wondering what his reaction would be if she told him that her preferred way to cook salmon is to season with salt and pepper, lay lemon slices and thyme on top, place in a dish and cover, and pop in the microwave for three minutes!

'Not as you do, I suspect.'

Thirty-Five

As they head back along the narrow track, Ellinor notices William scan the ground. Suddenly he stops and picks up a small round log, and a few yards further on he halts again.

'Ellinor, gather a handful of Wood Sorrel please.'

She gazes at the ground. 'Wood Sorrel?'

He indicates a large clump of delicate heart-shaped leaves growing amongst the leaf-litter on the woodland floor. Ellinor does as he requests and they continue on in companionable silence. As they approach the old landing stage, Branok is still in the same spot where they'd left him. Immediately, the dog gets to its feet, but with one reassuring word from William, the wolfhound quickly settles again.

'Put the Wood Sorrel on that rock over there,' William says, pointing to a boulder at the edge of the grass. He sets the fish down on the ground.

'What can I do?' she asks.

'We need dry firewood.'

Ellinor searches amongst the immediate woodland and holds up a branch. 'Is this the right size?'

'Yes, but also smaller branches and thinner twigs for kindling,' William says, looking up from collecting material suitable for tinder.

Once she has gathered sufficient firewood, Ellinor carries her bundle over to the landing stage, as William places a collection of dry mosses, plant, bark, leaves and feathers on the ground.

'These are good,' he says, glancing at her offerings, as he removes the flat stone and charred logs from the cold fire.

Ellinor watches in fascination.

Absorbed in his work, William resets the fire with branches. Next, he creates a small tinder nest, making an indent with his thumb in its centre. Then, with the tip of his knife, he carves a deep dimple in the fist-sized log he'd found in the woods, before finally selecting a straight stick and expertly whittling one end into a tapered point.

Glancing up, he smiles at Ellinor carefully observing him. 'You appear intrigued.'

'It's good to see a man hard at work,' she replies flippantly.

She's not going to admit that she's only ever seen fires started this way in the Bush Craft TV documentaries that interest Simon, or on YouTube.

William chuckles as he kneels and places the log on the ground. Inserting the stick into the dimple, he starts spinning the drill between his hands to create friction. Biting down hard on his lip, he concentrates on finding a rhythm, sawing ever-faster and exerting more pressure on the socket. After several minutes a wisp of smoke appears at the base. Adding a small amount of dry material, he blows gently to encourage a flame before quickly transferring it to the tinder nest. As the dry material catches, William squeezes the bundle and continues to fan the flame with his breath.

'That will suffice,' he says, straightening up.

The sight of fire being created from scratch makes Ellinor smile. There's something freeing and exhilarating about being in the company of someone so competent, and she feels more alive than she's felt for months, sitting here on the banks of the picturesque River Tamar with this capable man.

William adds small sticks to the bundle, and as these catch light, he feeds the fire with larger logs. Once the blaze is established, he places the flat granite rock on top and guts the fish.

Ellinor watches as William walks down to the river and rinses the salmon. Momentarily, she's spellbound by the light, fluffy clouds reflected in the clear blue water. Her gaze shifts to the opposite bank where a heron stands stock still in the shallows, and a sudden flash of turquoise announces a kingfisher skimming low over the water before swiftly disappearing upstream.

Picture perfect . . .

'Ellinor, perhaps you would shred the Wood Sorrel over the fish,' William says, walking back to the fire.

She nods, thankful that she's of some use at last. Crossing over to the rock where she'd left the three-leaved plant that reminds her of clover, she scoops it up in her hands.

William lays three wet salmon on the flat rock, which sizzles as their scales touch its hot surface. Roughly tearing the Wood Sorrel, Ellinor scatters its leaves over the silver bodies, and it's not long before a wonderful aroma fills the air. Once the fish are cooked, William skilfully removes the bones with the tip of his knife and cuts the salmon into portions.

'Here, Branok!' he says, throwing the dog a fistful.

Eagerly, the wolfhound gulps down the offerings.

'Can anyone fish in the river?' Ellinor asks, helping herself to a piece of salmon.

The piquant Wood Sorrel reminds her of lemon and apple peel as it hits her taste buds. It also takes away her thirst.

'No. Richard Edgcumbe owns the river, but I have permission.' Spearing a portion of fish with his knife, William takes a bite.

Curious about his relationship with the owner of the grand house, Ellinor asks, 'How do you know him?'

Intelligent eyes observe her. 'When Philippa and Ian took on the tenancy of the farm, Richard enquired if they knew of a forester. They proposed me.'

'So that's why you live in a cottage in the forest.'

'I have lodgings at the house when I need them, but I'm happiest at the edge of the woods.'

At the edge of the woods . . .

A shiver surges up Ellinor's spine and she rubs the back of her neck. 'What does your work entail, William?'

He considers her question. 'The most important duty

is to ensure the deer in my lord's forests are maintained for the hunts that he holds. I act as his assistant on such occasions. I also feed the deer in winter, take care of any new-born calves and deter poachers from killing too many. My other tasks are to prevent illegal grazing and logging in the woods.'

That explains why he's so practical, and judging by his impressive handling of the axe, no doubt he's handy with his crossbow, too! And as for the scars on his body, maybe they're the result of skirmishes with Cornish poachers.

'Do you perform any other duties for Richard?'

'Aye.' William eyes her curiously. 'As with all aristocracy, his household serves him and fights alongside when he goes to war. I am his mounted archer.'

Ellinor draws in a sharp breath. Is there little wonder he was so amused by her limited understanding? He hasn't received those *war wounds* from light-hearted skirmishes or drunken brawls . . . He has earned them from full-on battles!

The sun has slipped to the west and hangs low in the sky, and as the heat of the afternoon fades William places more logs on the fire.

'Come closer,' he says, drawing her to him.

Happily she obliges.

Placing his arm around her shoulder, he dips his head and drops a tender kiss on her lips.

He feels so good – masculine and strong – and as if viewing the scene from a safe distance, Ellinor observes how readily and enthusiastically she responds to his caresses. But there's nothing ethereal or otherworldly to the feel of his body beneath her fingertips, and as their passion grows she forgets about Simon and the spaniels, Pippa and Ian, Comfort Wood Farm, her life in Surrey . . . and *the incident*. All is captivating, sensuous, exciting, arousing, and as William swallows her heart and soul, she allows herself to drown in the feelings his masterful kisses call forth.

'Beautiful Ellinor,' he whispers, his voice thick and distorted.

A vision of Simon swims into her thoughts and with a prick of conscience she surfaces briefly from this dreamlike escape. But the next minute she's consumed by a surge of passion and an urgent need that cannot be denied. It's been so long since she and her husband have shared any intimacy, and if this version of him is the solution to finding her way back, then it's a wonderful gift.

Urgently, William unzips her jeans and plants a tender kiss on the soft skin of her lower belly. Impressed by his masterful handling of the unfamiliar device – he'd only *briefly* studied the zip on her fleece jacket! – Ellinor concludes that he must be a quick learner. As he slides her jeans down over her hips, she helpfully raises her pelvis, marvelling at the way she so willingly allows him to remove her clothes. Sitting up, she pulls her sweatshirt over her head and laughs at the look on his face as he surveys her bra.

'Your garments are a constant surprise,' he remarks.

Swiftly unhooking it, she removes the item and a thrill of excitement courses through her as she watches William's eyes darken.

'I have never seen one so fair,' he murmurs.

Lying back, she holds out her hands to him. 'Come to me, William.'

Teasingly, he works his way up her body, dropping butterfly kisses on every curve, dip and hollow, and by the time she feels his weight pressing urgently against her, Ellinor is on the point of exploding.

This man is well-practised in the art of seduction, but what did I expect? That he lived as a monk?

But the next minute all conscious thought is cast aside and as their bodies respond to a mutually growing need, Ellinor luxuriates in the feeling of pure abandonment.

Sometime later, with eyes closed, and resting her head on his chest, she listens to the comforting rhythmic beat of his heart. Gently, William weaves her silky hair through his fingers and she revels in the realisation that she's so easily and naturally overcome a major hurdle. Lying together, sated and at peace, they listen to the soothing sounds of the river as it laps the shoreline, heralding the return of the tide. And somewhere in the near distance, a duck quacks.

Ellinor can't recall the last time she's felt so relaxed, and opening her eyes she glances up at the full moon as it appears through a ring in the night clouds. Encircled by a moonbeam, softly it casts its silvery light upon the lovers.

'William.'

'Hmm?'

'Did you speak with Richard about what I told you?' Lifting her head off his chest, she props herself on one elbow and looks at him.

He doesn't answer immediately and she wonders if he hasn't heard her, but a few seconds later he responds.

'I did.' His voice is grave.

'What did he say?'

William sits up. Resting his elbows on his knees, he gazes out at the silver pathway leading across the river. All at once the atmosphere changes; no longer is it tranquil and peaceful. A sharp uncertainty hangs in the air.

'I didn't disclose who had told me, but I did outline your warnings,' he says in a serious tone. 'He said I'd allowed fear to infiltrate.'

'But as a military man surely he would consider the possibilities?'

William turns to her and the look in his eyes is guarded. 'The weather has been unseasonably good of late. It's hard to convince him that a bad storm will rob us of our victory.'

Ellinor frowns. She knows she shouldn't interfere with the course of history, but it's getting harder by the day to remember that *history* is what it is. This alternative existence feels more real to her than her own reality and she's desperate to keep William safe, if she can.

'Did you mention Kent prematurely launching their

rebellion and announcing that the Duke of Buckingham is their leader?'

'Not as such,' William says in a low voice. 'That would have raised far too many questions as to my source. But I did remark on the importance of all rebellions taking place simultaneously.'

History reports how the uprisings play out, so why does she think she can protect William from what will be? If only she could find some information about him. It would put her mind at rest, one way or the other. But what if something did happen to him? What would her life be without William? Her heart contracts painfully.

William turns to face her. 'Don't be sad, my love. We live for today.' He drops a gentle kiss on her lips and then gets to his feet. 'Promise me you won't disappear while I take a piss?'

'I'll do my best not to.' Turning her face up to the moon and closing her eyes, as if in prayer, softly she says, 'You witness it all. Please take care of William and show me the way.'

Suddenly Branok gives an urgent bark and her eyes fly open. Blinking in surprise, she gazes down at Rusty lying beside her with his head on his paws. Clouds fill the sky, and the grey river wends its way silently through the landscape. In the shallows, Rufus snuffles amongst the reeds.

How are the dogs still where she'd left them? She's been away for hours! But glancing down at her watch, she notices the clock-hands have hardly moved, and she also observes that she's fully dressed.

'Prruk-prruk.' Ellinor turns and her eyes widen. Sitting on the lower branch of a tree at the edge of the grass quay is the raven . . . In the exact spot where Branok had lain.

A whiff of wood smoke lingers in the air and Ellinor shakes her head, as if to rid herself of some enchantment. But as she gets to her feet, she knows that her time with William was no flight of the imagination because her body tells her that she has enjoyed hours of lovemaking.

Thirty-Six

'I'm so sorry, Elli.' Simon's voice is apologetic at the other end of the phone. 'I've been roped in to woo potential clients this weekend and Brian has booked two full-on days of winning-them-over entertainment. Even the golf clubs will be given an airing!'

'Two whole days . . . Poor you,' Ellinor says, in support. 'Mind you, knowing Brian, I'm sure the entertainment will be top-notch with no expense spared.'

Simon laughs. 'You know my boss too well!'

'Well, just enjoy it,' she says.

'I'd rather be in Cornwall.'

Why does the thought of not having her husband around this weekend bring on a sense of relief? Is it out of a perverse sense of guilt? Maybe it's simply that she'll have more time to process all that's happened before seeing him again.

'When's the new cider-making equipment arriving?' Simon asks. 'Is there a date yet?'

Ellinor thinks hard. Since her recent encounter with William, her head has been anywhere but in the present. Has she overheard Ian and Pippa discussing a delivery for the end of the week?

'Not sure. Possibly this Friday,' she says.

'Oh, well, I'll find out when I next come down.'

For some reason, she wonders when that will be.

'Counting the days!' Simon adds hurriedly.

But to Ellinor, his words don't ring true. Something is *off*. Perhaps he's having more fun socialising with the guys at work to want to travel down every weekend and spend time with her. Should she drive up to Surrey instead? But the thought of leaving Cornwall fills her with dismay.

'By the way,' she says. 'There's a theatre group visiting Cotehele on Saturday week and Pippa thought it would be fun if we went along. It's optional fancy dress, but she thinks we should make the effort.'

Simon chuckles. 'Any excuse to dress up!'

'I'll sort out an outfit for you. Apparently, it's a medieval romp – you know, dashing men in doublets and capes, and women in dresses with low bodices and heaving bosoms.'

'Love a heaving bosom.'

Ellinor gives a small laugh, which soon sticks in her throat as she recalls how her bosom had heaved under William's loving touch. Her face flushes crimson.

'Hope the weekend is a success,' she says.

'Thanks. See you soon.' Simon hangs up.

Ellinor frowns. He'd ended the call without the usual terms of endearment.

Rising off the bed, she walks to the window, opens the casement and stares out. It's not as if she's been unfaithful to her husband – William *is* Simon, only in a different time . . . Isn't he?

It's a fine day and cotton-wool clouds dot a sky the colour of cornflowers. She glances down into the courtyard and spots Ian encouraging the dogs into the back of the Land Rover.

'Morning,' she calls.

He turns and looks up at her. 'So it is, and a good one at that! I'm off to Truro but you'll find Pippa elbow-deep in flour in the kitchen.'

'So industrious,' Ellinor says with a smile. 'I'm visiting the local churchyard.'

'Whatever takes your fancy!'

Climbing into the car, he starts the engine, and she waves as the vehicle disappears down the drive. All is peaceful and still once again and Ellinor gazes around the yard. The two farm cats bask in the sun, washing themselves, and half-a-dozen chickens peck amongst the long grasses at the edge of the cart shed. But there's no sign of the raven. She's become accustomed to its comforting presence and it feels strange not to see it. She wonders what it does when it's not on *overseeing* duties. Is it flying amongst the valleys and hills of Dartmoor at this moment, or has it shape-shifted into a fifteenth-century Irish wolfhound to accompany William as he goes about his duties for the squire of the manor?

Ellinor sighs deeply. The more she researches Richard Edgcumbe's history, the pull of his time grows stronger, and she longs to revisit the people who inhabited this part of Cornwall. She purses her lips and raises a wry eyebrow.

Well . . . maybe just one particular person!

But this won't do, daydreaming of a time long ago, even though those people feel so very real to her. She has to get on with life in the *here and now*.

Ellinor turns away from the window and, grabbing her jacket and handbag from the back of the chair, she exits the bedroom and makes her way downstairs to the kitchen.

Pippa is kneading dough when Ellinor enters. 'Thought I'd make a batch of loaves and try them out at the farmers' market.'

'That's a good idea,' Ellinor says, crossing over to the kettle.

'It's just boiled,' comments Pippa.

Making herself a cup of instant coffee, Ellinor sits down at the kitchen island and watches Pippa divide the dough between half-a-dozen loaf tins.

'What do you have planned today?' her cousin's wife asks, sweeping away an errant lock of hair escaping from the scarf wrapped around her head.

'Continuing with research. I thought I'd visit the local churchyard and see if there's anything to discover about past occupants of Cotehele and this farm.'

Pippa slides the tins onto the oven shelves and closes the door. 'You've really taken the history of this place to heart, haven't you?'

'I find it fascinating,' Ellinor says with a nod. 'Which is the nearest church?'

'There are several in the area . . . not that we're avid churchgoers!' Pippa raises a wry eyebrow. 'I think the closest is St Andrew's Parish church but you'll have to drive there. It's just out of Calstock. Is there anyone in particular you're looking for?'

Ellinor swallows a mouthful of coffee before answering. 'As you know, I'm interested in the period around the time this farmhouse was built, so anyone who lived here during the fifteenth century.'

Pippa frowns. 'I believe the church is fourteenth century, so there may be some information. However, if you're looking for gravestones dating back to that era, I doubt you'll be lucky. The older memorials are more likely to be eighteenth and nineteenth century. The area, then, was buzzing with tin and copper mining activity, and other industries – accidents waiting to happen, if you ask me.'

'I'll check them out, anyway, just in case.' Downing the last of the coffee, Ellinor rises to her feet. 'Oh, I forgot to mention, Simon's not coming down this weekend. He's entertaining clients.'

'That's a shame.'

Ellinor nods. 'But he says he's up for the theatricals at Cotehele.'

'Good man,' says Pippa, turning back to her baking.

Located at the top of a hill, high above the village of Calstock, the tall tower of the church of St Andrew's is an impressive landmark. Ellinor parks the car in the quiet road and gets out. There's no one around and tranquillity permeates the air. Entering the grounds through a pair of gates under a slate-tiled canopy, she walks along a gravelled path towards the imposing tower. As she steps inside the porch, she notices the remains of a holy water stoup and imagines worshippers of past times dipping their fingers in and making the sign of the cross before entering God's house. Opposite this is an intriguing fireplace with a granite lintel and jamb, and she's considering why a porch would have one, when the wooden door to the church suddenly opens and a sweet-faced middle-aged vicar appears in the entrance.

'Hello,' he says. 'I hadn't realised anyone was here. I was just about to lock up, but I can stay a few minutes longer if you'd like to have a look around.'

'That's very kind, but only if you're sure,' she says with a smile.

'Absolutely,' he assures her.

'I wondered about this fireplace.'

'Its purpose is unclear,' the vicar explains. 'Possibly it was used for the kindling of the Easter fire, but it was more likely to be for hygiene reasons, keeping the building free of disease.'

Ellinor glances around. On the stone threshold are traces of brass nails embedded in the surface.

Noticing where her gaze has fallen, the man continues, 'We suspect an effigy was once positioned there and that it was part of an altar tomb.'

'There's so much to discover, if you understand what you're looking at,' Ellinor observes.

'And that, my child, can be applied to life itself.'

She glances at him. 'Are you sure I'm not keeping you?'

The vicar checks his watch. 'Not at all. I'm due at Mrs Chapman's for the parish council meeting at twelve, so I have some time yet.' He beams at Ellinor. 'Is there anything in particular you're interested in?'

She explains that she's researching the end of the fifteenth century and enquires if there are any graves dating to that period in the churchyard.

'That's quite some age.' His brow creases as he considers her question. 'There is evidence of building work in the church itself from that time. For example . . .' he points to several large granite blocks in the porch walls, '. . . these denote fifteenth-century work, and they also occur in the tower. But as far as graves are concerned?' He shakes his head. 'I can't recall any in the churchyard from that period, nor across the road in the cemetery.'

For the next half-hour, the vicar guides Ellinor around the church. She learns that the building was consecrated circa 1290, although nothing obvious remains from that period; it was re-roofed about 1420, when the south aisle was also added; and thoroughly restored in 1867. As they walk up the northern aisle, he points out a fifteenth-century turret projecting from the north wall and explains that it contains a rood staircase.

'And this is the Edgcumbe Chapel,' he announces, halting in front of a doorway, 'although it's no longer used as such. These days we use it to store religious items. As you can see, it is constructed from very different stonework.'

Ellinor glances up at the mould of the door, in which the initials *RE* have been inscribed. A fizz of excitement courses through her. 'Are those Richard Edgcumbe's initials?'

'They are indeed. He had the chapel built in 1558.'

'Oh!' she says, in disappointment. 'Not the first Richard Edgcumbe?'

'No. His grandson. It was he who built Mount Edgcumbe, at Cremyll, and moved his household from Cotehele to reside there. His descendants became barons and earls, and the earldom survives in a direct male line to this day.' The vicar glances at his watch. 'Apologies, dear lady, I have to leave. But please don't hurry away. You can stay and wander around the churchyard at your leisure. And if I can be of any further assistance in the future, please don't hesitate to return.'

Ellinor walks with him to the porch and waits as the vicar locks the door.

'Good day to you,' he says with a smile. 'I hope you find what you're looking for.'

She watches as he makes his way along the path towards the road. Then, turning back to the church, she lets out a sigh of frustration.

'Maybe the churchyard will be more forthcoming,' she mutters.

As she wanders through the church grounds, a granite cross catches her attention. Crossing over to it, she discovers that it's the site of the 1856 grave of Sir William Lewis Salusbury-Trelawny, 8th Baronet, of the adjacent Harewood Estate. Earlier, when the vicar showed her around the church, she'd noticed two plaques near the pulpit bearing inscriptions to the man, his wife and their five children. But this is not the period she's interested in. Infuriatingly, nothing in the graveyard provides her with the answers she's looking for, and in the cemetery on the opposite side of the road, she acknowledges that Pippa was right. Most of the graves date from the eighteenth and nineteenth centuries and tell a tale of folk lost to industrial and mining accidents.

Crushing disappointment consumes her, and feeling dejected, she returns to the car. Although it's been an interesting tour, no revelations have come to light from this visit, and she'd *so* hoped to find out more about William and what happened to him.

But, she reminds herself, it was only ever a long shot . . .

Thirty-Seven

Ellinor is still troubled by her last phone call with Simon. There had been a hint of distance between them and she's not sure why. She has no doubt that he *is* entertaining clients this weekend and that's the reason for him not to visit. But what if it's something else? She knows how attractive he is to other women – he was surrounded by them when she'd first met him, although he quickly transferred his attention to her. What if someone is taking advantage of the fact she's not around and moving in on him? She shakes her head.

My husband is a lot of things but he is not *an adulterer, of that I'm sure!*

Still, the thought of a division in their relationship makes her doubt her confidence in him and she can't help but wonder if their relationship is heading south. What, then, of their desire to start a family and a new life in Cornwall?

Desperate not to overthink things and create problems where perhaps there are none, she offers to help out again on the stall at the farmers' market. The loaves are a smash hit and soon sell out. Pippa decides to make them a regular feature, alongside the bottles of apple juice . . . and, of course, the cider, once the new equipment arrives, which she says is due to be delivered the following Thursday.

Once trading hours are over, Ellinor and Pippa load up the van and walk into town. Situated off the main street, up an alleyway, are a number of individual stores, and one offers fancy-dress hire. For the next hour or so, the friends happily search amongst the many outfits for something suitable for themselves and their husbands.

'This takes me right back to childhood,' announces Pippa.

209

'If I ever went missing, I was always found rifling through Mother's dressing-up box!'

Extracting a hanger from the rack, Ellinor holds a hooded, sleeveless dress with a plunging neckline against her body.

'What do you think of this?' she asks, striking a pose.

'Ooh, very Outlander!' Pippa says, lifting an eyebrow. 'Is it leather?'

'No, it's pleather – polyester leatherette,' the assistant announces from the other side of the shop. 'The costume comes with a bow, a suede quiver that attaches to the belt, a matching arm guard and a set of arrows.'

'Whoa!' Pippa exclaims. 'Not real arrows?'

The assistant grins. 'No. Rubber-tipped.'

Ellinor laughs. How typical that she's drawn to an archer's outfit. William *would* approve! Crossing over to a long mirror, she gazes at her reflection. There's something extremely sexy about the costume, but glancing at the alluring image one last time, she rejects it.

'Not going for it?' Pippa asks, discounting a large frilly dress and moving on to the next item on the clothes rack.

'No. I'd probably lose an arrow or two, or misplace the quiver.'

'Oh, this is nice,' Pippa says, extracting a dark-blue velvet dress with flared sleeves and a gold-and-black laced bodice. 'I'm going to try it on.'

'So regal!' Ellinor quips.

As the assistant shows Pippa to the changing room, Ellinor continues searching through the many outfits. Everything that catches her eye and warrants a second look has a plunging neckline or a slit up to the thigh, or is a goth-style outfit featuring masses of buttons and lace; perfect for the likes of Stevie Nicks. She sighs. If only she were half as confident as the singer; but she's determined not to draw any unwarranted attention to herself. At last, she finds a contender – a simple, moss-green, long-sleeved A-line dress with a beautifully tooled and embellished leather belt and matching purse, and faux-fur lined, leatherette wrist guards.

'Perfect,' says the assistant, coming up behind her. 'That colour complements your complexion. Would you like to try it on?'

Ellinor smiles. 'I would, thank you.'

'There's a lovely woodland elven diadem that goes with it,' the assistant continues. 'I'll get it for you so you can see the full effect.'

As Ellinor approaches the changing rooms, a cubicle curtain is briskly drawn back and Pippa steps out.

'Wow!' Ellinor exclaims, immediately dropping her friend a curtsey. 'Your Majesty . . .'

'Oh, stop it!' Pippa laughs. 'Is it too much? I mean, these medieval babes sure liked to show off their assets.' Pushing her boobs together, she accentuates a deep cleavage.

'No, it's wonderful!' Ellinor assures her. 'You'll have everyone jumping to your smallest command.'

'Watch out then,' teases Pippa. 'The power could easily go to my head.'

Ellinor enters the adjacent empty cubicle.

'Here you are.' The assistant approaches with the elven diadem. 'Handmade and inspired by the natural world.'

'This is lovely,' Ellinor says, examining the charming gold-and-green fairy crown, lushly decorated with glittering rhinestones, fabric leaves and flowers, and interlaced with satin.

'It appears delicate, but it's surprisingly robust,' the assistant comments. 'And it will look beautiful with your blonde hair.'

Ellinor closes the curtain and quickly changes into the costume. Placing the hair piece on her head, for a few moments she stares transfixed at her reflection in the mirror. The A-line dress flatters her figure without drawing attention to either her neckline or bust, and the diadem is the perfect accompaniment to the outfit. With her long hair tumbling over her shoulders, the whole effect casts her in the role of a medieval maiden.

Out of nowhere, unbidden words come to her: *child of the forest.*

She smiles at the young woman in the mirror, as if to a dear friend.

'How's it going?' The assistant's voice floats over the top of the curtain.

'Very well, I think.' Drawing back the curtain, Ellinor emerges from the cubicle.

'Lovely!' Pippa says, casting her vote. 'Feminine and practical, in equal measure.' She holds up two hangers. 'I've found these costumes for the boys – King Arthur and Robin Hood. What do you think?'

A while later, having hired the four fancy-dress outfits, the two women make their way through the town towards the car park. Ellinor takes a long look around at the buildings and their intriguing architectural features.

'This town is beautiful,' she remarks appreciatively.

Pippa glances across at her. 'Yes, we consider ourselves extremely lucky to have landed here. The area is full of interesting history.'

'All areas have history,' Ellinor says reflectively, 'but it's easy to get caught up in the process of living and it's often overlooked.'

'Very philosophical,' Pippa says, lifting an eyebrow.

'Must be something to do with all this research I'm doing!' Ellinor says.

'Well, I think it's wonderful that you've found something to immerse yourself in.'

'It's a funny thing, Pippa. I was never interested in history at school, and yet the more I investigate, it feels as though it's not something that happened in the past. It's as if it's occurring now, even as we walk along this street, only on a different plane.'

Pippa pulls a mystified face.

'I know that sounds crazy,' Ellinor continues. 'I can't really explain it, but where we tread now, others have trodden before – Druids, Romans, Saxons, Celts, Vikings . . . It's only a matter of folding back time to walk alongside them.'

'That's *waay* too deep,' Pippa says. 'You've really lost me.'

'Oh, ignore me. I don't know what I'm talking about.' Ellinor deflects Pippa from continuing the conversation, although she can't help but imagine that she and William are walking together now. 'You know, when I consider my life as a flight attendant it seems such a long time ago, and something that happened to someone else entirely.'

Pippa doesn't respond immediately. 'I think that's a good thing, Elli,' she says cautiously. 'It shows you're putting that period behind you and moving on.'

'Maybe.' Ellinor walks on, deep in thought.

'What did you find out from your visit to the church?' Pippa asks, changing the subject.

'Mainly what you told me – that the graveyard tells a story of loss through industrial mining accidents. The vicar said the area was full of tin and copper mining activity in the eighteenth and nineteenth centuries, as well as boat building, quarrying, brickmaking and lime burning.' Ellinor steps aside, allowing an approaching older couple to pass on the pavement. 'If we were able to travel back in time, we wouldn't recognise the area.'

Striding out to keep up with her friend, she suddenly stops as the enormity of what she's just said hits her.

That's exactly what I'm doing, isn't it?

Pippa turns back to her. 'What?'

Elinor shakes her head. 'Oh, nothing.'

'Come on then,' Pippa says. 'We still have time to grab a coffee before going back to the farm.'

Thirty-Eight

Despite Ellinor making daily visits to the building site, however hard she wishes to slip into that *other* world, it remains frustratingly elusive. The build is coming along well and the newly erected timber framework is now in situ, giving a skeletal impression of what the recreated cottage will look like once completed. In her mind's eye, she can already see the homely dwelling nestling secretively in the glade with a vegetable garden to one side and a rustic wooden bridge spanning the stream, granting access to the forest beyond for guests who care to take the path. But – and she can't help feeling sad – William is always present in her visions. How can that be? Maybe it's that his spirit will linger in this special place, and she will be aware of its presence.

At the sound of a car's engine, she turns, and as Jake brings the Range Rover to a stop she gives him a wave.

'Morning!' He climbs out and doffs an invisible cap to her.

She laughs. 'I see the cottage is coming along. Is all on schedule?'

He nods. 'We'll be digging trenches for the electrics next week. If all goes according to plan, and I don't see why it shouldn't, second fix will be complete by the end of the autumn. You and Simon can celebrate Christmas in your new home.'

'Oh, that would be wonderful, Jake,' she says, excitedly clapping her hands together. 'We'll throw an *open house* and you and Jess are invited.'

The big man smiles down at her with obvious affection. 'I'll let her know. She'll be right pleased.'

As they walk across the glade, Jake points to the newly dug foundations to the left of the two-storey timber frame.

'That's the glass walkway connecting to this new extension,' he says, arriving at an oblong area at right angles to it.

'It's larger than I thought it would be,' Ellinor comments, eyeing the concrete-filled trenches delineating the new living space.

'Interesting! Usually rooms appear smaller in layout, but I checked the dimensions before we started.' Jake's forehead creases and he rubs his chin.

'As long as the glazing measurements are spot-on, I have no objection to a larger space than I'd imagined!' Ellinor quickly assures him.

'It won't harm to re-check Graham's measurements.' Jake scrutinises the foundations.

Ellinor places a hand on his arm. 'I'm sure they're correct, Jake, but it may be best to check again.'

He nods. 'Come with me,' he says, motioning towards the main cottage. 'We found something interesting during the excavation.'

Giving him a quizzical look, Ellinor follows.

'When we extended the foundations we came across this in the spoil,' Jake explains, as he walks towards the folding table in the centre of the room. Selecting an item from a plastic box on the table, he turns to her and holds out his hand.

Ellinor approaches. A lump of mud is nestled in his palm, and she raises a curious eyebrow. Someone has rubbed away the soil, exposing a portion of dull, silver-coloured metal. Carefully, she takes the clump of earth from him, and as soon as she places her finger over the exposed object, a fizzing sensation shoots up her arms.

'Do you know what it is?' she asks.

Jake shakes his head. 'Not sure. Maybe a charm.'

'Where did you find it?'

'Over there.' He points to one of the concrete-filled trenches marking the foundations of the connecting glass walkway.

That's where William's outhouse is. Where he stores his equipment and hangs the game he's hunted.

'Have you found anything else?'

'Just a few rusty nails and bits of ironmongery, no doubt discarded by previous dwellers,' Jake replies. 'But other objects worthy of investigation may turn up.'

He's not going to suggest that she get an expert to check the piece, is he? That could delay the build for months, if it proved to be anything noteworthy. Her fingers close protectively around the mud-encrusted object.

'But we'll keep this to ourselves, if you know what I mean.' Jake taps his nose. 'We don't want anything holding up the build now, do we?' He gives her a wink.

Ellinor's eyes widen. 'I . . . I think I know what you mean, Jake.'

'Definitely not worth getting into a lather over.' He nods, as if confirming it to himself. 'Seems to me that this' – he waves his large hand around the glade – 'and all that's in it belongs to you now.'

A sudden thrill of excitement courses through her. She can't wait to get back to the farmhouse to investigate it further.

'Thank you, Jake,' she says, with a wide smile. 'Is there anything else you want to discuss with me?'

'Nah. We'll crack on with what we're best at.' He grins. 'But if there's anything grand inside that clump of sod, I expect to see you wearing it at the Christmas open house!' He turns away with a laugh.

Ellinor walks across the quiet clearing towards the track, her face flushed. He *does* suspect that whatever's hidden in the mud may be something of importance. As she starts walking towards the road, a movement on her left makes her glance at the hedge. Flying a metre above the hedge line is the raven.

'Have you been keeping an eye on me, Branok?'

The bird settles a few yards further on and gazes back at her inquisitively.

A sudden fluttering deep in her belly brings Ellinor to a halt; she's never experienced a sensation like it before.

Standing stock still, she waits for it to repeat, and when it doesn't she dismisses it as just *one of those things*.

'What was that?' she says out loud.

But if Branok knows the answer, he keeps it to himself.

'More exercise, that's what I need.'

Continuing on, she soon reaches the parish lane and as she turns onto it, she observes a lorry travelling slowly down the lane. It stops briefly at the entrance to Comfort Wood Farm and then turns into the drive.

'That must be the new cider equipment,' Ellinor informs the raven. She lets out a belly laugh. 'Goodness, Ellinor Forrester, you're turning into a right Doctor Dolittle!'

Whatever next?

Thirty-Nine

As Ellinor rounds the corner into the courtyard, the raven flies high into the pale blue sky and settles on the roof of the old cowshed. She's surprised to see Simon's Audi parked next to the lorry; she wasn't expecting him until later that evening. She's also relieved to feel a tremble of anticipation at the thought of seeing her husband again. Despite her obsession with that *other* world, the two weeks without Simon have stretched interminably and she's missed him. But when he and Ian emerge from the porch, she's immediately aware of his awkwardness as he catches sight of her. He looks tired – he's obviously been socialising hard and burning the candle at both ends. Once again, she wonders what's going on.

'I thought you weren't arriving until this evening,' she says, crossing the yard towards him.

'Ian messaged that the new equipment was arriving this morning, so I took the day off work.' Simon looks uncomfortable and unsure of what to do next.

'That's good,' she says, ignoring his stance and giving him a hug.

Standing back, his eyes narrow as he considers his wife. 'You look different, Elli.'

She makes a small face. 'What do you mean *different*?'

'I'm not sure,' he says. 'Definitely more relaxed . . .' He looks along the drive. 'Where have you come from?'

Ellinor balks, recalling William had asked something similar.

'I've been to the cottage for a catch-up with Jake. He found something when they were digging the trenches for the foundations. Look.' She produces the lump of mud from the depths of her pocket and holds it out to him, the dull silver-coloured metal clearly showing through where the soil has been rubbed away.

'That looks intriguing.'

'That's what I thought,' she says lightly. 'I'm going to prise away the mud and see what's hiding beneath.'

Unprepared for his sudden tender smile, Ellinor has the oddest notion that in that very moment they exist out of time. She glances around, but there's nothing altered to the courtyard scene. The Audi is still parked next to the lorry, and the delivery men are now carefully manoeuvring the new cider press onto the rear ramp while her cousin anxiously watches over proceedings.

'I said I'd give Ian a hand with setting up the equipment,' Simon explains. 'You don't mind, do you?'

'Of course not! Is there more than just that press to unload?'

Simon gives a small laugh. 'Everything on that lorry – vats, fermentation tanks, bottling equipment and other paraphernalia – all important for producing the future award-winning, Comfort Wood Orchards' cider. We may be sometime!'

'Well, you boys go and have fun.' She attempts an easy-going light-hearted tone, although oddly it feels as if she's just given him permission to slip further away.

With a puzzled frown, she watches him set off towards the lorry.

Suddenly Simon turns back. 'You know, Elli, I think Cornwall is good for you.'

'I think so, too,' she says quietly, glancing up at the old cowshed roof and observing the raven watching the unusual activity in the yard below.

Turning away, she walks towards the porch, pondering the uncharacteristic awkwardness between them. It seems as if they're trying too hard with each other. But as she enters the farmhouse a sweet aroma distracts her, and before going upstairs she makes a detour to the kitchen. Pippa stands at the counter with a wooden spoon in her hand, mixing ingredients in a bowl. Both dogs sit at her feet, their ears pricked as they inspect her every move.

'Something smells good,' Ellinor says from the doorway.

'Hope so. I've got a Victoria sponge and a coffee and walnut cake in the oven, and this is a fat-and-sugar-free chocolate log.'

'Wow!' Ellinor raises her eyebrows. 'Spoilt for choice.'

'If they survive the baking stage and aren't a total disaster, you can have whichever you like for tea. I thought if they're any good, we'd sell them at the next market.'

'We might have to sample them all,' Ellinor suggests hopefully. 'And it looks like Rufus and Rusty are tempted, too.'

Pippa laughs and glances down at the dogs. 'Sorry, boys. Not for you. But you can both have biscuits for being good and not pestering Mother while she weaves her magic.'

Eyebrows twitch, as two pairs of brown eyes gaze up at her in devotion.

'I'll let you get on,' Ellinor says, turning away.

As she crosses the dining room to the hallway she hears Pippa chatting to her dogs and smiles to herself. Another Doctor Dolittle! There must be something in the water . . .

Ellinor climbs the stairs and enters the bathroom. Extracting the lump of mud from her pocket, she places it carefully on the edge of the basin and considers how best to remove the object from its entrapment. The soil isn't hard-baked – more compacted – and she decides that probing with a pair of tweezers is probably the most effective way to loosen it. For several minutes she prods, pokes and teases, and at last the mud pie begins to loosen its hold. As more of the metal is revealed, an unfamiliar energy surges through Ellinor and a curious expectation mounts. Finally, the object is freed, and in the palm of her hand sits an exquisite silver Celtic love knot with a cabochon-cut semi-precious gemstone dangling precariously from a fragile link. The metal is dull and the amber cloudy, but it has survived.

A sudden giddiness overwhelms her and, perching on the edge of the bath, she waits for the sensation to pass. Strange notions and images come to her and suddenly she gasps, as absolute understanding consumes her. William gifted this necklace to her as a sign of his devotion. Of course, having lain hidden in the earth for goodness knows how long, the leather thong has long perished, but miraculously – against the odds – it has found its way back to her, and once more it is where it rightfully belongs.

She will *never* let it go again . . .

Ellinor wonders what a fifteenth-century silver and amber pendant is worth today. Of course, as a forester in the employ of Richard Edgcumbe, William isn't wealthy, and he can't possibly afford to give her anything expensive . . . can he?

No! It's unlikely to be worth much, only in sentimental value. But what if it is?

Ellinor holds back a sudden burst of hysteria. It's absurd, sitting here in Ian and Pippa's bathroom, knowing the artefact's provenance. It deserves to be presented to her at a richly spectacular and momentous ceremony, so huge is its discovery. But that will never be, unless she's prepared to hand it over to a museum and only ever view it from behind the ultraviolet-protected security glass of a display cabinet.

A sudden tapping at the window draws her away from her musings and she glances towards the obscure glass. A dark shape moves along the sill on the other side, and rising to her feet, she crosses over to the casement. As she opens it, the bird cocks its head and observes her with a beady eye.

'Well, Branok,' she says, 'you and I know the truth, don't we?'

Carefully holding the pendant between finger and thumb, she shows it to the raven.

'Prruk-prruk!'

'It will be our secret,' she whispers.

'Ellinor,' Pippa's voice carries along the landing, 'I'm making coffee for the boys. Do you want a cup?'

'Yes please. I'll be down in a minute,' she calls over her shoulder.

She glances back at the bird. Spreading its wings, it lifts into the air and flies off towards the trees bordering the fields at the back of the farmhouse.

Forty

'This is a good spot,' Ian says, surveying the lawn in front of the gatehouse tower.

'Perfect,' agrees Pippa, as she places the picnic basket on the grass.

Simon removes the picnic rug from under his arm and lays it out with a flourish. 'My lady,' he says to Ellinor, with a sparkle in his eyes.

Ellinor breathes out a silent sigh of relief. Since his arrival yesterday, they've circled each other with uncharacteristic wariness. At least, now, he's making an effort to enter into the spirit of the evening.

'You fool!' she responds. 'Just because you're dressed like that!'

'I don't know what you mean.' Simon pulls a mock-perplexed face. 'Dressed like what?'

'A right ponce, that's what,' Ian says with a grin.

'That makes the two of us, then,' Simon replies with a matching grin. He glances down at the hooded top falling barely to below his waist, the suede jerkin and arm cuffs, tight-fitting hose and boot covers.

'At least I'm regal,' Ian retorts, winking at Pippa. 'Thank you, dear wife, for finding me a costume that came with a crown.'

'I couldn't have you not matching my noble standing!' she replies with a laugh.

'I'll have you know,' Simon says, 'I find this outfit rather comfortable. In fact, I'm considering wearing it at all times.'

'Brian will never let you loose on potential clients if you do,' Ellinor remarks, taking containers of food from Pippa and setting them down on the rug.

'Well, that's not going to be an issue for much longer,' Simon comments.

Ellinor's head snaps up and she looks inquisitively at her husband.

'Ladies, we have something to celebrate this evening,' Ian announces, producing a bottle of bubbly from the picnic basket and deliberately prolonging the act of uncorking it.

'Go on. Don't keep us in suspense!' Pippa says, extracting champagne flutes and holding them out for him.

Ellinor holds her breath.

The cork pops loudly, and Ian fills the champagne glasses and hands them around.

'Tonight, you are looking at the new marketing director of Comfort Wood Orchards,' he says, nodding at Simon.

'Congratulations,' says Pippa, giving him a peck on the cheek.

So, he is continuing with their plans!

Realising it's a huge commitment and life-changing decision for her husband, Ellinor wonders if that's why he's been acting so strangely recently.

'That's wonderful!' she says, smiling broadly at him.

'It is,' Simon says, returning her smile. 'Thank you, Ian and Pippa, for offering the directorship to me, and here's to an increasingly healthy and prosperous business.'

'And a good harvest,' Pippa adds, raising her glass.

'To a good harvest,' they say in unison.

'Well done, Si,' Ellinor says quietly. 'It can't have been an easy decision.'

He pulls a face. 'Weighing up the pros and cons gave me a few headaches, but once I'd made up my mind, I knew it was the right thing to do.'

'Tuck in,' Pippa says, handing around plates. 'Don't hold back.'

Suddenly, a small flock of swallows flies overhead. Their long forked tail feathers stream out behind them as they swoop over the gathered crowd and amongst the ancient buildings, and their dark, glossy-blue backs, red throats and pale underparts show clearly as they agilely alter course.

'Oh, good,' Pippa comments. 'Our friends have returned from their winter sojourn in South Africa, but no doubt they're surprised to find Cotehele heaving with people this evening!'

Ellinor watches the birds a moment longer and then gazes around at the other picnickers waiting for the play to start. Most have embraced the request to come in fancy dress and the mood of the evening promises to be high-spirited. Suddenly a shadow falls across her and she looks up into the eyes of a middle-aged bearded man wearing doublet and hose, and sporting a cape, over-the-knee leather boots and holding a sword. With a smile, he welcomes the *fair ladies* to Cotehele and wishes them a pleasant evening, before engaging Ian and Simon in lively banter. After a while, he courteously takes his leave and wanders over to the next family of picnickers.

'Talk about swoon,' Pippa says with a smirk. 'You two men have your work cut out this evening if you expect to keep the attention of *these* fair ladies!' She helps herself to a smoked salmon sandwich.

Ellinor laughs.

A number of actors wander amongst the picnickers, chatting to the assembled audience, when suddenly a trumpet sounds. Immediately a hush descends, and a swash-buckling buccaneer appears at the entrance to the gatehouse tower.

'Welcome all!' His deep voice projects around the lawns. 'We hope you engage in the fun of this evening and enjoy our merry play. However, before we start, there are some rather *boooring . . .*' Stringing out the word, he gives an exaggerated yawn, which produces a laugh from the onlookers. '. . . but necessary health-and-safety requirements. Tonight we will take you on an interactive journey into the courtyard of Cotehele House and through some of the beautiful rooms. Should there be any need to urgently vacate the property for whatever reason – say, a fire or a sighting or two of the odd ghost . . .' He pauses.

On cue, the audience reacts. As ooh's and ah's fill the early evening air, the actor holds up his hands. Then, throwing his cape over one shoulder, he draws his sword from its scabbard.

'Fear not, ye good people of Cornwall, for my trusty sword and I will fight off any threat and defend the honour of those fair maidens amongst you.' Coughing noisily into his gloved fist, he adds, 'Maybe only the fairest amongst you!'

Laughter ripples amongst the gathered theatregoers, accompanied by a swell of dramatic booing.

'Joshing aside,' the actor continues, 'if there is any need to vacate the property, we are to meet on this lawn and a member of the National Trust team will mark off your name against an attendance list, so please don't just wander off. Now, without further ado, let the fun begin!'

Flourishing his cape, the man turns away and strides into the archway leading to the courtyard. A group of actors pour through in the opposite direction towards the audience, and the performance begins.

A while later – amidst a particularly loud burst of laughter from the spectators at the actors' antics – Pippa holds out a Tupperware container. 'Chicken drumstick, anyone?'

Ian and Simon help themselves, but Ellinor shakes her head. 'It looks like the play's moving into the courtyard,' she says. 'Come on, we'd better follow if we want to keep up with the story.'

Getting to her feet, she walks towards the entrance and is immediately surrounded by actors laughing and dancing in circles around her. She glances back at her party who are preparing to follow and attempts to extricate herself from the throng of people encircling her and wait for them, but all at once she's swept along on a wave of merriment into the inner yard. Despite this, she has enough wits about her to register that the house appears altered and the elegant two-storey building is now a simple hall house, with an adjacent chapel, wider than the one in present day. Turning her head, she peers through the mass of waving arms and swirling bodies. Gone are the charming courtyard stone elevations with the mullioned diamond-paned windows on two floors, and in their place are simple, rough walls rising to only one-storey high. She glances back at the gatehouse tower, but this, too, has vanished, along with the upper storeys that flank it. Anxiously, she looks around at the people carrying her along on a sea of high spirits, but she can't see Simon, Ian or Pippa anywhere, and she finds herself transported into the hall, which has also changed. Simpler and narrower, its magnificent arch-braced timber roof appears lower and less embellished. Weapons are still displayed on the stone walls, which she notices are in their natural state and not painted white, and rush matting covers the floor.

A young man, little older than a boy, suddenly approaches. He thrusts a tankard of ale into her hands, which Ellinor accepts without fuss, and as if in a stupor, she raises it to her lips and takes a large gulp. A feast is taking place and the hall is filled with noise and laughter. Lit only by candles, it's a much darker room than the one she visited with Simon, Ian and Pippa. At the lighter end of the hall is a long wooden table laid with pewter platters and tankards, while at the other end, a fire glows fiercely in the hearth of a large inglenook, around which several men and women sit or stand. All are dressed in fine velvet and satin with fur trimmings, and sporting elaborate headwear. Minstrels sing and play, and the evocative music floats above the sounds of good cheer. Amongst the instruments, Ellinor recognises a lute, a dulcimer, flute, pipe and tabor.

As she glances around the hall, her gaze comes to rest on a familiar figure standing on the far side. Leaning against the wall with one arm outstretched, William supports the weight of his body while talking to someone. But he, or she, is blocked from view, and taking a step to get a better look, immediately Ellinor wishes she hadn't. A pretty, young woman stands against the wall smiling up into William's face.

Instantly Ellinor is consumed with jealousy. Quickly, she reminds herself that, of course, he has an entirely different life; one she knows nothing about. But like a moth drawn to a flame, she can't help but look, and his body language suggests he is open to this woman.

Placing her tankard down on a convenient chest at the side of the room, Ellinor is about to turn away when William glances over in her direction and his eyes open wide. Without hesitation, he pushes himself off the wall, says a few words to the woman and strides across the room towards her. Hurriedly, Ellinor heads for the door leading out into the courtyard, but he reaches her before she's made her escape.

Catching her arm, he turns her towards him. 'Ellinor!' His eyes are troubled. 'You're here?'

'So it would appear,' she answers frostily.

Silently, she reprimands herself for being cold towards him. Their times together are so short-lived and unplanned. She should be warm and light-hearted, and grateful for the joy and respite that he brings.

'Are you well?' He asks, standing back to survey her.

'I am, thank you,' she replies stiffly.

'Again, your robe is most . . .' his mouth twitches in amusement, '*distracting*!'

She glances down at the fancy-dress costume. At least she's not wearing her usual jeans and sweatshirt. What would this lot make of her if she'd appeared dressed like that?

She looks up almost shyly. 'I didn't know when I'd see you again.'

His eyes soften. 'Nor I. Your sudden disappearance from the riverbank bemused me, but I remembered you warned that you had no control over it.'

He smiles down at her with such tenderness and compassion that all at once the party-goers and their exuberant voices fade into the background. It's as if she and William are the only people in the hall. As a definite flutter takes hold, deep in her belly, Ellinor gazes into his bright blue eyes. Suddenly there's a flash of light, and it seems to her that a thousand fireworks simultaneously explode.

William glances over her shoulder towards the door. 'Come,' he says, taking her hand. 'Let us escape this madness.'

She allows him to lead her out into the yard, into a throng of people. Some are dancing, while others perform acrobatics; and over in the far corner Ellinor is aware of a small crowd watching a play in full swing. She searches amongst the sea of faces for Simon, Ian and Pippa, but they're not with the onlookers, and as William's warm hand leads her towards a doorway in the side wall, she willingly follows.

Pushing open the wooden door, William pulls her inside a small room. At once, he wraps her in an intense embrace and Ellinor succumbs to glorious emotions as his lips meet hers. After a while, she draws back.

'I have missed you fearfully,' he murmurs huskily.

'As I have you, William,' she says softly.

And it's true. She can no longer deny it.

He kisses her again with a passion that takes her breath away. 'I have urgent need of you, Ellinor. There is no time to lose. The uprising is but a week away. God willing, we will be successful, but should we not . . .' His voice trails away.

Anxiety floors her, and a fear of his unknown fate propels her into a decision.

'Then let's away to your cottage,' she says, starting towards the door.

'I cannot leave,' he says, catching her hand. 'I am in attendance this evening. But these are my lodgings.'

'Your lodgings?' She looks around the sparsely furnished room, and recalls that he'd mentioned it in passing.

'My home is in the woods, but I have this room,' he continues. 'It's convenient and it means Richard can avail himself of my services, other than forestry, when required.'

The room is simple, little more than a cell, and apart from one arrow-slit window, the only light comes from a tallow candle in a small wall alcove. Caught by a sudden draught, the flame throws its flickering light across a bed, a simple desk and a wooden chest.

'No one will disturb us here.' Taking her hands, William raises them to his lips and slowly kisses each knuckle. 'Please stay a while.'

'I promise to stay as long as I can.'

He squeezes her fingers and then reluctantly lets her go. 'And that will never be long enough.'

She gazes at him, only now fully taking in his splendid attire – the broad, padded shoulders, the full-shirted tunic, cut so extremely short that it only just reaches a few inches below his waist, the colourful hose and his long pointed shoes, which make her want to giggle.

'You wouldn't look out of place where I've just come from,' she says, raising an eyebrow.

'And where would that be?' he asks, regarding her curiously.

'We are attending a medieval play at Cotehele.'

He frowns. 'Is that why you are attired so?'

She grins. 'Yes. I've gone as Maid Marion.'

'And are you with . . . Simon?' His voice falters as he speaks her husband's name.

'I am,' she replies softly. 'He's Robin Hood.'

His eyes darken and abruptly he turns away.

'Come here, William,' she says, holding out her hand. 'Let's not talk of such things. We have so little time.'

All at once they're in each other's arms again, powerless to control their shared rising passion.

Suddenly William steps away from her. Taking off his tunic, he throws it on the chest. Ellinor removes her diadem and wrist guards, and undoes her belt, laying all the items alongside his tunic.

William groans. 'If only your garments always lay next to mine.'

Raising herself onto tiptoes, she kisses him tenderly. 'Can you help me out of this dress?'

'It would be my pleasure, my love.'

She laughs softly. 'It's one of those modern zips, but I'm sure you can manage.'

She turns and holds her hair aloft, feeling William's breath teasing the nape of her neck as he slowly . . . deliciously . . . unzips her dress. Turning back to face him, she allows it to fall in a puddle at her feet.

The eyes that survey her body are full of hunger and she delights at the sound William makes in the back of his throat.

'Ellinor . . .' With one swift move, he picks her up and carries her to the bed.

Forty-One

'Now you can see why zips are so much more convenient!' Ellinor says, as she loosens the laces that attach his hose to his gipon.

William gives a throaty laugh. 'I think I would like to live in your time.'

She considers him thoughtfully. 'I think you may already.'

He raises an eyebrow. 'If that is so, I would like to remember.'

She sighs deeply. 'Oh, it's all too complicated to comprehend.'

As William impatiently kicks away his tangle of clothes, Ellinor watches with widening eyes. If it wasn't for the surroundings that testify to the earlier period, she'd believe it was the twenty-first century, so familiar is the man standing naked before her. Slowly she scans his body, savouring the muscular contours, and her stomach muscles contract sweetly at the sight of his obvious arousal.

'Come here, William. Take me.'

Again . . . that groan in the back of his throat.

'Love me . . . all of me,' she whispers.

Sometime later, with the sound of the celebrations taking place in the yard filtering into their sanctuary, they lie together, sated, in a tangle of limbs and fingers entwined. Despite not wanting to consider anything other than the present moment, Ellinor is unable to prevent the face of the young woman she'd seen him with from entering her thoughts.

'William,' she says, raising herself onto one elbow and

gazing at him. 'When I saw you earlier in the hall you were talking to a young woman.'

Opening his eyes, William meets her gaze.

'She is very pretty,' Ellinor continues.

He doesn't respond immediately. 'No one is as fair as you, my lovely Ellinor.'

A smile twists her lips.

'Lie with me a while longer,' he says, reaching for her.

She snuggles against his chest and attempts to quieten her tumultuous thoughts. But it's hopeless . . . She wants to know more.

'Who is she?'

'No one of any consequence,' William says, gently combing his fingers through her long, silky hair. 'A true lover does not desire to embrace in love anyone except his beloved.'

Lifting her head, she gazes at him again. 'That's comforting, but nevertheless I'd like to know.'

He considers her for a long heartbeat. 'She is John's sister and her name is Juliana. She is attendant to Richard's wife, Joan.'

'So does she live at Cotehele?' Ellinor asks slowly, processing the information.

'She does. But let's not talk of her.' Gently, William rolls Ellinor onto her back. Nuzzling her neck, he drops a tender kiss on her scar. 'This is no longer so angry.'

He runs a finger lightly along its length and Ellinor shivers – not from the memories the scar still demands, but from his touch.

'I thought that the other day,' she says, casting her mind back to earlier in the week, when she'd examined it in the mirror.

'You and I, we're battle-worn,' he says, looking deep into her eyes. 'Both resilient and focused beyond adversity.'

She smiles warmly. 'I like that.'

He kisses her again, long and hard, and soon their passion reignites. But before the world has had a chance to recede, three loud knocks on the door force their attention back to the present.

'William, are you within?' a boy's voice enquires.

William groans. Taking his weight on his elbows, he calls out, 'Yes. What is it?'

'The master asks for you in the hall.'

William sighs. 'I'll be there shortly.' As the boy scuttles away, he gazes down at Ellinor. 'It is not to be, you and I.'

'Don't say that,' she says swiftly, as despondency threatens to claim her. 'The time we have together is so very sweet.'

He nods. 'But it leaves me a starving man! I hunger for more.'

She kisses him softly. 'So do I, William.'

Briefly he closes his eyes. 'Argh . . . I am bewitched!'

In one swift movement, he gets off the bed and starts the laborious process of putting on his clothes, only pausing to help Ellinor with the zip of her dress.

The candle has burnt low and all is in shadow. Glancing around, Ellinor realises that of course there's no mirror, and placing the diadem on her head, she hopes her appearance is not too dishevelled.

At last, William is presentable, but before leaving their refuge and venturing forth into the wider world, he draws Ellinor to him once again and kisses her softly.

'You are all things to me, Ellinor.' He rests his forehead lightly against hers. 'I desired you from the moment I first set eyes on you.'

She smiles up into his tender gaze. 'You have me, William. Heart and soul.'

He kisses her again. 'Please stay.'

She knows there's no way she can promise him that. 'I am here now. Let's be content for the time we can have together.'

Sadness clouds his eyes and she hates herself for being the cause of it. But suddenly his mood shifts – focused once more.

'Come. I must attend my lord.' Opening the door, he checks the surroundings before stepping outside.

The feast is in full swing when they enter the hall, and it's even noisier and more boisterous than before. Ellinor scans the room and observes Richard Edgcumbe sitting at the long table with a woman beside him, who she presumes must be his wife, Joan. Sitting next to her is a young girl, aged about six, and seated beside her in line are the three older girls and the boy whom she'd seen in the terraced gardens on the day she'd discovered the tunnel leading from the medieval stew pond and dovecote. Other men and women are seated around the table, and servants deliver a seemingly never-ending array of platters. Ellinor watches as the food is brought out from the kitchen – herons, pheasants, swans, a whole roast boar and pies that appear to be filled with layers of pigeon, rabbit and pork, and taking pride of place in the centre of the table are two peacocks, their lovely plumages reattached.

'Apologies, but I must attend Richard,' William says.

'Of course! Duty calls,' she says light-heartedly, though her heart is heavy. Reassuringly, she squeezes his arm. 'Go!'

Hesitating briefly, he bends his head and she feels his lips against her ear. 'Ellinor, if you stay, I promise to be loyal and honest to you all my days.'

Before she can respond, he turns away.

Ellinor's heart pounds as she watches him stride across the hall through the throng of party-goers towards the high table. If only she could stay . . . But Simon, Ian and Pippa trickle into her thoughts and she turns towards the entrance door. If she steps through it, will she be transported back to her own time? Torn, she turns towards the table again and observes William talking to Richard, who suddenly looks across the hall in her direction, and acknowledges her with a nod. She returns his acknowledgement and wonders what's being said, but the next minute the thought is forgotten as she's rudely knocked sideways.

'Forgive me,' says a woman. 'I did not see you there.'

'No damage done,' Ellinor responds automatically. But when she sees who has bowled into her, it occurs to her that it may not have been by accident.

Close up, the young woman is even prettier than at a distance. Petite, with curly brown hair and hazel eyes, a button nose and rosebud lips – the complete opposite to Ellinor's taller stature and more pronounced features, her long blonde hair and blue eyes.

'It's Juliana, isn't it?' Ellinor queries.

The young woman's gaze turns wary. 'Do I know you?'

'No,' she replies, swallowing hard. 'Just promise me that you will be good to him.'

'Who?' Juliana says in an innocent voice.

But the fierce blush spreading across the young woman's cheeks gives her away, and Ellinor knows that her adversary for William's affections knows only too well to whom she refers. She glances over at the table again. Head bowed, William stands at Richard's shoulder, listening intently to the words of his lord. Oh, how she longs to stay . . . but already she can feel the pull of her time whispering in her ear.

'He's an honourable and brave man,' she says to Juliana with a sorrowful smile. 'He will make you very happy.'

She glances back at the table one last time. As if sensing her eyes upon him, William looks up and she sends him a loving smile, before quickly turning towards the door and stepping outside.

The throng of revellers are still there and it appears that nothing has changed, although she notices that fire-eaters and jugglers have joined the other entertainers and now move amongst the crowd. But as Ellinor walks further into the courtyard, the night air ripples like water disturbed by the toss of a pebble. Through the darkness, the vague outline of the gatehouse tower and its adjacent buildings appear – faint at first, but quickly gaining structure and solidity.

'So what's happening here?' Simon asks, emerging from the gloom.

She takes a moment to drink him in before stepping forward and kissing him firmly on the mouth.

'Ellinor!' he exclaims. 'What's brought this on?'

'Just you . . .' she says, linking her arm through his, 'being here with me.'

'Where else would I be?'

She smiles, thinking of William attending his lord, and recalls the voice in her head that had assured her everything was connected and all would be well.

'I love you, Simon Forrester.'

'And I love you,' he softly confirms.

'Come on,' she says. 'Let's see what those actors are getting up to.'

Forty-Two

Early the next morning, Ellinor comes to. Feeling rested and at peace with the world after an undisturbed night's sleep, she stretches languorously. The previous evening had been fun and she's so relieved that things appear to have eased between her and Simon. It's as if whatever awkwardness that had threatened their relationship was unable to crescendo and simply dispersed. She turns and gazes at her husband's strong, handsome face. It never fails to amaze her how soundly he sleeps, regardless of what's going on in his life. And even though she's spent the past seven years with him, the attraction is still strong. She feels a frisson of excitement. Maybe now is the time to rise above her need to control everything, brought on by her trauma, and let him in. Moving closer, she places her hands on his body and starts to gently massage.

Simon's eyes open. 'Elli?'

'This is your early morning wake-up call,' she purrs.

She slides her hands down over his stomach and his gaze turns to one of disbelief.

'Elli?' he repeats.

'Shhh . . .' she says, quietly.

Lying back, Simon watches her closely as he allows her free rein of his body, and his breathing soon turns ragged. Feeling his immediate response to her touch, Ellinor breathes out a sigh of relief and acknowledges her own mounting needs.

All will be well . . .

With a groan in the back of his throat, Simon holds her hands still. 'Elli, are you sure?'

'Perfectly sure,' she says with a smile.

Raising herself up, Ellinor straddles her husband, savouring every moment as she slowly lowers herself onto him.

Later, with the sky an impossible blue and the sun beating down on their backs, husband and wife walk along the track to the cottage. Before long, they've peeled off their sweatshirts and Simon drapes his casually around his shoulders. Ellinor ties hers around her waist.

Suddenly she stops. 'Listen to that.'

He halts, and his face breaks into a smile at the sound of birdsong in the air. 'Can't wait to live here full-time.'

'Any idea when that's likely?'

He turns to her. 'I want to see how the cider business shapes up first before making any rash decisions, but I don't expect to be in London this time next year.'

'Jake thinks we can be in the cottage by Christmas,' she says.

'Christmas in Cornwall! Now that's something to look forward to. All those log fires and windswept walks along empty beaches.'

'We'll have to get a dog,' Ellinor enthuses.

They continue on and soon reach the glade. Despite the work taking place in the clearing, wildflowers still show their heads in the long grass. No workmen are present, it being Sunday, and they walk leisurely around the site, checking the overall layout.

'When I first saw the foundations for the new living area, the room appeared larger than I'd anticipated,' Ellinor says, pacing the boundary of the newly erected structure. 'I thought Jake had made a mistake, but he re-checked the architect's measurements and he'd interpreted them correctly. With these uprights in place, it looks just right.'

'I agree.' Simon says. 'Not so large that it overshadows the footprint of the original cottage, and the two-storey windows will bring the outside in. It will be like living deep in the woods.'

'Or *at the edge* . . .' Ellinor says under her breath.

The sudden harsh, metallic call of a pheasant and the sound of flapping wings make them turn as a cock pheasant lands in the clearing. Caught in the sunlight, its feathers are a magnificent sheen of vibrant colours.

'This place has been a haven for wild animals and birds for so many years,' she says. 'I'd like to keep it that way. I'd hate it if they felt it wasn't their home once we move in.'

Simon glances at her affectionately.

'What?' she asks.

'Honestly, Elli. You are *so* different now that I wonder what you've done with my wife!'

'Oh, she's still here, but she's evolving into someone she was always meant to be.'

'Lucky me! Two for the price of one,' he says with a wink.

Ellinor laughs. 'What a bargain . . .'

Entering the skeletal timber-framed building, Simon crosses over to her. 'I'd pay double for you any day.' He puts his arm around her shoulders, still cautiously. 'You do know that, don't you?'

She hugs him closely.

'And, Elli,' – he turns to face her – 'thank you for this morning. I know what a milestone that must have been.'

She looks up into his bright blue eyes, filled with compassion.

'I can't deny it. The longer we didn't make love, the more of a hurdle it became in my mind. I'm just so grateful that you allowed me the time and space, and stuck around long enough.'

'Why wouldn't I have stuck around?' he asks in a bemused voice.

'Oh, you know.' She shakes her head. 'You've been so patient, waiting for me to *return*. I thought you might have grown impatient and started looking elsewhere.'

His hold tightens. 'Of course I wouldn't go elsewhere, Elli. When we made our marriage vows it was for better or worse. I prayed . . . no . . . I *knew* it was only a matter of time before you found your way back.'

'Then, thank you for having faith in me,' she says quietly.

Bending his head, Simon drops a gentle kiss on her lips. 'I've always had faith in you, Elli. From the moment we first met I recognised how resilient you were and that whatever life threw at you, you would always find the strength to push forward and never quit.'

'Goodness!' Her cheeks turn pink. 'I hardly recognise myself from that description. *Didn't* I stray far?'

'It's hardly surprising after what you've endured.'

'That man robbed me of so much,' Ellinor says, briefly allowing herself to think back to *the incident*. 'He made me feel powerless and I was so angry with him for doing that. I've felt broken and such a failure ever since.'

Simon holds her gaze. 'Not once did I ever doubt that my battle-worn warrior would pull through.'

'Battle-worn?' Eleanor's senses snap to attention and she looks searchingly into his eyes.

'Yes, battle-worn. Understanding that failure is not a bad thing, but instead a necessary step in shaping and building us to become stronger.'

'I know what it means,' she says. 'I'm just surprised that you used that word. I've not heard it in your vocabulary before.'

'You should sit in on one of my marketing meetings,' he says with a grin. 'You'd be amazed at what I come up with. Sometimes I even surprise myself!'

She smiles uncertainly. Is this really Simon standing before her?

'Come on, Mrs Forrester, let's see what Jake and his trusty assistant have accomplished in the old cottage. Then I'd like to walk to the quay and check out the sailing barge Ian told us about, and if the tearoom's open I think we should celebrate our reunion with coffee and cake.'

As it turns out, little has changed in the adjacent cottage

since Ellinor's previous visit, but telltale marks show that a start has been made to remove the granite lintel from the fireplace.

'I've asked Jake to install it over the main door, or possibly in the porch . . . wherever it fits best.'

Approaching the stone, Simon runs his fingers over its surface, tracing each witch mark. Ellinor smiles. It's what she does, every time she visits, and it's good that he's drawn to it, too; only, her fingers always linger over the inverted triangle. She's not sure why.

'I suppose when the old cottage was built it was common practice for people to protect their property with witch marks,' Simon says, as his fingertips follow the indentations of the daisy wheel in the centre of the stone.

'Do you know what they mean?' Ellinor asks.

He shakes his head. 'I know that people considered them to be protection from evil spirits, witches or their animal familiars.' He straightens up and smiles at her. 'We should find out.'

'I would like to know what protection is in place for our cottage,' she agrees.

Simon checks his watch. 'Well, it seems that Jake has everything under control.' He holds out his hand to his wife. 'Let us stroll hand-in-hand through the woods as lovers do.'

She chuckles.

His eyes soften. 'It's good to hear that sound again.'

'It feels pretty good, too,' she says, slipping her hand into his.

Exiting the cottage, they head off through the woods and follow the track leading down to the main path, and it's not long before they reach the fork where the upper route leads to Cotehele House via the Valley Garden. But, ignoring it, they take the path bordering the river, which, today, reflects the colour of the sky and offers tantalising glimpses of blue through the trees. A rhythmic voice calling out gains their attention and they watch as a pale green gig glides silently downstream on the mirror-like surface of the water, its six oarsmen rowing in harmony. On the path ahead, a middle-aged man rounds the corner with an elderly black Labrador, sporting a red collar, following a few paces behind. As the man approaches, Ellinor greets him.

'Good morning,' he responds. 'It's not much further to the chapel.'

'The chapel?'

'I assumed that's where you were heading,' the man says. 'My mistake. Never assume!'

'Isn't it rather out of the way for a chapel?' Simon comments.

'Ah, there's a rather wonderful story attached to it,' the man says cryptically, and with a knowing smile. 'But I won't spoil it. I'll let you discover that for yourselves.'

Calling to his dog, he continues up the path.

'Did you know about a chapel?' Simon asks, as they walk on.

Ellinor shakes her head. 'Missed that detail! It's odd, though. Cotehele has a chapel, so why would there be the need for another?'

'I suppose,' Simon considers, 'through the centuries there were several dwellings scattered along the river that weren't part of the estate. But I'd have thought places of worship in Calstock would have catered for those homesteads.'

As they follow the path high above the river, dappled light filters through the leafy canopy above them, casting its softness on the carpet of bluebells that now cloak the forest floor. Presently, a small stone building with a simple iron Celtic cross on its roof comes into view.

'That must be the chapel,' Ellinor remarks. 'It looks charming.'

'I see your friend waits for you,' Simon says.

For one disorientating moment Ellinor thinks he's referring to William, but then she gazes up, and there, on the roof of the building, is the familiar black silhouette of the raven. A smile spreads across her face. He's never far away.

'Hello, Branok,' she whispers to the bird, as they near the chapel.

Hopping along the ridge tiles, the raven watches their approach.

The chapel is positioned to one side of the path on a plateau above the river, and its windows look both ways along the waterway. With a sudden thrill, Ellinor recognises its location: the serenely quiet and peaceful site on the bend of the river, where William trapped the salmon they had for their impromptu riverbank supper. He feels so close, it's as if she could reach out and touch him. She glances at her husband, who is studying a plaque at the side of the ancient building, and wonders . . .

'This is interesting,' Simon comments. 'It says here, *The chapel, dedicated to Saints George and Thomas A Becket, was built by Sir Richard Edgcumbe as a thank offering for his preservation from his enemies, from whom he escaped on this spot in the year 1483.*'

A tease tiptoes up Ellinor's spine.

'Fourteen eighty-three! Buckingham's Rebellion,' she announces excitedly. 'It must have something to do with that.'

So, the failed attempt had resulted in Richard's persecution, too, not just Harry Stafford's. What, then, had befallen William? Heat rises in her face and her heart starts to pound. It's so frustrating not knowing what happened to him, but as forester and archer in the employ of the Edgcumbes, any mention of him seems to have evaporated into thin air.

Forty-Three

Over the course of the following week, Ian and Pippa spend time assessing the various barns on the farm, working out which one is the best size and location for the new farm shop, and designing its layout. Ellinor busies herself with daily inspections of the building site, giving her cousin and his wife the space and privacy to discuss their visions of bringing the business to life. Although impatient for the cottage to be finished and ready to move into, she doesn't want Jake and Pete thinking she's checking up on their work, so mainly visits when she knows they won't be there.

One morning, just before daybreak, she lets herself out of the farmhouse so quietly that even the spaniels asleep in their beds are undisturbed. As she makes her way across the courtyard and along the drive towards the lane, a grey pre-dawn light fills the air. Away to the east, she notices a shimmer of pale cream lighting the horizon; it won't be long before the sunrise reaches this corner of Cornwall. As Ellinor turns onto the parish lane, the raven joins her, flitting from one hedgerow to the next. Her ever-faithful, shape-shifting friend!

A hundred yards further on, she heads down the track leading to the site. The early morning dawn chorus is all around her, and from somewhere deep in the forest she hears the muffled sound of a woodpecker.

Perhaps it's not a woodpecker. Maybe it's William chopping wood.

The thought makes her stomach tighten, and again she's aware of a flutter deep in her belly, although this time it's more intense. With increasing excitement she picks up her pace. Soon, she turns onto the newly formed driveway leading to the clearing and the raven flies high into the air, away over the treetops. As she reaches the edge of the forest, Ellinor stops and listens. All is silent and disappointment swamps her, but suddenly she senses a tremble of air through the trees, and a flash of grey morphs into the Irish wolfhound loping towards her.

'Branok,' she calls softly, as the dog comes to a halt in front of her.

And then she hears the sound again, resounding around the clearing in evenly spaced intervals. She frowns.

What is that noise? It's not the drumming of a woodpecker. It's heavier and deeper.

Smoke rises from the chimney of the simple thatched cottage, and Ellinor notices the leaves are turning golden and russet. She glances up at the sky. Heavy cloud cover – and there's a sharpness in the air. Rubbing her arms and sternly dispelling any dark notions, she emerges through the trees, feeling the crunch of fallen leaves beneath her feet. As she steps onto the grass and sets off across the glade, she's aware that Branok falls into step beside her.

Reaching the far corner of the building, Ellinor peers round. At the far side of the clearing stand three tripods made from long branches bound together with hemp, and with large rounds fashioned from straw and other natural materials securely tied to each. A movement to her left makes her turn. William draws back an arrow, the muscles of his right arm taking the strain and displaying high strength. Perfectly toned and balanced, his concentration is intense. Although his body is turned towards her, his eyes face forward, focused on the target. Suddenly he releases the arrow and it flies through the air with a whoosh, quickly followed by a deep thud as it finds the centre of the round of straw. Without taking his eyes from the adjacent tripod, William reaches into his leather quiver, extracts another arrow and positions it on the bow. Drawing back his arm, he releases it. Again, the arrow slices through the air and its tip buries deep in the target. Ellinor watches in awe as William reaches for yet another arrow, and then another; she counts twenty, drawn in quick succession, in less than a minute. When his quiver is empty, William looks over in her direction.

'Ellinor! How long have you been there?'

'Not long.'

Glancing briefly at the arrow-filled targets, he walks towards her. 'That's enough for now.'

Sudden, acute anxiety besieges her and she smiles weakly. 'Are you preparing, William?'

'It's required of archers to practise every Sunday, but it's wise to put in the extra work. My lord's army leaves for Exeter in a few days.'

Ellinor's face falls and her anxiety turns to fear.

He draws her to him and kisses her softly. 'Worry not, my love. All will be well.'

'But it won't, will it, William? And look!' She points up to the sky. 'The weather turns.'

He frowns. Without saying a word, he takes her hand and leads her to the entrance of the cottage. As soon as they enter, Branok lies down across the threshold. William hangs the longbow and empty quiver on a peg on the wall, and removing his leather finger tab and bracer, he throws them onto the top of the wooden chest before approaching her. Urgently, he draws her to him. His kisses are deep and filled with passion, and she can't resist. His body is battle-ready, and she knows the hardness of him.

'William,' she says breathlessly. 'You must persuade Richard to abandon the uprising. You just have to . . .' But again she realises she cannot change the course of history, and her voice trails away.

'I have done all that I can,' he says, with a sad smile.

From out of the corner of her eye she notices Branok get to his feet, his hackles raised. Softly he growls. She peers through the open doorway as William walks to the door.

Stepping outside, he glances around, but after a few minutes he places a reassuring hand on the hound's neck.

'It is nothing, Branok, though it's good to be vigilant.'

'What was it?' Ellinor asks.

'I thought it may be wolves or wild boar, but it was only the wind in the trees.'

Wolves! Wild boar!

She, too, must be vigilant when she finds herself in this alternative world. Ellinor gazes anxiously out of the open door, but as Branok settles once more, she turns back to William.

Crossing over to the sack cloth and drawing it aside, he rummages in a small wooden box before walking over to her. In his hand is an object that makes her draw in a sharp breath. Dangling between his fingers, in pristine condition, is a length of dark green plaited leather on which hangs the silver Celtic love knot and amber gemstone pendant.

'I had this made for you,' he says, 'as proof of my devotion.'

Ellinor gazes up at him and it's all she can do to whisper, 'Thank you.'

She holds up her hair as William fastens the pendant around her neck.

'I offer you true, steadfast and virtuous love, which will never wane,' he says in a low voice. 'And I pledge to defend your honour and be loyal to you to the end of my days. You have my heart, beautiful Ellinor. This I wish you to know.'

A sharp pain stabs at Ellinor's own heart and she blinks back tears.

'Don't cry, my love.' Gently, William cups her face and lovingly strokes her cheek.

She can hardly breathe. This man, so strong and yet tender in equal measure, is the embodiment of Simon. Is it coincidence, or are she and William destined to continually find each other?

'William, I am humbled by your words,' she says, gently fingering the pendant. 'This is beautiful and I shall cherish it always.'

He smiles down at her. 'Now, let us eat.'

* * *

Much later, oblivious to the lumpy, straw mattress, they lie together in contentment. Their lovemaking has been urgent and full of passion, yet tinged with a longing that Ellinor instinctively knows will never be satisfied . . . not in this lifetime.

'William,' she says softly, as she teases her fingers through the hairs on his chest.

'Yes, my love?'

She bites her lip. Is it wise to tell him, or should she let history unfold?

When she doesn't answer, he opens his eyes and glances at her. 'What troubles you?'

She *has* to tell him. She takes a deep breath. 'I found out more about what happens to Richard Edgcumbe after the unsuccessful rebellion.'

William's brow furrows.

'He returns to Cotehele,' she continues quickly, 'pursued by Richard III's agent, Henry Trenowth of Bodrugan, who places him under house arrest.'

William's frown deepens.

'But Richard escapes by killing a sentry, and he finds a boat that takes him to Brittany and Henry Tudor.'

'That's hopeful,' William says. 'Sir Henry de Bodrugan is a powerful man. He has a fierce reputation and is notoriously brutal.'

Ellinor shivers. 'In two years' time, when Henry Tudor is crowned King, Richard is knighted and ordered to arrest Bodrugan. Historical accounts record that Sir Henry is chased to the edge of the cliffs near his home, where he leaps off and manages to get to a ship sailing to Ireland. Many of his lands and houses are forfeited and, subsequently, some are given to Sir Richard, who is elevated to the Privy Council and becomes a trusted member of the new King's court.'

William turns to her with a troubled expression. 'Your

foresight puts you in grave danger, Ellinor. Do not repeat what you have told me to anyone, not even Philippa or Ian.'

She shakes her head. 'I only share my knowledge with you, William, in the hope that it may help you in some way.'

He regards her for a long moment and then kisses her lightly on the tip of her nose. Suddenly rising from the bed, he pulls on his loose-fitting trousers.

'Are you getting up?' she asks in surprise.

'Yes. This is the first sleep.'

She frowns. 'What's that?'

'The *first* sleep,' he repeats, as if she should know. 'Don't you do this in your time?'

'No. We sleep through until morning.'

'There is much to learn of the twenty-first century.' He shrugs on his shirt and proceeds to lace up the front. 'This period is called the Watch, and is followed by the second sleep.'

Walking over to the fire, he prods the embers with a poker and throws on a couple of logs.

Ellinor extends out an arm from under the blanket and instantly recoils. As the cold air bites and goosebumps prick her bare skin, she reaches for her jeans and sweatshirt and hurriedly puts them on.

Crossing to the wooden counter, William pours ale into a cauldron and hangs it on an iron hook over the fire.

'Something to warm you,' he says, glancing at her.

'It's a bit on the cold side!' she says with a grimace.

He laughs, and her heart squeezes at the sound.

'Come here,' he says.

As she walks towards him, he picks up a sharp-edged stone and starts to score the right-hand side of the granite lintel. It's only then that Ellinor notices the difference between this rubbing stone and the one in her cottage – one of the witch marks is missing. As William works away at the granite, a horizontal line slowly appears. With a sudden rush of recognition, she realises he's making the inverted triangle – the mark she's compelled to touch each time she's anywhere near the granite stone.

'What are you inscribing?' she asks.

'The symbol for Earth,' he says. 'It draws attention to nourishment, endurance, the body and nature.'

She watches in fascination. He stops briefly to pour warmed ale into two tankards and passes one to Ellinor, but as the end of the Watch draws near, an inverted triangle is plain to see.

'Now you,' William says, holding out the sharp-edged stone to Ellinor. 'Inscribe a horizontal line towards the lower end of the symbol.'

Now she understands why she's instinctively drawn to the carving – she had a hand in its creation! As she concentrates on scoring the line, William moves behind her and wraps his arms around her. Tenderly, he places his hands over her stomach and she leans back into his embrace, aware of a deep fluttering sensation beneath the warmth of his palms.

'We draw this symbol as a prayer to the divine feminine,' he says softly, 'and pray for the gift of motherhood, fertility, growth and life.'

Suddenly Ellinor lets out a gasp, as all becomes crystal clear.

Forty-Four

As she turns in William's arms, the room beyond distorts into a realm of swirling greyness and her heart plummets. She knows only too well what that means.

'No!' Ellinor moans. 'Not yet, please.'

She tries to hold on to William, but even as her hands grab at his shirt sleeves he loses clarity and definition, and as if trying to grasp something as insubstantial as sand running through her fingers, she finds herself clutching at thin air. Wildly, she stares around at the cottage's timber framework, now enclosed by weatherboarding, and in despair she turns back to the chimney. The hearth is bare and clean, and shows no signs of a recent fire having been lit. As her rational brain kicks in, Ellinor notices the fireplace has been extended and that a substantial oak beam now spans the widened opening, replacing the former granite lintel that had graced it for centuries.

'William,' she says with a heartfelt sob, 'I wasn't ready to leave.'

A sudden noise puts her on high alert.

'Ellinor? Is everything OK?' Jake's voice comes from someway behind her.

Composing herself, she plasters a smile on her face and turns. 'Yes, all fine. I see you've found a replacement for the granite lintel.'

Leaving the entrance, he crosses the room towards her. 'I found it in one of the sheds on Father's farm and cleaned it up. I think it looks good here.'

Ellinor agrees. Sensing that he still eyes her with uncertainty, she quickly moves the subject on to the newly installed weatherboarding.

'Doesn't take long, once the framework's up,' Jake says. 'I've got a couple of roofers arriving later in the week and the solar panels can be installed. We'll soon have the building watertight and then we can start on the internals.'

She nods. 'That's good.'

He frowns. 'Are you sure you're OK?'

'Yes, I'm sure.' To divert his attention she glances at her watch. 'Gosh, is that the time? I must be on my way.'

She doesn't want Jake to scrutinise her too closely. Her heart is breaking and she's not sure how much longer she'll be able to keep her emotions in check.

Ellinor exits the building and steps out into early morning sunlight. She never gets used to the fact that when she time travels she can be away for hours and lead a completely different life, and yet she always returns to the exact moment she was transported from, as if time is suspended. Her hand flies to her chest, but the Celtic love knot necklace isn't there. At least she has it in safe keeping at the farmhouse. It may be battered and worn down by time, but it's in her possession once again. She glances back at the timber-framed cottage. Even with the newly installed weatherboarding it still looks skeletal, as if it's a temporary building quickly erected for the purposes of a film set. No doubt, once the roof is on it will appear more substantial. But, oh how she yearns to see that other, older thatched cottage with William at the door and Branok lying across the threshold. She sighs. Yet another reminder that although the past feels forever near, however dear it is to her, all she can do is hold the memories close to her heart.

Ellinor is still standing at the edge of the forest when Jake appears in the doorway. Seeing her there, he strides across the grass towards her.

'Glad you haven't gone yet.' He beams at her. 'I've just remembered I've got something in the car for you.'

A small frown puckers her forehead as she accompanies him to the Range Rover. Opening the passenger door, Jake extracts a battered leather-bound book from the glove compartment.

'After you questioned me the other day about my ancestors, I spoke to the family and Great Aunt Maud handed me this. It was her late husband, Ted, who carried out the research, and even though I say it myself he did a fantastic job. He wasn't a historian, but he was a damn fine amateur and he's made loads of notes. Fascinating reading . . . for me, at least. Not sure how interesting it will be for you, mind! But you never know, it may throw some light on what you've been searching for.'

Ellinor's heart pounds. 'That's so kind of you to do this for me,' she says, taking the well-thumbed notebook from him. 'I promise to take great care of it.'

'I have no doubt of that.'

'And I'll let you have it back as soon as I've read it.'

'Sure,' the big man says. 'If there's anything you want to know about any of the entries let me know. It goes way back to Saxon times. As I said, Great Uncle Ted did a sterling job.'

Turning away, Ellinor hugs the book close to her chest, and it's all she can do not to break into a run. As she hurries back to the farm, she can hardly contain herself. Her heart races at an alarming rate and she can feel the blood fizzing through her veins.

Maybe . . . just maybe . . . today I will have some answers.

Ellinor turns up the drive leading to Comfort Wood Farm. As she enters the courtyard, a couple of swallows swoop low over her head and disappear through the open door of the old cowshed, where Pippa suddenly appears.

'Hi, Elli. You're up early!'

'I went to the cottage for a catch-up with Jake.' Ellinor colours at the memory of what had really taken place. But she *had* caught up with Jake, so it's only a teeny white lie.

'All OK down there?' Pippa asks.

'Great. The roofers are in later this week,' Ellinor replies. 'How are your plans for the farm shop shaping up?'

'Oh, you know me. Brimming with ideas and ideally wanting it done yesterday. However, dear husband – voice of reason – has pointed out a few logistical problems in using this old barn, so we're rethinking the location. We may get Jake to build a log cabin affair in Penrose Orchard and use that . . . Once he's finished building your place, of course.'

'That sounds a good idea,' Ellinor says supportively. 'I thought I'd visit the orchard and read this.' She holds up the notebook. 'Jake's lent it to me. Apparently, his great uncle researched the family tree and his findings are in here.'

Pippa smiles. 'That's great. It's a beautiful day to sit amongst the apple trees and blossoms. I'll rock by at lunchtime with a picnic if you're still there and share a glass of wine or two with you.'

'Perfect!' Ellinor gives Pippa a wave as she sets off across the yard towards the orchards.

'See you later,' Pippa calls out, turning back inside the barn.

Ellinor opens the wooden five-bar gate and walks up the grassy track, pausing to look across the traditional orchard. The mid-morning sun is warm and the chickens scratch for grubs beneath the boughs of the shady trees. As she gazes out over the valley towards the river that snakes unhurriedly through the picturesque landscape towards Plymouth in the far distance, she spots a barn owl flying silently and low over the peacefully grazing sheep in the adjacent field, a vole gripped in its claws. Perhaps it has young to feed, and she wonders if it's the one that lives in the hayloft next to the farmhouse.

The air is clear and the panoramic vista is in sharp detail. The sea beyond the city shimmers a deep blue, and on the opposite side of the valley, the tors of Dartmoor rise majestically skywards. How different would the landscape have been in the fifteenth century when Richard Edgcumbe escaped house arrest and fled to France in a boat? Ellinor considers the type of vessel it might have been, and for a moment – a trick of the light – she envisages a three-masted sailing ship making its way down the central channel, its rigging glinting silver in the sun. But with a blink of the eye, the vision evaporates, and she knows that in reality it was probably a small boat that had taken him downstream.

Turning to her left, she gazes towards the location of the cottage and is surprised to see how obvious it is from this viewpoint. She remembers Ian explaining that the old, dilapidated chimney was only visible from the orchard because a tree had recently come down. However, with the addition of a second floor and the subsequent new height of the roof, the property now shows up quite clearly above the treeline. When she and Simon finally move in, they will enjoy a pleasant view from the bedrooms across Ian and Pippa's orchards and wild meadows, but how fortuitous that no houses will look in on them!

Ellinor walks to a tree whose boughs are weighed down with blossom, and sits amongst the wildflowers at its base and leans against its trunk. It feels good to have the bark at her back. It brings about a sense of being in the *here and now*, not slipping back to the time where she cannot stay.

Sighing deeply, she opens the notebook and very soon she has no time to wistfully daydream, as Great Uncle Ted's revelations ignite her interest. Not only has Jake's ancestor listed a relatively comprehensive family tree reaching back centuries, but he has also noted brief information about each of the family members he's managed to discover. Ellinor's eyebrows lift as she reads the impressive number of trades that Jake's family have been involved in over the years. Blacksmithing, carpentry, salmon fishing – presumably because the family farm is situated on the banks of the River Tamar – boat building, and tin and copper mining. And it's fascinating to learn of the Saxon invasion and the coming together of Danish and Celts in an attempt to thwart the attack on lands in the Tamar Valley. But the entry that steals the breath from her throat and sends shivers down her spine is a simple recording of fact.

In the winter of 1484, Juliana, youngest daughter of Gilbert and Alice Pascoe of Greenbank Farm, married William Bowman, archer and forester to Richard Edgcumbe of Cotehele. The couple had five children, of which three survived – Ellinor, Julia and James.

Forty-Five

Ellinor sits on the edge of the bath, her left foot tapping impatiently on the floorboards as a strange mix of nerves and apprehension descends.

What the hell is wrong with me? Why didn't I immediately pick up on the signs?

She checks the digital result in the clear plastic window and gasps at what she sees. Elation overwhelms her and a huge smile lights her face. Simon will be delighted! They've been trying for a baby for *so* long. But suddenly she stills as her eyes focus on the number 2, clearly displaying. Two weeks since conception. Rapidly, she thinks back and her cheeks turn crimson with the realisation.

'Oh. My. God!' She stares at her reflection in the mirror. Face flushed and eyes wide. 'But that can't be!'

She checks the results again – the word 'Pregnant' and the number 2. Immediately, her mind goes into overdrive. Two weeks is close enough, but any fragmented remaining belief that her escapes to the *other* world are conjured up from her imaginings is blown straight out of the water. Ellinor takes a deep, calming breath, and as her emotions begin to settle, another feeling takes shape and she hugs her arms across her stomach. How very precious – not to say *unique* – this baby is. She thinks of Simon . . .

Unable to face herself in the mirror, she places the testing kit back in its packaging and carries it through to her bedroom. No one must see it before she's had a chance to break the wonderful news to her husband. However complicated it is, she has to believe that everything is falling into place exactly as it's meant to.

A sudden clattering in the yard draws her over to the window and Ellinor's jaw drops. Night has closed in, and yet it's only mid-afternoon! She glances at her wrist but her watch is no longer there. Turning, she surveys the bedroom. Somehow, between crossing the hallway from the bathroom to the bedroom, she has slipped through time. She turns back to the window. The wooden shutters are open wide and angry gusts of wind whistle into the room, seeking out its many hidden corners, as storm clouds rage across a darkened sky. Outside, rain beats down hard, and within minutes the surface of the yard has turned to a quagmire. Through the darkness, Ellinor can just make out the shadowy figures of four horsemen sitting huddled in their saddles, their charges stamping impatient hooves and tossing heads in the torrential downpour. Behind the barns on the opposite side of the yard, the gale blows through the tops of the trees, mercilessly swaying them one way and then the other, stripping whatever leaves remain on the branches. Glancing to her right, she sees a ghostly image sitting in the entrance to the hayloft – a solitary barn owl with ruffled feathers, observing the goings-on in the yard below.

Suddenly, Philippa emerges from the shelter of the farmhouse beneath her window, holding aloft a lantern. Acute anxiety besieges Ellinor. As the lantern's light casts upon the riders, she recognises William, Ian and John, and her eyebrows shoot up in surprise – present-day Ian would never get that close to a horse. The fourth man is a stranger. She strains her ears to catch the exchange taking place, but the ferocious wind sends the men's words scuttling off into the night. She's never witnessed weather like it! Where has it sprung from? As a figure rushes across the yard from one of the barns, the riders quickly dismount and hand their horses' reins over to the man. Then, William and the other men make their way towards the farmhouse, their bodies bent low against the gale.

Ellinor closes the wooden shutters and blocks out the

weather, but she can still hear its angry roar outside. Glancing down, momentarily she's taken aback to see that she wears a white linen chemise with a sky-blue, black-laced damask kirtle.

Have I been here for a while?

But she doesn't have time to consider this, as urgent voices sound along the passageway. Quickly refocusing, she makes her way across the room and opens the door a few inches, listening intently before exiting and descending the wooden stairs.

Following the sound of voices, Ellinor enters the open hall. It's dark and cold, and she shivers. The shutters of the tall windows are closed to keep out the worst of the weather, and caught in the numerous draughts, candlelight flickers from the wall sconces, casting fantastical shifting shadows across the room. In the centre is a roaring open fire with a cauldron suspended above it, but despite this, freezing air circulates around the room and into the massive timbers and trusses of the cavernous roof space. Sitting at the long table are several men and she notices a further group standing huddled together at the far end. Suddenly, one of the figures peels away and strides across the room towards her.

'Ellinor!' Throwing the sodden mantle back over his shoulder, William encloses her in a damp but loving embrace.

As she breathes in his masculine scent she detects a hint of something else.

Is it fear?

'William, what's happened?' she asks urgently.

Putting his arm around her, he leads her out of earshot of the others seated at the table.

'You were correct,' he says in a harsh whisper. 'The uprising was a complete disaster. The weather was against us, and word reached us that all of Buckingham's followers deserted. The mutinous cowards!'

She holds him tightly. 'But you are safe.'

His kiss is hard and urgent. 'I am alive, but we are not

safe.' Holding her at arm's length, he stares deep into her eyes. 'And neither are you, Ellinor. Can you not return to your time?'

'I don't know,' she says uncertainly.

He hugs her to him again and whispers in her ear. 'As you forewarned, Bodrugan and his men have pursued us, and Richard is under house arrest.'

Of course he is! History tells it so.

Nevertheless, Ellinor gasps, caught up by the heightened emotions swirling around the room.

'We were lucky to slip away,' William continues, 'but we are not out of danger. Our followers have scattered, but it's only a matter of time before Bodrugan's men cast their net wide to the surrounding areas.'

'What of the rest of the household? Are Joan and the children also under house arrest?'

He nods, his expression grave.

Desperately, Ellinor tries to think of something she can do, but she is powerless. What she told William would happen is playing out . . . just as history records it. Only she hadn't imagined she'd be caught up in the danger.

Philippa approaches from across the room, holding a wooden tray filled with steaming tankards. 'William, drink this. It will warm your cold, aching bones.'

'Thank you, madam.' He takes a flagon from the tray.

Phillipa glances at Ellinor but makes no comment. Quickly, she moves away to another man and offers him the same.

'What are you going to do?' Ellinor asks William.

'We'll keep low for a while. Ian has a change of horses and John's family farm is further downriver. They will give us safe harbour.'

He kisses her again.

'William, don't forget that Richard escapes,' she says, quietly.

'I have not forgotten,' he says with a frown. 'Is that of his own doing?'

Ellinor thinks hard. 'There's no mention of anyone else in the history books,' she says, with a shake of her head. 'But that doesn't mean he didn't have help.'

'The horses are ready,' Ian suddenly announces from the other side of the room. 'Let us away.'

As the men at the table rise to their feet, Ellinor hugs William close and whispers, 'Please keep safe, William. I am pregnant.'

His hand tightens on her waist and she feels his heart hammering against her chest.

'You are with child!' he exclaims quietly in her ear.

She nods, taken aback by the tears pooling in her eyes. 'Your child.'

He stares at her, eyes shining. 'Then you *must* find your way back to your own time. Not just for yourself, but for our child.'

Ellinor smiles sadly, and when William kisses her again there's no denying the depth of his love.

'I promise you, my beautiful Ellinor, if it should take a thousand years I will find my way back to you.'

Forty-Six

'What are you up to?' Simon asks on the other end of the phone.

'I've just visited the cottage,' Ellinor replies. 'It's progressing well and you'll notice one hell of a difference. Now, I'm on my way to the chapel, so I may lose signal. It's a beautiful day. The woods are alive with new growth and the sounds of wildlife, and you'll never guess who's accompanying me!'

'That's not hard!' Simon laughs. 'Branok?'

'Yes,' she says, glancing at the bird hopping through the undergrowth and flitting from branch to branch.

'Good to hear he's taking his guardianship duties so seriously, although he has double the work now that he has the two of you to keep a watchful eye over!'

She smiles and places a protective hand over her stomach. 'Where are you now, Si?'

'Just approaching . . .' His voice cuts out.

Removing the mobile from her ear, Ellinor checks the signal. 'You're breaking up. What did you say?'

'I should be with you . . .' His voice fades again.

Ellinor stares at the mobile screen. Barely one bar. 'Missed that. How long?'

'Within the hour.'

'Can't wait to see you, Simon.'

No reply.

With a sigh, Ellinor stuffs the phone in her back pocket and carries on down the track, and a short while later the charming stone chapel comes into view. Although it's an understated building, she considers it the perfect offering that Richard Edgcumbe commissioned in thanks for his narrow escape. Suddenly, the raven swoops low over her head and she feels the air currents from its fly-past. Landing effortlessly on the roof, the bird turns to face her. Cocking its head, it stares back up the path. Ellinor turns and gazes along the track but there's no one around.

'What do you see, Branok?' she asks.

The raven continues to keep an eye on the path, tilting its head first one way and then the other.

Ellinor listens intently, but apart from a now gentle breeze rustling through the trees, there's no other sound. She walks around the building and gazes in both directions along the languid, tidal river that winds its way through the burgeoning landscape on its journey to the sea. A movement amongst the reed beds on the Devon bank catches her attention and as a little egret emerges and wades out onto a mudflat in search of food, she marvels at the elegance of the bird with its whiter-than-white body, slender black beak and long black legs. She watches for a while longer, absorbing the serenity, before continuing around the small building and arriving at the wooden entrance door. Lifting the latch, she steps over the threshold of the moulded granite doorway and enters the historic chapel.

The interior is peaceful and unadorned with bright whitewashed walls, and Ellinor has the place to herself. As she walks around the small space, reverently she examines the few wooden benches with their original, fifteenth-century carved bench-ends. Pausing at a plain wooden altar table positioned beneath an attractive window, she observes the medieval-stonework statue niche, the only adornment in the building, before walking back to the door. Above it, displayed in an alcove, is a painted wooden plaque informing visitors of the tale of the chapel's foundation.

Suddenly the raven sounds a warning. 'Prruk-prruk!'

Stepping into the open doorway, Ellinor peers out. All is still, but as she exits the building and closes the door behind her, dark clouds swirl overhead and she's certain that shadowy shapes flit amongst the trees. Immediately she's on high alert, and anxiety and fear catch at her throat. All her senses warn that something is coming, and with hammering heart she holds her breath and listens. Snapping branches, heavy crashes and shouts come from the surrounding woodland and along the riverbank.

Whatever's happening, I don't want to be part of it.

Quickly she turns to re-enter the chapel, but to her alarm the building has disappeared, as has the path leading back through the woods. In their place is a heavily wooded, untamed area above a fiercely swirling, brown river.

'Oh, God,' she moans.

Crashing sounds again. Whatever's in the woods is getting closer, and instinctively Ellinor knows it's not friendly. Perhaps it's a hunt. If so, she's in danger of being mistaken for the prey.

I can't stay here. I have to move!

But gripped by fear, she remains frozen to the spot.

All at once, a herd of deer rush through the trees, the whites of their terrified eyes standing out starkly against the deepening gloom, and following not far behind are a dozen wild boar, squealing and grunting as they flee for their lives. Figures loom out of the woodland and suddenly Ellinor is surrounded by a handful of sweating men, all fired up and looking for a fight. Adrenalin and testosterone flow freely, and she looks on in horror at their outfits – gambesons and gauntlets, chain-mail vests, brigandines and sallet helmets. More terrifying still are the weapons they wield.

'Why are you abroad in the forest?' one of the soldier's shouts at her.

Ellinor's voice has deserted her and she can't stop shaking.

'Speak,' the man demands, thrusting a poleaxe at her.

'I got lost,' she manages to croak.

The other foot soldiers laugh.

'That's not good,' the first soldier replies. 'You don't want to be lost in these woods today.'

She shakes her head. 'No. I can see that.'

He eyes her keenly then looks around at the others. 'So,men, what shall we do with this fair maid?'

'I know what I'd like to do,' says a swordsman, lasciviously leering at her.

More laughter.

Swords and daggers threaten to prod her and, egging each other on, the men force Ellinor into a spin. As she reels into one soldier, he propels her onto the next, and so on around the circle. Jeers and laughter erupt, accompanied by the reek of high excitement. Casting around wildly for any means of escape, she tells herself sternly that she will not fall foul to this rabble of men. Then, more shouts from the woodland, and a harsh whistle from somewhere further up the hillside, focuses the warriors' attention.

'You're lucky . . . for now,' the first soldier says, jabbing his poleaxe towards her again, as if to ram home his words. 'But you won't escape so easily should we find you here when we come back.'

As the small group of soldiers set off at a steady jog, Ellinor tries to stop shaking, but this exchange has only increased her fear. She has nowhere to go. William's homestead is in the same direction as the men have gone, and anyway, he won't be there. But she realises the soldiers' threats are not idle and if they come across her again they won't spare her. Willing her legs to move, she forces her way through the undergrowth, pushing aside the foliage and stumbling over fallen logs as she frantically scans the landscape for a thick, shrubby bush to hide in. The air is filled with a cacophony of sound and her breathing is laboured – it's as if the sky is falling and closing in, ready to crush her.

All of a sudden a hand reaches out and grabs her, and Ellinor stifles a scream.

'Quiet!' a man's voice commands.

As she peers into the dark interior of a large clump of bushes, her panic builds.

'Mistress Eleanora, come quietly.'

The grip on her wrist increases, forcibly pulling her towards the dense cover. All her instincts tell Ellinor to tear herself away from this unknown assailant, but suddenly the leaves part. On his knees in the centre of the bush is Richard Edgcumbe.

'What are you doing here?' he demands in a harsh whisper, drawing her into the centre.

'I was walking in the woods,' she explains, as the foliage falls back into place and conceals her.

His look is incredulous. 'It is not wise to be abroad in the forest.'

Her thoughts go into freefall. With sudden, shocking certainty, Ellinor realises what she's stumbled upon and she tries hard to rein in her emotions. She's about to speak when footsteps thunder by and Richard clamps a gloved hand over her mouth. Feeling faint, Ellinor shrinks back and concentrates on even breathing through her nose. She *cannot* have a panic attack now! More shouts. But all at once, as quickly as they had intruded in on the tranquillity of the woodland, the sounds fade into the distance.

'I beg your forgiveness,' Richard says, removing his hand from her face, 'but we must not be found.'

'I understand,' she says quietly.

He stares at her, his expression revealing a mix of high anxiety and determination.

'Bodrugan's men search for me,' he explains gravely.

'I know,' she says. 'Fill your cap with stones and throw it in the water. His men will think you've drowned while attempting to escape via the river.'

His eyes widen. 'Mistress, you have read my exact thoughts!'

She smiles weakly. 'Do it now.'

His hands sweep the ground, searching for suitably sized rocks. Finding some, he removes his cap and wraps them in it.

With one last peek through the foliage, he turns to her. 'If I make it to freedom you will be handsomely rewarded, Mistress Eleanora.'

'Go,' she whispers, 'and may the gods be with you.'

She wonders if that's the right thing to say – is a belief in the gods blasphemous in fifteenth-century England?

Without hesitating, Richard slips silently from the bush and makes his way precariously down the hillside towards the water, and Ellinor is left alone in the hiding place with a pounding heart and the blood roaring in her ears. A minute later, she hears a splash, followed by a series of urgent shouts, and she cowers as four soldiers rush by. Standing at the edge of the plateau, they peer down into the murky river. They're so close, she can smell the stench rising from their bodies. Desperate not to gag, she covers her nose with her hand.

'Look!' one of the men exclaims. 'Over there! A cap.'

Keeping as silent and as still as a hunted mouse, Ellinor watches wide-eyed through the bush as the foot soldiers lean over the edge of the embankment and scan the swirling waters below. In broad Cornish accents they discuss whether Richard Edgcumbe is attempting to escape by swimming to safety. But eventually, with no signs of the wanted man, they give up their search.

'The traitor must have drowned,' one soldier proclaims.

'Good riddance,' says another. 'Saves the cost of an execution.'

'I was looking forward to that!' retorts another.

'God has done us a favour,' adds the fourth man.

Turning away from the river, the soldiers head off into the surrounding woodland and Ellinor lets out a long, shuddering breath. As the enormity of what she's just witnessed kicks in, adrenalin courses through her body and she starts shaking again, and she remains hidden in the thicket for a long time, too cautious to venture out. The hiding place feels insubstantial and Bodrugan's men may still be searching the woodland. It wouldn't do to be discovered. But after a while, realising she can't stay here forever and with cramp setting in, she moves.

'And what have we here?'

It takes a moment for the man's voice to penetrate through to her brain, but when it does, she freezes. As the point of a sword is thrust into the bush, parting the branches and exposing her, Ellinor looks on in horror at the dark shape rearing above her, like some demonic figure.

'A handsome maid indeed, and all a-tremble!' The man's accent is thick and regional.

Pressing the tip of his blade into the skin beneath her chin, he forces her to tilt her head and look up. Ellinor's eyes open wide in terror as they meet his, and memories of *the incident* that so easily could have ended in disaster come flooding back. The helmeted figure towering over her is none other than the deranged assailant on board that flight. But how is he here? Has fear caused this hallucination?

'Maybe I'll have my way with you before I run you through.' He gives a callous laugh as he puts pressure on the hilt of the sword. 'Come, my pretty. On your feet.'

Ellinor winces as the blade presses her skin to breaking point. Desperately, her eyes search for an escape, but with a twitch of the sword the man forces her to scramble up from her crouching position, despite the excruciating cramp in her right leg. Madness lurks in his eyes, and as his free hand fumbles with the buckle of his belt, he swears loudly. She wonders if this is enough of a distraction to give her the chance to run, but the next moment he slides the sharp edge of the sword's blade from her chin, teasing it over the soft skin of her neck, and pointing the tip at just below her ear . . . at the top of her scar. As if he knows its position!

What Godforsaken nightmare have I landed in? And how the hell am I going to evade this man's obvious intentions? No burly rugby player is going to come to the rescue this time.

Relishing the tease, the man moves the sword slowly down her scar and as the blade bites deep, the wound reopens. Suddenly realising what he's doing, she lets out a shriek.

'Shh . . . my pretty!' he says with a grin. 'Don't spoil the fun.'

Ellinor feels sick, and as the blood flows down her neck and her stress levels rise, she experiences a terrifying sensation of ice sliding into her bowels. Automatically, her hands protectively cover her stomach. She *can't* lose the baby! Feeling powerless against her adversary, she tries to remember all the calming techniques her therapist had showed her, but however she considers her predicament, it is dire. But she cannot die here. What would happen to her body in her own time? Would it be found and her death simply written off as unexplained? She *must* not die! She has too much to live for. She cannot leave Simon, not when they've only just rediscovered each other. And she certainly won't allow this deranged assailant to threaten her liberty again.

The man grunts as he makes clumsy attempts to remove his trousers, and cursing loudly, he glances down. Taking advantage of his momentary lapse in concentration, Ellinor tries to escape but immediately his eyes snap back to her.

'So . . . a feisty mare. Just as I like 'em.'

Removing his helmet, he takes a step towards her and Ellinor screams. The sound echoes chillingly around the dark woodland and she hears the raven call a harsh warning signal. And then, from some way off, a loud and insolent whistle. As the man glances in the direction of the noise, a cold rush of air darts past Ellinor's right ear.

'What the—' But her assailant's sentence is cut short.

Uncomprehendingly, Ellinor looks on as his lascivious expression turns to one of utter astonishment and shock. As the sword drops from his hand, the man's eyes open wide and a trickle of blood oozes down the centre of his face from where the arrow has found its mark, embedded deep in his forehead. Gloved hands flail as they try and fail to grasp the shaft of the weapon, and his body sways. Suddenly his eyes roll back into their sockets, and moments later the man keels over backwards, and straight as a ramrod, he crashes to the ground. As the life drains from his twitching body, Ellinor's hand flies to the wet scar on her neck. It throbs badly and blood oozes between her fingers, and all at once her legs buckle. Collapsing to the forest floor, she gulps back sobs and tries to quell her terror.

'Ellinor!'

Hands reach for her and William's face swims into focus, as she glances up through misted eyes.

'The bastard hasn't injured you, has he?' His voice is harsh with concern.

The lump in Ellinor's throat makes it impossible for her to answer, and she simply reaches for him. Anger pools in William's eyes, as he notices the blood on her hand. But as soon as his fingers close around her wrists, the surrounding woodland fades and the scene slides to an undulating, watery world. She tries to hold on to him, even though she knows it's pointless, because there's nothing she can do to prevent him from disappearing.

'William,' she mouths silently.

His look turns from anger to frustration, and then despair, and as the swirling greyness encroaches, she hears his words.

'I promise you, my beautiful Ellinor. Even if it should take many centuries, I *will* find my way back to you.' His eyes bore into hers, as unwittingly she is pulled away.

Ellinor cries out. Closing her eyes, she lets out a sob.

'It's OK, Elli. I've got you.'

Instantly her eyes snap open and she gazes up into Simon's smiling face.

'Can't have you disappearing down that mudslide into the water.'

As nausea and keen yearning claim her, she bends over and retches.

'Are you all right?' Simon asks with concern. 'I saw you fall.'

She retches again. It's as if her body tries to expel all that it's been through. If only her mind will expel it too. Clinging to her husband's firm grip, she glances towards the river meandering untroubled some way below. The ground where she sits is scuffed and disturbed, as if an animal has either scrambled up the bank or slid down to enter the river.

'What are you doing here?' she asks in bewilderment.

'You said you were visiting the chapel, so I thought I'd come and look for you.' Simon pulls her to her feet.

Ellinor gazes at the little stone building sitting peacefully in its tranquil setting. On the slate roof standing sentinel next to the Celtic cross is the raven.

'Prruk-prruk,' it croons softly, looking her straight in the eye.

'Are you OK?' Simon asks, brushing mud from her jeans.

Her hand flies to her neck.

'Does your scar hurt? Here, let me take a look.' He gently prises away her fingers. 'It's very raw. We should put some aloe vera on that.'

'Is it bleeding?'

'No, but it looks angry and red.'

So, the reopened wound hasn't accompanied me into this timeline.

'I'm OK, Si,' she says, resting her hands on his shoulders. 'But I'd like to go back to the farmhouse now.'

Epilogue

As her pregnancy progresses, Ellinor experiences no further timeslip episodes to that *other* world. Whether it's due to hormonal changes or something else, she's unsure; it's as if she's lost the capacity to visit that time. But sometimes, in dreams, through a heavy veil she catches glimpses of William, and occasionally – in the moments between sleep and waking – she hears his voice.

'Never fear, my love. Whatever may come, I will always walk with you on distant paths.'

Each time she wakes to keen longing, but she soon refocuses on the present. Watching the changes to her body is exciting, and because of her medical history Ellinor attends many appointments with various health professionals, which keeps her firmly in the *here and now*. She also picks up a paintbrush again and is surprised at how her paintings have transformed. No longer are her canvases and sketchbooks covered in dark, jagged, brutal images, full of anger, but, instead, peaceful, pastoral scenes of the surrounding Tamar Valley countryside. One day, while cajoling Rufus and Rusty to pose for her, she further surprises herself by discovering a talent for creating whimsical animal characters, full of charm.

Comfort Wood Orchards officially launches its cider and the business takes off, with interest coming in from many different quarters – not only Michelin-starred restaurants in the county, but also countrywide. Simon sets up a successful meeting with the head of Harrods Food Halls, and based on the number of crates the company orders, he brings forward his departure from his marketing job in London and decamps full-time to Cornwall. Both he and Ellinor agree not to hurry their decision over the Surrey house, and they have no trouble renting it out through an executive letting agency.

'OK, Mrs Forrester. How shall we do this?' Simon asks with a grin.

'What do you mean?'

'Well, I *have* to carry you over the threshold of our new home.'

'No way!' she exclaims. 'You'll give yourself a hernia getting this Heffalump into the cottage. And anyway, that's for newly-weds.'

'But I insist,' he says, attempting to sweep her off her feet. 'And it is as though we're newly-weds. It's a new start for the both of us.'

She laughs. 'You'll do yourself a mischief.'

Valiantly attempting not to drop her, Simon staggers a few steps towards the door before admitting defeat.

'Maybe I was being a tad optimistic,' he says, carefully putting her down.

'Told you so.' Ellinor laughs again. 'But you do realise you've created a rod for your own back, Simon Forrester. Now that you've shown your chivalrous side, I expect to see it more often.'

He pulls a mock-horrified face.

Spotting something over her shoulder, he says, 'Look, Elli. Branok's brought a friend to welcome us.'

She turns and smiles. Hopping into the centre of the clearing is the raven, and with him is another.

'Did you know they pair for life?' she remarks.

'As I've said before . . . you, dear wife, amaze me with your newfound knowledge.'

Ellinor turns towards him. 'I hope they stick around.'

'I can't imagine for one moment that Branok will let you out of his sight.'

As they enter the cottage beneath the granite lintel – its witch marks clearly displayed – Ellinor stops and glances around. A huge smile lights her face as she takes in the white-washed walls, the honey-coloured wooden flooring and the substantial oak beams spanning the room. It's cosy, comforting and homely – just as she'd envisioned it would be once the build was complete. Jake and his army of men pulled out all the stops so that the cottage would be ready in time for Christmas; they've even managed to finish with a week to spare. Glancing at the enlarged inglenook, Ellinor crosses over to it, remembering how she and William had stood in this very spot, and, together, carved the fertility witch mark into the granite lintel when it had spanned the smaller fireplace. Suddenly Simon's arms encircle her.

'I can no longer touch my fingers around your middle!' he teases, dropping a tender kiss beneath her ear.

She smiles. 'See, I told you I'd morphed into a Heffalump!'

'And a blooming beautiful one at that.'

Her smile broadens.

Tonight will be the first time they've stayed in their new home, and tomorrow they will put up Christmas decorations in the cottage and the connecting glassed living area. After all, being seven months pregnant won't stop her from throwing the 'open house' she'd promised Jake back in the spring. Ellinor fingers the restored Celtic love-knot pendant and amber stone, which she wears all the time, now that she has a plaited green-leather necklace for it.

Simon drops his arms. Walking to the far end of the room, he opens the door to the kitchen and peers in at the bespoke wooden kitchen units.

'The craftsmanship in this place is second to none. Jake has really come up trumps for us, hasn't he, Elli?'

'He certainly has,' she replies, noticing that someone has thoughtfully laid a fire in the hearth, just waiting to be lit. 'If it hadn't been for his numerous trade contacts, I'm sure we'd still be relying on Ian and Pippa's generosity to provide a roof over our heads.'

Simon gazes down the room at his wife. 'It's curious how things have fallen into place. I mean, I hadn't planned on being here until next spring but with the cider business taking off so spectacularly, it seems as if I was meant to be here sooner.'

'All things happen at the right time,' she says quietly, listening to the sound of her husband's footsteps crossing the wooden floor to the front door.

'This old granite lintel looks brilliant here at the entrance.'

Ellinor smiles to herself. 'I agree.'

'May the road rise up to meet you; may the wind be always at your back; may the sun shine warm upon your face; the rains fall soft upon your fields; and until we meet again, may God hold you in the palm of His hand.'

His voice sounds muffled, as if coming from a very great distance, and a sudden tingle teases its way up Ellinor's spine.

She turns. 'What was that?'

'Oh, it's an old Celtic blessing,' he says, running his hand over the witch marks.

She stares at her husband's back. 'But you don't know any Celtic blessings . . . Or at least, I didn't think you did.'

He turns towards her. 'Oh, there's much to discover about me.'

'What do you mean?' she asks in bemusement.

'Don't you remember?' He walks towards her, eyes twinkling with mischief. 'I once made a promise that if it should take a thousand years I would find my way back to you, my beautiful Ellinor.'

'Simon!' she exclaims, deeply searching his bright blue eyes.

He holds her gaze.

As incredible possibilities gallop through Ellinor's mind, like the synchronising cogs of a wheel, a fantastical idea falls flawlessly into place.

'William?'

Acknowledgements

When I started writing this book, I had no idea what a Herculean task I had set myself. The amount of historical research and necessary fact-checking was quite something! I am in awe of those authors who write historical fiction and I hope that I have done justice to this period.

Huge thanks to Team Embla for their ongoing dedication in producing and marketing my books. To my editor, Melanie Hayes, for not only providing excellent constructive criticism and teasing out the best in this novel, but also for her understanding and flexible attitude during a time when my health was not at its best; Emma Rodgers for the enchanting cover design that so cleverly captures the essence of the story; Emily Thomas, copy editor, for her thorough and proficient suggestions and guidance; and Michelle Bullock and Robin Seavill for their eagle-eyed proofreading. As always, many thanks to my agent, Hannah Todd, of the Madeleine Milburn Literary & TV Agency – serendipity was certainly at play the day our paths crossed.

And big thanks must also go to:

My beta readers, Helena Ancil, Sally Tunley and Shelagh Clowe, who had the huge task of reassuring me that the first draft wasn't as hopeless as I believed!

Chris Whaley (friend and retired pilot) for his advice on airline procedures.

Louise Horrod and Nick Stokes, respectively Collections and House Officer and Manager, Cotehele National Trust, for their assistance in providing historical details of this glorious property.

Special thanks must go to Jules Chabeaux, Intuitive Wildlife Artist, for sharing her amazing talents and insights into the animal kingdom, from which the raven stepped forward and asked to feature – https://instagram.com/juleschabeauxartist

And finally, heartfelt thanks to my husband, Martin, whose constant support and belief in my writing journey is a wonderful comfort. Knowing that I won't starve or suffer dehydration while wrestling words into something worth reading is one less thing to worry about. Thank you!

Turn the page for an exclusive extract from the
wonderfully romantic and captivating novel,
Into a Cornish Wind . . .

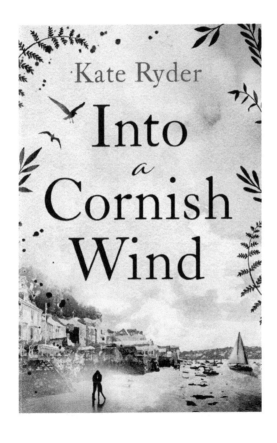

1

'You know he's married, don't you?'

The blood drains from Kat's face. Clutching the phone, she concentrates on steady, even breathing. In for three, hold for four, out for five . . .

'You didn't. I'm so sorry.' The woman's voice holds no guile.

Kat closes her eyes. How could she have been so stupid – falling for the oldest trick in the book? She usually prides herself on her savviness, but Colin has successfully undermined that particular accomplishment.

'Are you OK?' The voice at the other end sounds concerned.

Opening her eyes, Kat summons the ability to speak. 'Who did you say you were?'

The woman gives a soft laugh. 'I didn't, but I thought you should know before you're too deeply entrenched.'

'A well-wisher then?' A frown creases Kat's brow.

'Yes. I've known Colin for a while. He's a lovely guy, but he's *taken*.'

Kat shuts her eyes and pinches the bridge of her nose. Why hadn't she read the signs? During the course of their seven-month relationship, Colin has rarely stayed over during the week. Foolishly, she believed it was because he felt uncomfortable in her flat, and whenever she suggested staying over at his place he's always made the excuse of a loud and messy housemate. How stupid is she? She should have heard the warning bells, but she was falling in love and so deaf to their clanging.

Pushing back her chair, Kat gets to her feet. 'Do I know you?'

'We have met, briefly.'

'Where?' Kat's voice is insistent.

The moment stretches before the woman answers. 'The Old Swan.'

'What? Last Wednesday?'

'Yes.'

Kat casts her mind back. Colin had arranged to meet her after work for a quiet drink, although it had turned into anything but when several of his workmates suddenly appeared and hijacked the evening. Now she thinks about it, Colin had seemed uncomfortable when his colleagues approached their table. Recalling the women among them, she wonders which one she's talking to now.

Suddenly, the room is plunged into deep gloom as black clouds obliterate the sun. Kat shivers.

'Looks like we're in for a storm,' comments Kat's colleague, Gemma, sitting at the only other desk in the narrow office. Rising to her feet, she walks towards the door and switches on the headache-inducing, overhead fluorescent light, which snaps into life with a loud buzz.

Kat turns and gazes out of the window at a bank of menacing clouds sweeping across the sky that only five minutes earlier held the promise of a beautiful, early spring day. Raindrops fall and swiftly gather force. In the road below, an array of umbrellas spring open under the deluge unleashed from the sky and people scurry along the pavements heading for the nearest cover. Absent-mindedly tapping the phone against her chin, Kat watches the city street quickly turn into a river.

A man dressed in casual attire catches her eye. Incongruous in the busy London square, and seemingly unconcerned by the onslaught of rain, he holds a briefcase above his head and calmly hails a taxi. This is no city gent or office worker. His deep, early tan and the wild dark hair curling at the nape of his neck speak of foreign holidays, distant shores and an altogether more abandoned existence; not one confined to office hours and endless meetings. As a black cab slews across the road in deepening water, the man takes an unhurried step back from the spray that threatens to soak him. Kat watches as he opens the car door and climbs in.

A sudden clap of thunder sounds overhead and the fluorescent light flickers.

Crap! That's all she needs . . . a power cut.

She still has to complete the illustration pinned to her easel before the day is through.

As rivulets of water stream down the windowpane, obscuring the street scene below, Kat becomes aware that she is still holding her phone in a vice-like grip.

'Hello?' The woman's voice cuts into her thoughts. 'Is everything OK?'

'Oh . . . Yes.' Kat frowns. 'Just how married is Colin?' she asks quietly.

The woman sighs. 'His second son is due any day.'

Kat's eyes widen. *Second* son! He's covered his tracks well. She had no idea he wasn't single, let alone a father . . .

'Are you sure we're talking about the same man?'

'Absolutely. Colin Andrews is my brother-in-law.'

Kat inhales sharply.

'When I saw you two together the other evening,' the woman continues, 'and how you were with him, I knew I had to say something. I couldn't let you be drawn deeper into the deception. You see, it's not the first time this has happened. He's prone to wandering during my sister's pregnancies. This will be the third time.'

'Third?' Kat's voice is barely more than a whisper.

'Yes. This is child number three.'

Good God! He's definitely packing them in.

'Thank you for the heads up,' she says stiffly.

'I'm sorry if this has come as a shock but it's unfair of him to take advantage of you. I've seen it happen too many times.'

Aware of intense curiosity coming from the other end of the

room, Kat stares straight ahead at the numerous illustrations plastering the walls of her workspace.

'Anyway, I wish you luck,' the woman says. 'You seem nice and you don't deserve to be treated like this.' She ends the call.

The complete and utter BASTARD!

No wonder Colin has never invited her to his place. Seven months she's wasted on him!

Sitting down again, Kat slowly replaces the handset.

'You all right, Kat?' Gemma enquires. 'You look as if you've had some bad news.'

'I have.' She glances over at her colleague. 'And, no, I'm not all right, but I will be . . .'

The girl rises to her feet. 'I'll grab us some coffees.'

Kat throws her a weak smile. 'Black please . . . strong.'

As Gemma exits the room, Kat's mobile alerts her to an incoming message. In disbelief, she stares at the screen.

See you at Luigi's at seven. Don't be late. Col xx

'Bastard!' she shouts.

'You OK, Kat?' The art director's disembodied voice drifts over the partial screens dividing their offices.

'Bloody men!' she exclaims in response, quickly adding, 'No disrespect, Hugo.'

'None taken. They can't all be like me.'

Despite her tumultuous feelings, Kat's mouth twitches into a smile. 'Sadly, it seems all the best ones are taken.'

'Now, that's where you're wrong,' Hugo assures her. 'Somewhere out there . . .'

She considers Colin's message. What should she do? Not turn up and leave him wondering where she is, or respond with a short, sharp text saying she's aware of his sneaky assignations with her? No, let the sodding man stew.

She glances out of the window again. Flash floods, but the rain has stopped and the sun is doing its best to disperse the ominous clouds. She checks the time on her mobile – 11.40 – and rises to her feet. The unfinished illustration beckons but it can wait; there will be time this afternoon to put the finishing touches to it.

Grabbing her jacket from the back of the chair, she turns and sees Gemma in the doorway holding two steaming mugs.

'Sorry, Gem. Change of plan.' She smiles apologetically. 'I'm taking an early lunchbreak.'

2

Kat climbs the steps to Tate Britain, and as she enters the marble foyer, a sense of calm descends. Art always does this for her, helping to put whatever challenges she faces into perspective. However troubled or anxious she feels, being surrounded by masterpieces carrying centuries of history within them reminds her that life goes on and she is but a mere speck in the overall scheme of things.

Her heart rate settles further as she wanders through rooms filled with important art dating from the 1500s to the present day. Gazing at the incredible talent on display, she knows she can only ever hope to emulate this in her own small way, but is comforted by the knowledge that she is part of a greater whole. Fortunately, there are not too many people about and, unhurried, she enjoys the masterpieces of such eminent artists as Turner and Constable. However, mindful of her lunch *hour*, it's not long before she makes her way through to the Pre-Raphaelite section.

Apart from half-a-dozen chattering Japanese tourists, Kat is alone in this gallery. Immediately she crosses over to Sir John Everett Millais' painting of a scene from Shakespeare's *Hamlet – 'Ophelia'*. Upon discovering Hamlet had murdered her father, poor Ophelia turned insane with grief, and in her distraught state fell into a brook and drowned. Kat grimaces. With her latest, less-than-successful relationship with Colin to add to her disastrously long list of exes, this painting hits a nerve. But refusing to dwell on such grim thoughts, she examines the background of the masterpiece that Millais had created from real life. At the time, it was thought to be one of the most accurate studies of nature ever painted. Her gaze alights on Ophelia's face. Dante Gabriel Rossetti's lover, wife and muse, Elizabeth Siddal, had posed for the painting and in her hands are flowers that include poppies, symbolising death.

Poor Lizzie Siddal, having to lie for hours on end in a bath of cooling water.

Kat knows the painting was created in the artist's studio, and that lamps placed beneath the bath to keep the water warm had gone out. Subsequently, Millais' model had become dangerously ill.

Continuing around the gallery, Kat gazes at each painting in turn until reaching the works of Rossetti, in front of which a bench is conveniently placed, and she sits down to study the portrait, *Sancta Lilias;* the abandoned first version of one of the artist's most important pictures, *The Blessed Damozel.* It's the only one of Rossetti's paired pictures and poems, in which the poem was completed first. She contemplates its neighbour – *The Beloved ('The Bride')* – the best known of his poems and inspired by the biblical *Song of Solomon.* The painting tells the story of a young woman preparing to marry. Rossetti has portrayed her surrounded by attendants, with a young, black child in the foreground holding a gold vase of roses, and as the bride lifts the head covering away from her face, her eyes are fixed directly on the beholder.

Oh Dante, you did have a liking for redheads!

Kat glances down at her own lustrous locks falling over her shoulders. She'd hated the colour growing up. Children can be *so* callous. Carrot-top, ginga, ginger nut, firecracker, tomato . . . She'd been called them all and made to feel like a freak. But as the years passed, the name-calling naturally receded, and thanks to a certain young actress exploding onto the nation's TV screens as Demelza Poldark, Kat's colouring has caught on, and numerous women now dye their hair shades of fire-red through to autumn. No longer does she stand out.

A movement at the entrance makes her look up and as a couple enter, Kat's eyes widen. It's the man she'd spied from her office window only half an hour before! He's ditched the briefcase . . . but it's definitely him. She observes the woman at his side. Smartly dressed in a navy pinstriped skirt-suit, her high heels elevate her to almost his height. They make a striking couple, even though he's casually dressed by comparison. His linen jacket is crumpled, no doubt from having been caught out in the rain and then sitting in a taxi, and there are watermark stains at the ankles of his pale blue trousers. But a sense of freedom envelops him and, as before, Kat is reminded of sunnier climes.

She watches a while longer. The man and the woman are obviously at ease in each other's company and the overriding impression Kat has is one of mutual respect. Oh, how she longs for a relationship like that, not some sordid fumble after work knowing that Colin will rarely, if ever, stay the night to welcome in the morning with her. Why has she been so foolish? As she thinks of her deceitful lover, Kat decides not to stoop to his level. She will let him know she won't be meeting him tonight for a cosy supper at his favourite bistro. She's about to text him when the man glances over in her direction. The inquisitive look from a pair of hazel eyes lasts no more than a few seconds, but as his attention returns to the woman at his side and they move on to the next exhibit, Kat takes a deep, shuddering breath.

As the couple work their way around the gallery she is unable to tear her eyes away. Everything about the man speaks of capable masculinity. His movements are easy yet controlled, reminding her of a panther, and the hushed conversations he has with his companion reveal a delightfully deep, warm voice. An air of confidence surrounds him and she can imagine him taking calculated risks whilst leading an adventurous life.

As her senses heighten, Kat's fingers begin to tingle, and she feels the blood start to fizz in her veins. A dazzling light suddenly falls upon him and as she glances up at the ceiling to find its source, she thinks she hears a seagull's cry and the snap of a sail caught by a gust of wind. And there's another distinct noise, too. *Wap, wap, wap.* What is that – rigging lines slapping against a mast? Kat shakes her head. She's always been accused of being ultra-sensitive and having an overactive imagination, and growing up she was constantly reprimanded for embellishing the facts. She'd learnt to keep her thoughts to herself. However, as her artistic skills developed and her imagination conjured up images that translated into her drawings and paintings, her tutors had despaired and questioned why she was unable to simply draw what was in front of her. She'd never understood and would look back at the subject she was tasked to paint and wonder why her teachers were unable to see the living, breathing scene as she could.

Dragging her eyes away from the man, with a shaking hand Kat responds to Colin's text.

No go tonight or any other night. Thinking of your family.
She hits 'send' and glances up again.

The atmosphere has returned to normal and no strange lights or unusual sounds invade the hushed space. Kat knows she should head back to work but decides to sit for a few minutes longer, absorbing the peace and serenity of the gallery.

The couple are about to exit the room, when suddenly the man turns and silently observes her sitting motionless on the bench, like a statue. Kat stops breathing, stilled by the depth of his gaze.

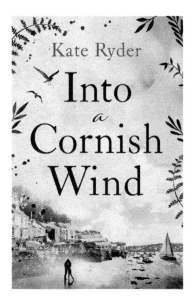

Kat Maddox has had her fair share of terrible relationships. And after discovering that her latest boyfriend has been hiding an entire other life from her, it's time for a fresh start.

Accepting a job on the Cornish coast, Kat begins a new chapter in Fowey. She is immediately drawn to the beautiful Cornish landscapes and swiftly an old feeling begins to emerge. Ever since she was young, Kat's had a 'gift' – when her paintbrush touches canvas, she's able to see the history of her subject as if by magic.

Consumed with trying to discover what this could mean, she crosses paths with local sailor, Mac. Though this isn't the first, or the last time, they're destined to meet. As Mac and Kat grow closer, she begins to wonder whether she should open her heart to love one more time . . .

Available to buy now!

About Kate Ryder

Kate Ryder is an international bestselling author of romantic suspense and timeslip. Her writing incorporates nature and history with a hint of the otherworldly/supernatural.

Originally from the south-east of England, today Kate lives on the 'jam-first' Cornish side of the beautiful Tamar Valley with her husband and a rehomed Bengal-cross cat. When not writing she gravitates towards the coast, theatre, music and art, although the latter always makes her yearn to pick up a paintbrush. But – as there are only so many hours in a day – instead, she paints pictures with words!

About Embla Books

Embla Books is a digital-first publisher of standout commercial adult fiction. Passionate about storytelling, the team at Embla publish books that will make you 'laugh, love, look over your shoulder and lose sleep'. Launched by Bonnier Books UK in 2021, the imprint is named after the first woman from the creation myth in Norse mythology, who was carved by the gods from a tree trunk found on the seashore – an image of the kind of creative work and crafting that writers do, and a symbol of how stories shape our lives.

Find out about some of our other books and stay in touch:

Twitter, Facebook, Instagram: @emblabooks
Newsletter: https://bit.ly/emblanewsletter

Printed in Great Britain
by Amazon

37700668R00172